PRINCESS SISTER

PRINCESS SISTER

Sheila Copeland

sepia
★BET
BOOKS

BET Publications, LLC
http://www.bet.com

SEPIA BOOKS are published by

BET Publications, LLC
c/o BET BOOKS
One BET Plaza
1900 W Place NE
Washington, DC 20018-1211

All Kensington Titles, Imprints, and Distributed Lines are available at special quantity discounts for bulk purchases for sales promotions, premiums, fund-raising, and educational or institutional use. Special book excerpts or customized printings can also be created to fit specific needs. For details, write or phone the office of the Kensington special sales manager: Kensington Publishing Corp., 850 Third Avenue, New York, NY 10022, attn: Special Sales Department, Phone: 1-800-221-2647.

ISBN: 1-58314-235-5

First Trade Paperback Printing: October 2002
10 9 8 7 6 5 4 3 2

Printed in the United States of America

For Princess Sisters everywhere,
you know who you are.
Especially my sister, Michele Adams,
and for you, Big Head, for recognizing
and loving me, your Princess Sister.

.

THANK YOU

Father, I continually praise You for choosing me before the foundation of the world to bring my Lord and Savoir, Jesus Christ, glory with this gift through the anointing of the Holy Spirit. What an honor!

Always my mother, Georgia Copeland. The Lord sure knew what He was doing when He gave me you.

The Adams, Bowens, Johnson, and McCoy families for your love and support. My love is your love.

My Pastor, Dr. Beverly "Bam" Crawford, for your commitment to knowing the Lord Jesus Christ and the fellowship of His sufferings and BEFIC for your prayers and support.

Erma Byrd for helping me run with the vision. Shirley Hogan, Gwen Holdness, Lynn Wynn, Felicia Pelton, the Pettis family, Percy Holden, Henry Holmes, Frances Hunter, Christopher Lee, Rosalind Lee, Dr. Raul Mena, Iola Noah, Helen Sutton, Maurice Taylor, and Bill Whitten . . . my peeps . . . for your guidance, wisdom, and listening ears.

Linda Gill, my publisher, and Glenda Howard-King, my editor. You are gifts from God and you are my friends. Kicheko Driggins, what would we do without you?

Leroy Bobbitt and Virgil Roberts for getting my act together.

Robi Reed-Humes, for your excellence that continually inspires me. We've only just begun to work God's Plan.

Olivia Ose-Sarfo and The Norfolk Public Library, and Portia Hamilton for helping me to bring Paris and New Orleans into the souls of my readers.

My readers . . . for enjoying my stories. Your support encourages me to continue.

From the bottom of my heart, thank you very much.

And though I have the gift of prophecy and understand all mysteries and all knowledge, and though I have all faith so that I could remove mountains, but have not love, I am nothing.

I Corinthians 13:2

PRELUDE

It was nearly dusk when the ship docked in Port New Orleans. The boy watched the anchor sink into the deep, murky water and his heart sank with it. He didn't want to go. When the men had unloaded the last crate of seafood, his father stood in front of him.

"It's time to go now, son."

He slowly picked up the small suitcase that contained a few items of clothing, took the hand his father extended to him, and climbed out of the fishing boat onto the dock.

"It will be dark in less than an hour and the streets will be unfamiliar."

"I know, Papá."

They stood in silence listening to the sound of the river lapping against the boat. Strains of music and laughter floated up into the air from the city beyond them.

"Do you have the directions your mother gave you to her sister's house?"

"Oui, Papá."

"Good. They are family and they will take care of you. You will have a better life here. Your mother's family has more to offer you than life as a fisherman. Your mamá is expecting you to follow in the Prideaux tradition and become a very important attorney. How she wound up on an island with somebody like me is still a mystery, but I guess that's why we call it love."

"I don't mind staying on the island and working as a fisherman. If it's good enough for you, then it's enough for me."

"No, son. Now you must not disappoint your mother. If I took you back to Haiti she would hate me."

"All right, Papá." He shook his father's hand and headed toward the city.

"Good-bye, son. Shall I give Felicite your regards?"

"Yes, Papá." He wouldn't turn around to look at his father because he didn't want him to see that he was crying. He had to be a man now, even if he was only seventeen.

He followed the map his mother had drawn as he walked through the city past cafés, juke joints, restaurants, and clubs.

"Happy Mardis Gras!" a stranger called out to him as he continued walking through the narrow, cobblestoned streets.

Festive music filled the air seasoned with laughter, as Mardis Gras revelers prepared for the dance.

He made his way through the French Quarter to a quieter side of town, and walked down Claiburne Street until he found the address. It was one of the prettiest and biggest houses on the street, powder blue trimmed in ivory. He pushed open the black wrought-iron gate, walked up the stairs, and lifted the shiny brass knocker on the door. Several moments later, a woman with vanilla skin and auburn hair pushed aside the white lace curtains, frowned, and motioned for him to go around to the back.

His spirits lifted at the sight of his mother's older sister, Marie Prideaux. He had never met her, but there was a strong family resemblance. She pulled open the door and he smiled, happy to have located his family in this strange new town. No one had informed her that he was coming.

"Hello, Aunt Marie."

"I beg your pardon?" Her cold hazel eyes looked him up and down with contempt.

"I'm Pierre Chevalier, your sister Jacqueline's son."

Her thin pale lips pursed as her eyes glazed over with hate.

"Come in." She opened the door and Pierre thought twice about entering.

"I said come in." She grabbed his jacket sleeve, yanked him into the canary-yellow kitchen, and quickly shut the door.

"What did you say your name was?"

"Pierre. Pierre Chevalier." He didn't know why he was whispering.

"Well, if you are my sister's son . . . you sure are black. But your father was certainly one black nigger. You are Felipe's boy?"

"Yes." He was whispering again. Black nigger . . . He had never felt so humiliated in his life. He wanted to turn and run from the mean, hateful woman and her big, fancy house, but he had nowhere else to go.

"I still don't know why Jacqueline held such a fascination for him. She thought he was handsome. But that was my sister, hanging out with the hired help. What a waste for all her lovely French blood, because it certainly didn't help you."

Pierre stared at his small suitcase and felt even smaller. This woman would never give him a place to stay, nor would she help him get into college. He didn't want her help either because he despised everything about her.

"It's just like your kind to want a white woman. You need to stay with your own. You have a suitcase. . . . Did you think you were going to stay here?"

"No." He had found his voice and he was no longer whispering. "Mamá said to give you her regards."

He picked up the suitcase and headed toward the door.

"Well, you've given them. Now I don't ever want to see your face again. Jacqueline is no longer my sister. She turned her back on this family when she married your father. How she lives on that god-awful island with you savages is beyond me."

He heard the door slam behind him as he quickly walked away and found his way back into town where the Mardis Gras carnival celebrations were in full swing.

ONE

The golden glow of the floodlit Arc de Triomphe bathed the heavens as the Seine River, shimmering and metallic, flowed through the city dividing it in half. On the Right Bank, huge red and gold bows and tiny twinkling bulbs adorned the windows of the shops and boutiques along the elegant Champs Elysées. Fir trees decked with shiny gold ornaments and hundreds of miniature white lights glittered and sparkled. It was Christmas in Paris and the night air was crisp with excitement as shoppers rushed to make last-minute purchases.

Vadé Chevalier watched her warm breath form wisps of smoke and disappear as she walked hand in hand with her father. Her hand-tailored black cashmere coat felt good that evening. Swinging her shopping bag filled with special gifts for her younger brother, Laurent, she skipped an extra step to keep up with her father's cool, lean stride. She couldn't wait to see her brother's face when he opened the tin of new paints, charcoals, and pad she had purchased for him.

"Look, Papá!" She removed a gloved hand from her father's large, strong one and pointed to a crucifix encrusted with diamonds on a delicate gold filigree chain in the store window."Do you think Mamá would like it?"

Without further discussion, the two of them turned and walked into the brightly lit shop.

"Welcome, monsieur! Mademoiselle!" An impeccably dressed sales-lady handed them each a glass of champagne. "Merry Christmas!"

"Merci, madame." Vadé giggled as she sipped the sparkling wine that she was allowed to sample only during the holidays. "Papá! The bubbles tickle my nose."

She removed the butter-soft leather gloves and carefully tucked them into her Louis Vuitton shoulder bag and selected a square of spinach quiche from the silver tray before her. From a mirror behind the counter she caught a glimpse of her cocoa face and long black braid and turned to face her father again.

"Is this the necklace you wanted, Princess?" Her father smiled as the clerk displayed the cross she had shown him in the window.

"*Oui*, Papá!" She smiled and took a tiny sip of the champagne as he chatted in French with the clerk. She was so proud of her handsome father. A black silky beard covered his smooth mocha skin. He was internationally renowned as a jazz pianist, with his own group, Amour.

"Here is another treasure for your bag." He placed a box wrapped in purple foil, tied with a gold bow, in her bag while he tucked another small box in the pocket of his cashmere coat.

"What was that, Papá?" She pointed to his coat pocket.

"What was what?" He tried to suppress a smile.

"What did you put into your pocket?"

"*Je n'ais sais pas*, Princess. What other shopping do we have?"

Vadé smiled and took a list from her purse. "Did you get a gift for Big Claude?"

He looked through the stack of beautifully wrapped packages he was carrying. "Yes, I did."

"*Bien.* Then we are done."

"Good. We still have to make beignet for our Christmas Eve party after midnight Mass."

"Beignet," Vadé repeated, smacking her lips. "My favorite."

Beignet were delicious sweet square-shaped doughnuts lavishly sprinkled with powdered sugar, served warm with café au lait. Pierre made a batch every year at Christmas. He had learned a special recipe while working as a waiter in a restaurant in New Orleans. The guests would be sorely disappointed if there were none of her father's famous beignet and Desiree's Creole gumbo and rice. Vadé could taste the savory seafood stew already.

"I can't wait. Let's go home, Papá."

They walked several blocks through the busy square to a quiet residential area and up the walkway of a magnificent seventeenth-century five-story town house. Pierre pushed open the delicate black wrought-iron gate decorated with foliage and chimera into a courtyard tiled in black and ivory marble. Stairs of dressed stone, lit by hanging lanterns, curved graciously up an elegant staircase. Pierre took Vadé's shopping bag, pulled her tam from her head, and ran his hand across her silky black hair, the same texture and color of his own.

"A gentleman always carries his lady's packages."

"I don't need a gentleman to carry my packages as long as I have you and Lar," she teased. "I'll have them do other things for me."

"I bet you will." Her father was laughing now.

A blaze of light and warmth greeted them as the cutest golden boy with bronze skin and hair and copper eyes threw open the front door.

"Mamá! They're here! Papá, what is in all of those packages? Are any of those for me?"

"Yes. And don't ask us any more questions or you won't get anything." Vadé laughed.

"Yes, I will! Day, Papá! Guess what?" he continued, even more excited than before.

"What?" Vadé was almost as excited as her brother.

They were in the entrance hall. A massive Louis III table sat opposite two upholstered benches. An engraving by the French painter Nicolas Poussin hung over the table.

"Mamá and I wrote a song. We're going to sing it tonight at the *reveilion.*"

In the salon, the main reception room, a fire was roaring in the fireplace and a Christmas tree stood waiting to be decorated.

"The tree." Vadé sighed with pleasure. She quickly unbuttoned her coat, tossed it on the end of the sofa, and ran across the room to the large fir.

"You better get busy, young lady."

Vadé was the spitting image of her mother, Desiree Chevalier, except she was cocoa, and Desiree was golden vanilla. Her blond silky straight hair was pinned up into a huge bun on the top of her head. A

mere five feet, she made up for what she lacked in height by her cap-
tivating beauty. Her voluptuous curves were unable to hide beneath
her cook's apron. She stared into her daughter's green eyes with an
identical set.

"Vadé, hang that coat up!"

Pierre picked up his daughter's coat, pulled his wife into his arms,
and kissed her.

"And you better get to those beignets or else you get no gumbo,
she said."

"That's what you think, woman. I'm getting a sample now."

He laughed as he tossed Vadé's coat back onto the couch, and ran
into the kitchen. Desiree ran behind him laughing, as Laurent sat
down next to his sister in front of a huge box of Christmas decorations. Vadé and Laurent always decorated the tree while their parents
cooked, kissed, and drank champagne in the kitchen. It was a family
tradition.

"That's nice that you and Mamá have a new song for tonight, Lar."

Lar was Vadé's own special pet name for her younger brother. She
started calling him that the day he came home from the hospital four-
teen years ago. No one called him Lar but Vadé, and the family.

The children took out a set of colored lights and strung them on
the tree. Laurent, a talented artist, was the master craftsman and
Vadé, his assistant. By the time they had hung the last bulb and string
of tinsel on the tree, their noses led them into the kitchen where their
father was sprinkling powdered sugar on a sheet of beignet. Desiree
poured everyone tall steaming cups of vanilla *latte* sprinkled with cinnamon and the family lit into the hot pastry.

"I hate this time of year." Desiree groaned as she picked up the last
piece, pulled it in half, and gave the largest portion to her son. "I always have to go on a diet in January."

"You're beautiful, Mamá," Laurent assured her.

"Thank you, sweetheart." She patted her hips and laughed. "It's the
only place where that African blood really shows," she reminded her
husband. "Vadé, Laurent, it's time for you to get dressed for Mass.
And, Vadé, clear those dishes from the table."

"*Oui*, Mamá." Vadé picked up her brother's dishes and added them
to her own.

"I'll help." Laurent jumped up and collected his parents' dishes for
his sister.

The only time she talks to me is when she's telling me what to do. Vadé placed the dishes in a black stone sink and rinsed out the cups.

"Did you get a present for JP?" Laurent teased, bringing her into the present. "I heard he has one for you." Laurent's eyes sparkled with mischief as he smiled at his sister.

"Where did you hear that? Did Little Claude tell you?"

"I'm not telling where I heard what, but JP does have a gift for you. You bought him a gift, didn't you, Day?"

"Yes." She smiled. "You know I did."

Little Claude was her brother's best friend. He was the son of their father's best friend, Big Claude, with whom he had started the jazz group. Laurent and Little Claude were the same age, born only days apart. The men had been in America handling business with the record company while their wives were in Paris. Desiree and Big Claude's wife, Giselle, were pregnant together. They swore the men had planned it that way.

Jean Paul, affectionately known as JP, was Little Claude's first cousin from America. He was eighteen, and had recently joined them for a year of classes at the University of Paris. He would continue his international relations degree at Grambling. He had been smitten with fifteen-year-old Vadé, as all the boys were. However, JP was older, American, and therefore a novelty to Vadé.

"I bought him a Dallas Cowboys jersey. You know he's always talking about that American football team."

"Good, he'll like that. I'm just glad you got him something, because I wouldn't want to see a grown man cry."

Vadé laughed and couldn't help smiling now that her brother had brought up JP. She saw her shopping bag on her canopy bed and slipped back into the living room to arrange her presents for the family under the tree. Her father's gifts were still sitting on the huge round coffee table. It was the centerpiece for a sofa and several Queen Anne chairs placed in a square. A huge brass chandelier hung from the ceiling over the table where two large candelabras sat ready for lighting. It was a beautiful room offering the same view of the garden as her boudoir, a story below.

She retreated to her room and entered a huge walk-in closet filled with all sorts of clothing and shoes. *I wonder how JP will like this.* She pulled a forest-green silk velvet dress out of the closet and held it in front of her as she went to stand in front of a mirror in the gleaming mahogany armoire.

Vadé chose her own clothes. She enjoyed the trips on the Metro to Les Halles, a multistoried glass and concrete shopping complex that housed some of the best boutiques in the city. She had purchased the dress especially for tonight but now she was doubtful. Maybe it wasn't sexy enough.

She walked across glistening parquet floors, past her favorite impressionist painting, out of her bedroom, and into her brother's.

"Lar, do you think this dress is sexy?"

"Day!" He blushed. He was in the middle of putting on a pair of crisp black trousers.

"Sorry. But you haven't got anything I haven't already seen. Do you think JP will like this?" She held up the short after-five dress in front of her as she stood in the mirror. "Is it sexy enough?"

"Sexy? You?" Her brother laughed.

"Never mind." She glanced up at her brother's *Purple Rain* poster as she left his room. "I should have known better than to ask you."

She could hear her brother still laughing as she went back into her room. She lit a fire in the fireplace and turned on Charlie Parker as she ran a bath in her sunken stone tub.

Bathed and dressed, she applied the pale copper lip gloss she was allowed to wear and placed it with her compact in her shoulder bag. Part of her hair was drawn up into an elegant bun and pinned with a diamond barrette in the front, while the rest of it hung down her back to her waist.

"You must never cut your hair, Vadé," her mother constantly reminded her. "A woman's hair is her glory." She fastened a strand of genuine pearls around her neck and a pair of teardrops to her ears and went into the living room, where she found her mother admiring herself in one of the room's numerous mirrors. She was striking in an emerald-green silk gown. A tiara diamond necklace sparkled at her throat and her hair was swept up into a chignon.

"You look beautiful, Mamá."

"Thank you, Vadé. Now run and get your brother. If we don't leave right now, we're going to be late for Mass."

As she headed toward the stairs, she heard her father come into the room and whistle.

"Look at my little princess."

Vadé stopped and twirled around so her father could see the front of the dress.

"Little?" Desiree repeated. "She's taller than me."

"Sweetheart, you look delightful, but isn't that dress a little too short?"

"It's fine, honey," Desiree interrupted. "That's how the girls are wearing them now."

"All right. I just better not see that JP drooling over you tonight."

"Papá!" she squealed, embarrassed by her father's interest and knowledge of her love life.

They usually walked to La Madeleine, a rather unusual-looking Catholic church named in honor of Mary Magdalene, but tonight they drove over in the family's Rolls.

Vadé loved the church with its dark, foreboding interior. Candles lit the building now and she could smell the lingering scent of the holy incense. When she was younger, she used to imagine that her childhood heroine, Madeleine, from her favorite books, was sitting next to her. They would beg Madame not to punish them for some mishap they had just caused. She used to tell Madeleine all her secrets and they would pray and ask God to make them good little girls.

She returned to the present when she heard everyone around her singing "Adeste Fideles," and she stood and sang from the hymnal with Laurent and her father. Her mother was up front, singing in the choir.

Vadé sighed happily, seated between the men she loved. JP was sitting in front of her with his family. He turned around to smile just as Desiree stood up to sing "Ave Maria." Her mother's rich clear alto voice was strong and beautiful. She looked at her brother who was rapt with attention as they all listened to the words of the song about Mother and Son, Mary and Jesus.

I love Christmas with the family.

TWO

Nearly everyone attending Mass was a guest of the Chevaliers' Christmas Eve soiree. This group of Parisians was part of the city's elite. Everyone was married or would be married at La Madeleine. They were extremely wealthy and they were artists . . . musicians, writers, painters, designers, or bankers and diplomats.

Laurent stood by his mother outside with their backs to Las Tuileries, the beautiful floral gardens adjacent to the church. The fresh-air market was open and doing big business. Customers were scooping up bouquets of freshly cut tulips, camellias, orchids, and palmariums. Laurent smiled as he watched Vadé and JP stroll off toward home so they could have a chance to be alone before the rest of the family and guests arrived.

"Come along, Mamá." He took his mother by the hand and led her over to his father. "The night air is not good for your voice, especially when you have to sing tonight and tomorrow. I'll make you some tea when we get home."

"All right, Laurent." She brushed her hand across her son's cheek and smiled. "Come, let's go sing and dance."

Desiree, always the center of attention, laughed as she chatted with her two adoring men. Little Claude joined them, whispered something to Laurent, and the two boys raced toward the house, laughing the entire time. They nearly ran Vadé over, who was just arriving with JP.

"Lar, be careful."

"What are the two of you doing?" Little Claude grinned impishly.

"Be cool, little brother, and tell Vadé you're sorry." JP spoke with a streetwise American accent. Vadé shivered in her mink coat at the sound of his voice.

"Sorry, Day."

"It's okay, Little Claude." Vadé kissed the boy on the cheek and smiled. "Look what JP gave me for Christmas." She extended a slender arm to expose a charm bracelet with a heart and a tiny diamond. The heart was engraved with the words *My Day*.

"Ooh," the boys cooed together.

"Shush," Vadé warned as all of their parents walked up, together.

The boys ran up the stairs laughing. They loved the way Vadé told them her secrets, and they would never betray her confidence.

"Vadé, go inside and put on some Christmas music. I want everyone to hear music as they come into the house."

"*Oui*, Mamá." She turned and ran up the stairs before her mother began giving her additional orders.

"I'll help you." JP ran up the steps behind her.

"I swear, every time I tell that girl to do something, some man rushes to do it for her."

"Like mother, like daughter." Pierre laughed.

"Pierre, you spoil her terribly."

"Guilty as charged."

"It's like the two of you have something going on."

"We do."

"Giselle, did you make the crawfish étoufée?" Desiree deliberately changed the subject.

"The crawfish and shrimp arrived this morning. We'll have a fine dinner at the club tomorrow." Big Claude smiled at his wife and kissed her.

Nat King Cole's classic Christmas music greeted everyone as they entered the main salon. The candelabras were lit and the Christmas tree blinked on and off to a beat of its own. The smell of freshly brewed coffee, vanilla, and sweet beignet filled the house. Waiters began dishing up gumbo over bowls of steamed rice. There was also roast duck, fish in a delectable cream sauce stuffed in lobster shells, and a sparkling punch.

Little Claude sat on a stool in the huge kitchen finishing off a bowl of gumbo while Laurent put a kettle of water on to boil. He lined up a cup and saucer, lemon slices, and honey in assembly-line fashion on the gunmetal granite counter. When the water was hot, he prepared a cup of tea for his mother and then made one for himself. He carefully set the cups on a silver tray with a doily and carried the tray into the salon.

"My little man, always taking care of me." Desiree picked up the cup and winked at her son. "Pierre, honey, will you introduce us?"

As Pierre made his way over to the grand piano, Desiree summoned her daughter to turn off the music.

"There's a lot of family tradition surrounding our annual *reveilion*. And now it's time for my favorite, after my wife's gumbo." Pierre was striking in a black Italian-cut suit. He flashed a Denzel Washington smile and had every female in the room swooning. "Ladies and gentlemen, Desiree and Laurent Chevalier."

Desiree extended her hand to her son and the two of them marched across the room together as everyone applauded. She loved entertaining and performing. She nodded to Pierre, who played a stanza of "Baby, It's Cold Outside."

It was effortless for Laurent to remain in step with his mother. He was the perfect dance partner. He carefully twirled her around. They were both wonderful dancers. She had taught him to dance by the time he learned to walk. His first performance was at the age of three, when he wandered out of Giselle's reach and onto the stage with his mother. Desiree, ever the consummate performer, made him a part of the act when she picked him up and held the microphone for him to sing.

Pierre played his last note and the room thundered with applause.

"Encore, encore!" everyone was yelling. Next they sang a duet in French. Normally, Laurent could have sung for their guests all night, but now he had other plans. He found Vadé and JP in the kitchen.

"Let's go downstairs and dance."

"Okay, Lar. We'll round up some more people and meet you downstairs."

The children were not allowed to have televisions in their rooms, but their parents had provided them with a media room, complete with a large-screen TV and a powerful music system. The room held thirty people quite comfortably.

Laurent and Little Claude put on a German disco record, cranked the volume, and hit the floor imitating Michael Jackson. They barely noticed Vadé and the others enter the room.

"What is that music you guys are trying to dance to?" JP laughed. "It's horrible."

"Something Lar found over in the Latin Quarter. He buys all of his music over there. He's always hanging out with those crazy college kids. They love it."

"You guys dance like white people." JP laughed, speaking loudly enough for only Vadé to hear.

"What do you mean?"

"You got anything else to play?"

"Sure." She led him over to Lar's collection of albums and CDs. "These are his treasures."

"I'll bring some of my music next time I come over."

They flipped through the discs until JP found an Isley Brothers CD. "This will work." He quickly changed the music while Laurent and Little Claude protested.

"Be cool, little brothers," he said in that tone that set Vadé's heart racing. "I'm going to teach you an American dance. Everyone lined up next to JP as he executed the latest hip-hop steps. Laurent stood directly behind him, watching his every move, before doing his own smooth version.

"Lar, stop showing out." Vadé laughed as she danced over to her brother. By now, everyone was standing around watching. "You know I taught you everything you know."

"You're the one who's showing out." He grinned as his sister spun around and everyone screamed.

Everyone was so noisy that Desiree and Pierre came to investigate. She made her way to the front of the circle that had formed around her children.

"Go, baby," she shouted to Laurent. The music ended and everyone cheered. Pierre put on Donny Hathaway's "This Christmas" and the media room was now a small disco as guys and girls partnered off. Laurent danced with one of his college friends. He could go from being a kid to charming in seconds.

"Your little brother is too smooth." JP laughed as he and Vadé danced around in a small circle. She could feel his warm breath as he whispered into her ear, and kissed him gently on the cheek.

"Thank you for my beautiful bracelet, JP."

Everyone left around four in the morning. Not a drop of gumbo was left in the house, except a pot Desiree managed to stash away for the family dinner at the club.

"Day, wake up." Laurent shook his sister gently around noon. "Let's go open our presents."

"Presents!" She jumped out of bed and they raced up the back stairs and through the kitchen. The house was silent as they tiptoed over to the Christmas tree overflowing with presents. They always opened their presents to each other while their parents were still asleep.

"Here, Day." He handed his sister a box. "Maybe this will help you be sexy." She squealed and handed him a gift, too.

"Go!" she yelled as they ripped through ribbons and paper.

"Day, these are great!" He was already reading the colors listed on a tin of forty paints. She also gave him pastels, pads of special drawing paper, an easel, and a Janet Jackson CD. She knew he loved American music.

"Where did you find this?" He held up the CD. "I've been looking for this everywhere." They had explored the Left Bank together, attending music and dance concerts and plays. The Sorbonne constantly kept them exposed to French pop culture.

"The same place you found this." She held up a gold metallic bikini. "Lar, this is fabulous." She was already imagining the look on JP's face when he saw her in it.

"Merry Christmas, Papá."

She looked up as her father sat down between her and Laurent.

"Merry Christmas, Papá!" She kissed his cheek and laughed as he rubbed his silky beard across her face.

"Here, Papá." Laurent handed his father a package and grinned.

They laughed as Pierre ripped off the paper like a child. "This is exactly the one that I told Santa Claus to bring me." He stuck the pipe he had unwrapped between his lips.

"And he told me!" Laurent beamed at his father, pleased because he was happy with his gift. He had examined pipes and sniffed various blends of tobacco for hours before he selected the perfect combination.

"Santa said you wanted this, too." Vadé watched him rip into her selections of Parisian and American novels. He was an avid reader, although he had never advanced his education past high school.

"Thank you, Princess." He handed her a box wrapped in the same paper as her mother's gift from the jewelry store.

"I knew you bought something else!" She gasped when she saw a pair of one-carat diamond stud earrings. "Papá!" She immediately placed them in her ears. "I feel beautiful!"

"You are beautiful, Princess."

"Pierre! You didn't buy that child those extravagant earrings."

"Merry Christmas, Mamá!" Laurent rushed to his mother's side. "Look what I have for you!" He always knew the right thing to say.

Vadé sometimes wondered if her brother was running interference between her and their mother, but she never said anything to him about it. She watched her mother smile and coo over her brother and stroke his bronzed hair as she removed the wrapping paper from a case of lipsticks and nail polishes.

"Here, Mamá. Merry Christmas." Vadé handed her mother the crucifix she had first spotted last summer. She had wanted it for herself, but decided to give it to her mother.

Desiree looked at her daughter and carefully tore off the elegant foil wrapping. "It's too pretty to open, *mon ami.*"

Vadé felt herself choke up at the endearment. She loved her mother dearly and wished she would lavish her with the same attention she constantly gave her brother, instead of always making demands.

"This is the most beautiful thing I have ever seen." She looked at her daughter, amazed. "Come here."

She pulled Vadé into her arms and kissed her on the cheek. Vadé struggled against the tears that wanted to flow, and fastened the chain around her mother's slender long neck.

"Stand next to Mamá!" Laurent twisted the lens on his 35mm camera. "I want to take a picture."

Mother and daughter focused identical gray-green eyes on him and smiled.

"A queen and a princess." Laurent snapped the photograph and smiled at them.

"A queen and a princess." Pierre smiled at his two favorite ladies, and silently prayed that the color of his daughter's beautiful sepia skin would never bring her the pain that his had brought him.

THREE

The club, Olivier's, was on the Left Bank in Montparnasse, an area of Paris well known for its fabulous nightlife. During the late 1940s when the constraints of German occupation were over, Boboino's music hall, popularized by Josephine Baker, gave Parisians the opportunity to talk openly again . . . to drink, dance, and make noise, love, and enjoy music as they had longed to since 1940. Decades later, crowded jazz cellars and select private clubs still did great business.

Pierre paused to light a *gauloises,* his favorite French cigarette, and blew out the match with a blast of smoke. He loved the rich, acrid tobacco for its strong, mellow taste. There was a spot etched on his smooth lips where the cigarette would dangle while he played. He would close his eyes and feel the coolness of the ivory keys as the sound of his own musical creation filled his soul.

"Chevalier, let's eat, man." Claude Olivier, a good-looking Creole with olive skin and black, curly hair, was Pierre's oldest and best friend. He had been a horn player in Beau's band that performed nightly at Richoux's, a restaurant in the French Quarter of New Orleans where Pierre used to wait tables.

"Get a plate for that sandwich, Little Claude. And bring plates for all of us, too."

"Yes sir." He took an additional bite from a steak sandwich and went into the kitchen as Laurent set four bottles of Coke on the table. Pierre gulped down the entire bottle in a matter of seconds.

"Go get your Uncle Claude and me a beer, son. You ready for tonight, man?" Pierre looked at his friend and grinned.

"I was born ready. Remember that New Year's Eve bash at Richoux's? Man, you wore us out that night."

"How can I forget that night, man?

"I can see Beau's face now." Big Claude laughed. "He wanted to kill you."

"Tell us again, Uncle Claude." Laurent never grew tired of hearing the stories about the good old days.

"That was the night Amour was born." Big Claude spoke solemnly.

"Tell us," Little Claude urged. "Please?"

"The first time I saw your father, he was playing the heck out of Richoux's old piano. It was the middle of the day and I dropped by the restaurant early, to leave my suit that I had just picked up from the cleaners. At first, I thought it was Beau until he started playing Beau's music, better than Beau. And then he started playing some pieces I had never heard."

"I used to fool around on the piano when I was in high school on the island," Pierre added. "I could play anything I heard, including the songs playing in my head."

"Songs playing in your head?" Little Claude popped the last bite of his sandwich into his mouth.

"Yes," Laurent explained quickly. "I always hear songs in my head, too. Mamá gave me a tape recorder to sing into so I won't forget them."

"Well, all of your daddy's songs were in his head. Some of the most beautiful arrangements and melodies I ever heard."

"Big Claude went to college and he knew how to read and write music," Pierre said. "I would play my tunes for him, and he put them down on paper. He scored pages and pages of music. He did arrangements for every instrument in the band and we had them copywritten. Your mother added words to many of them years later."

Big Claude continued the story. "We worked as often as we could. We had done at least twenty songs by the end of the year. Richoux's, like every other club with a band, did big business on New Year's Eve. Beau's piano player came down with the flu and couldn't play. You don't have a band without a piano."

"Couldn't Beau play?" Little Claude looked at his father.

"Beau could play a little bit. But he was always much better at standing in front of us and waving that baton around, like he was the Duke or Count Basie, than playing the piano."

Both men laughed as they traveled the road to yesteryear.

"So he had to let you play, didn't he, Papá?" Laurent smiled at his father proudly.

"Sure did. No one knew he could play like that except me and old man Richoux, who told Beau he had to let Chevalier play because there was no time to find another band." Big Claude paused to finish his beer. Laurent pushed another toward him so the men would continue talking.

"Chevalier lit into that piano like never before. It had to be the crowd giving him all that extra energy."

"I know exactly what you mean." Laurent, in another world, spoke softly.

"Beau fired me that night," Big Claude reflected. "Said we were trying to steal his band from him."

"We put our own band together and we've been partners ever since," Pierre finished. "Happy New Year, my friend."

The men clicked empty beer bottles together, toasting their years of friendship, music, and success. They were coowners of the group and club.

They had modernized a bistro, retaining the long sinuous bar and covering its sides and the walls of the club with various patterns of gleaming brass. White marble with flecks of black and gold capped the bar. Tables covered with white linen cloths were positioned around the room, offering an unhindered view of the bandstand, but still leaving enough room on the mosaic-tiled floor for dancing. Bouillabaisse, *croque-monsieurs*—grilled ham and cheese sandwiches made with goat cheese and cinnamon—and music were Olivier's specialties.

By ten that night, the club was filled to capacity. Tuxedoed waiters moved about the room ensuring that everyone had a glass of champagne. The band outfitted in crisp white dinner jackets played softly while couples swayed back and forth to the music.

Desiree sat at a table reserved for the family and special guests. She was radiant in a chartreuse beaded evening gown. Giselle, her best friend and first cousin, was beside her fashionably attired in the latest Parisian creation in black. They had spent the afternoon in and out of boutiques until they found the perfect thing for Giselle, who had decided at the last minute to go shopping. Like their men, they too shared a history. They had always been close growing up, but after four years of college in Paris, their intertwined destinies were sealed forever.

They had vowed never to tell each other's secrets. They were wild women, on the loose. They hung out in jazz clubs every night once they hit Parisian soil. Desiree's voice wooed countless audiences while Giselle drank expensive French champagne with other local performers who were part of the artist set known around the city as *les posh*. They frequented the finest cafés, bistros, and nightclubs. When any of the American R&B funk bands played in Paris, you would always find them at a *les posh* soiree.

During the day, the girls attended the University of Paris. Desiree's curriculum consisted of ballet, literature, and painting. If her father had ever suspected she was onstage singing, she knew she would be ordered home, but he had never found out.

"Those men look good tonight." Giselle lit a cigarette and smiled at her cousin.

"They sure do." Desiree watched a waiter refill her champagne flute. Vadé, seated near her mother and Giselle, focused her attention on their conversation.

"Remember the first time we saw them play?"

"The dance at the college."

The champagne made them both giddy as they sat there laughing like teenagers.

"Pierre was the finest thing I ever laid eyes on. I made my mind up right then that I was going to marry that fine, French-speaking man, or die trying. His accent drove me crazy."

"You and everybody else."

Vadé covered her mouth with her hand to suppress a smile. Her mother must have consumed a great deal of champagne to speak so freely.

"Uncle Maurice must have suspected something after the two of you met because days later we were on our way to Paris."

"I know. We had begged our fathers to send us away to school and suddenly we were on a plane. I should never have asked my brother to introduce us to Pierre. I know he told Father."

"You should have known better. You know how they feel about . . ."

Giselle looked up to see Vadé hanging on to her every word. She tried to appear uninterested but Giselle had caught her listening.

"Vadé, sweetie, go out to the kitchen and tell Cook to fry up a basket of shrimp. I'm hungry."

Desiree nodded her approval and Vadé dragged herself away from the table. *Just when we were getting to the good part.*

She knew there was some mystery surrounding her parents' marriage, but whatever it was, it was never discussed in front of the children. She had never met her grandparents from either side of the family. She knew her parents had married in Harlem and lived in Paris ever since. She had never been to America. Giselle and Little Claude flew over every year, but the Chevaliers never left Paris, except Pierre, for an occasional business trip to New York City.

She paused to look at her father's awards housed in a glass case. Her favorites were the miniature gold phonographs. He called them Grammies. The kitchen was extremely busy. She saw Cook and rattled off Giselle's order in French. None of the staff spoke English.

JP appeared out of nowhere, catching her by the waist. "You can speak French to me any time, baby."

She smiled at the sound of his voice and before she knew what was happening, he whisked her into a nearby closet and kissed her.

"Happy New Year, Day."

It was the first time a boy had ever kissed her. She felt her insides melt like hot butter.

"Happy New Year, Jean Paul." She spoke in French. He kissed her again, and she thought she would die. "Come." She took him by the hand and led him out of the closet. "We don't want to miss the New Year."

Giselle nudged her cousin and pointed to Vadé and JP as they found a place on the dance floor. "They look so cute together. Is that a Dior Vadé is wearing?"

"Yes. Can you believe her? That child dresses better than me."

"Did Pierre get it for her?"

"Who else? But she picked it out herself. You know I've been letting her do her own shopping since she was ten. She even goes to view the Collections."

"She has a wonderful sense of style, Dez. We should have sent her shopping for my dress. . . . And she's going to be tall like Pierre, not a shorty with big hips like you. You should let her model for the Collections. She'd be fabulous."

"No way. I catch her in the mirror all the time now."

"That sounds familiar."

"Giselle, I was never as bad as her. Pierre has her so spoiled that no man will ever be able to meet her expectations, let alone afford her."

"Dez, please. She's just like you. Where do you think she gets it? Little Claude says all the boys at school are crazy about her."

Desiree shook her head as she watched her daughter. "No, G . . . I was never that sophisticated nor that beautiful."

A waiter brought Giselle's shrimp. Laurent and Little Claude, also dressed in black tuxedo pants and white dinner jackets like their fathers, appeared at the table seconds later. She sprinkled the jumbo golden-fried shrimp with Louisiana hot sauce and pushed the basket toward the boys.

"Like mother, like daughter," Giselle taunted with twinkling eyes.

Desiree bit into a plump shrimp. "I don't have time for you now, girl. It's time for me to go sing with my husband."

She held out her hand to Laurent. It was his cue to escort her onstage. Pierre smiled when he saw her stand in front of the microphone that stood waiting for her.

"Bonsoir," she cooed into the mike. She closed her eyes and sang a Chevalier classic. She had recorded vocals with the group and performed nightly when she was younger. But now they performed only three or four nights a week, leaving the others for dancing and private parties. Applause filled the room and Pierre joined her at the microphone to count down the New Year.

"*Trois, deux, un* . . . Happy New Year!" they shouted into the mike together. Pierre kissed her until the infectious beat of "Billie Jean" had everyone on the floor.

Laurent, dancing and singing in a world of his own, had gathered a crowd around himself as usual. Vadé, Little Claude, and JP were cheering him on.

"Chevalier, that son of yours is going to steal our band." Big Claude laughed. "Look at him."

"Go, Laurent, go, Laurent!" Everyone in the club was shouting his name.

Vadé looked around the room relishing the looks of joy on the people's faces as they watched him dance. Everyone was having a great time. She looked up on the bandstand to see her parents' reactions. As usual, Mamá was smiling and applauding, but she had to look twice when she saw the intense frown clouding her father's handsome face.

FOUR

The house was abnormally quiet for a Saturday morning. Vadé moved around the kitchen in silence as she placed a steaming pot of café au lait, croissants, and various dishes of strawberry, blackberry, and apricot preserves on a tray. She added fresh cream, sugar, and an extra sprinkle of cinnamon to the coffee and carried the tray downstairs to the media room.

She turned her favorite Charlie Parker CD on low before she peeked in her brother's room and found him still asleep. He had stayed up most of the night with the new Playstation. Vadé took a bite of the buttery pastry and smiled knowingly . . . Charlie Parker and fresh coffee with frothy steamed milk would have her brother out of bed in no time. Minutes later he was standing over her.

"What's that, Day?" Laurent poured himself a cup of *creme* and spread a croissant with apricot jam.

"Just an idea I had for a dress and jacket." She hummed softly as she stared at the tray of chalks, selected the perfect shade of orange and yellow, and filled in the outline of the dress with an intricate design.

"That looks good. I didn't know you could draw."

"I can't. At least not like you and Mamá." She added a few additional strokes to the pad and pushed it aside. "I was experimenting with your pastels while you showered. You'd better hurry so we won't be late."

Saturday mornings were always spent at the Louvre. When Vadé and Laurent were younger, the nanny would take them to the museum to keep them from waking their parents. Now that they were older, they attended art classes.

Laurent poured the last of the coffee into his cup. "I'm almost done with my interpretation of a Monet work for class. Let's go over to the Latin Quarter after lunch and see a movie."

"Aren't you the daring one, living on the edge," she teased. "What do you want to see?"

"*The Sound of Music.*"

"Again?"

"You know how I love that movie."

"I know. I love it too."

"We've seen everything else worth seeing. I wish we lived in America so we could get all of the good things when they premiere and not several months later."

"Lar, you really want to live in America?" Vadé knew her brother was in love with American pop culture, but he had never expressed a desire to live there.

"I don't know yet. I might like to live in New York or LA."

"That's interesting. . . ." She had never thought about living anywhere but Paris. She loved Paris and knew in her heart that she'd never be happy anywhere else. Paris was her home. "I'll take these dishes upstairs, get some money, and meet you downstairs in the courtyard."

She counted out a wad of francs from the stash that Desiree kept in the cookie jar. They were used to planning their own adventures. Family activities were limited to holidays and vacations. By the time they returned from the cinema, her parents would be at the club again.

Laurent was waiting for her by the fountain in the courtyard. He stood there watching the water splash down a small waterfall into a garden pond with goldfish. His leather schoolbag was draped over his shoulder. It contained art pads and pastels for his Saturday morning impressionist art class at the Louvre. He joined his sister as she pushed open the gate and they walked together in silence the short distance to the museum, their thoughts focused on the three-hour workshops ahead.

"Lar, let's eat at the Rue Mouffetard market." Vadé turned up the walkway toward the art deco section of the Louvre to the interior design studio. "I'll meet you by the Metro after class."

She swung her long legs over a stool and flipped open her old Madeleine lunch tin and removed various swatches of fabric and wallpaper. She was furnishing and decorating the living room of her villa. She had already spent weeks visiting antique stores snapping Polaroids. She sifted through a pile of tapestries, brocades, and satins searching for the perfect color. It was like putting together a puzzle. All the pieces were there. She just had to find them.

Before Vadé knew it, class was over. She stopped to pick up her notebook from her teacher on the way out. It was filled with detailed notes on various types of furniture, fabric swatches, wallpaper, and paint selections. She had even taped in pictures from magazines of various rooms as additional samples of flooring and furniture. A class project called for her to decorate a Mediterranean villa.

"Mademoiselle Chevalier, your notebook was magnificent and you have impeccable taste. One day you shall be the most sought-after interior decorator in all of Paris."

"Really, monsieur?" Her instructor was never one to give such a lavish compliment.

"*Oui*, mademoiselle. I am anxious to see what you do with such an extraordinary gift."

Vadé smiled all the way to the subway. *Imagine me . . . a great Parisian interior decorator.* She could hardly wait to tell Papá.

Laurent was already waiting for her at the Metro. She dashed up to the train moments before the doors closed and the two of them scooted in just as the warning siren sounded. She wanted to share her good news with Lar, but he was listening to his Sony Walkman so she stared out of the window and daydreamed of Vadé's House of Interior Design as the train zipped along.

The ride to the market was brief. Vadé and Laurent exited the train and trotted up a steep narrow street to the Rue Mouffetard. They would have lunch first. They strolled down the aisles past stands of shiny fresh fruit and vegetables, meat, cheese, and seafood so fresh it was still squirming in buckets of ice water, to an American restaurant.

"We already know what we want," Laurent informed the waiter before he handed them menus. "We'd like two double-decker cheeseburgers with the works, french fries, and onion rings."

"And two chocolate malts," Vadé added.

"With whipped cream."

"This is going to be so good. I wonder if I should get chili on my cheeseburger."

Vadé shook her head and laughed. Lar loved to eat and he loved cheeseburgers. A waitress set two chocolate malts on the table, so thick that they had to be eaten with a spoon.

"I got an A on my impressionist painting. Look."

Vadé gasped when Laurent exposed a watercolor drawing of the fountain and garden pond in the courtyard of their town house. He had even drawn in the pattern of the mosaics.

"Lar . . . this is so good! Can I have it, please? I know the exact place for it in my room. Over my Louis the Third desk."

"You can have *this* one, but I'm going to sell them to you from now on." He smiled at her with twinkling eyes and she laughed.

"Guess what?" She spooned a dab of the malt and cream into her mouth. "My instructor said I could become the most sought-after interior designer in Paris!"

"That's really great, Day. You'll be a famous designer and I'll be a famous singer. We'll be known all over the world."

Vadé laughed at the thought. "Laurent Chevalier. You'll have to change your name. That sounds so conservative. You'll have to think of something cool."

"I'm going to use Lar Legrande."

"Lar Legrande . . . That just might work."

"I know, Vadé Chevalier. Now, that sounds like the name of an interior designer. You'll be rich and JP can take care of your money."

"Now, why do you think I'll need JP to take care of my money?"

"Because every woman needs a good man, and every man needs a good woman." He swirled several fries through ketchup and popped them into his mouth.

"Oh . . . and where did you get this information?"

"From Big Claude. And Papá agreed. They say it's important for a man to have a good woman. And I intend to have someone who'll be good to me."

Vadé chewed her burger thoughtfully. Lar was always saying things like that lately. "And are you and this good woman going to live in America?" she inquired, not really wanting to hear his answer. She didn't care for all these plans of Lar's. She wanted things to stay just like they were.

"Maybe . . . I'm not sure yet. You ready to go?"

She counted out francs for their lunch and left a generous tip for the waiter. They still had several hours before the cinema, so Lar phoned Little Claude and made plans for them to meet later.

The shopping mall of choice today was Le Galerie, a wonderful collection of interesting shops, perfect for browsing. They strolled down cobblestone passages to Lar's favorite music store hidden behind a crumbling facade.

Aretha Franklin was blasting and Lar headed straight for the pop music CDs. Vadé flipped through a bin of jazz on vinyl. Her father still preferred his old albums.

"I can't spend all my money on music," Lar said. *I better get out of here.* "You ready, Day?" He knew she would be. She didn't buy many CDs herself. She liked whatever he and Papá enjoyed. She joined her brother at the cash register while he paid for his treasures.

"What's that?"

"The Funkadelics, an American R and B band."

"Lar, you always have money. I know you get it from Mamá."

"So? You get yours from Papá."

She watched him count from a neatly clipped wad and laughed when she saw the paper clip. *I'll get him a real money clip from the Chanel boutique for his birthday on St. Valentine's Day.* Their birthdays were only a week apart.

The siblings strolled through the passage inspecting hand-painted china for Vadé's villa, Playstation cartridges, perfumes, and books. Vadé carefully examined the section of new releases while Lar flipped through poetry books.

She moaned with pleasure when she found signed copies of several different *Babar* classics in a bin of old children's books. A closer inspection rewarded her with *Le Petit Prince* and a Laura Ingalls Wilder title.

"We'd better get going." Vadé found Laurent was immersed in a volume of French poetry. "I'll buy that for you."

He closed the book and returned it to the shelf. "I have that book at home. But you can buy this for me." He handed her a copy of Maya Angelou poems. "JP was telling me about her. You know he likes poetry, too."

"I cannot wait until you have a girlfriend. I'm going to tell her how you sleep with that stupid teddy bear if you don't leave me alone."

"Okay, Day. Okay. I'll stop. I promise." He was laughing hard because she knew he still slept with Monsieur Bear.

"But what makes you think I don't have a girlfriend now? Actually I have several."

"Who?" Vadé was shocked. "That Celeste Vivienne from L'Ecole?" Celeste, a gorgeous French girl, was in her class. She was very popular and Vadé hated her because she had the hots for her brother. Celeste was too old to be serious about Lar. She had even tried to become Vadé's friend to get closer to Lar.

"Oh, she likes me . . . a lot. But I like this girl at the university."

"The university? How old is *she?* And how come you didn't tell me?"

"Because I knew you would react this way. She's only seventeen."

"Seventeen? Does Mamá know? What's her name?"

"Mamá and Papá met her. She was at the Christmas *reveilion.*"

"Why didn't you introduce her to me?"

"Because you were too busy with JP."

They stepped onto an escalator that took them to the last level of Les Halles where the movie theaters were located.

Lar sure has lots of secrets these days. Her mind wandered with thoughts of her brother. He would be fifteen next month, but he was still too young to date. Vadé couldn't officially date JP until she turned sixteen in February.

"Little Claude's already here and look who's with him." Laurent sprinted the remaining stairs on the escalator to his best friend.

Vadé, back in the present, felt her heart beating under her heavy sweater the moment she laid eyes on JP. She was glad that she had taken a moment to put on lipstick and smooth her hair. She was wearing designer jeans and a white silk shirt. The diamond studs sparkled at her ears.

"We already purchased the tickets. You can buy the snacks, Laurent."

The cousins grinned in agreement and rushed to make their candy selections before the movie started.

"I've got your snacks right here," JP whispered into Vadé's ear. She blushed as JP kissed her in front of the boys.

"I like your snacks." She smiled.

JP purchased chocolates, popcorn, and drinks for them to eat in the movies. Seated several rows behind her brother and Little Claude, they saw very little of the movie. They kissed through the entire thing. JP's breath was sweet and it tasted like strawberry bubble gum.

"You are so beautiful," he whispered. "My sweet, chocolate girl."

Vadé smiled and rested her head on his shoulder. She really did like JP. He was her best friend after Lar. *Maybe Lar is right about me needing a good man. . . .*

"Lar? What did you think of the movie?" JP asked as they rode down the escalator.

Lar . . . That's my name for Laurent. No one calls him Lar but me . . . and Little Claude. She looked sideways at JP. *I guess it's okay. He is family.*

Her brother's response prompted a heated conversation on musicals and American films.

Later, as they watched music videos while waiting for the Metro, JP rubbed her hands to keep them from getting cold. It was an unusually chilly, damp night. She looked at her brother laughing with Little Claude and wondered if they were talking about Lar's mystery girl.

JP snuggled closer and kissed her on the cheek, but her thoughts were back on her brother. *I can't believe Lar has a girlfriend and he didn't tell me.*

FIVE

Today is May 7, Mamá and Papá's eighteenth wedding anniversary. Everyone is so excited. There's a big party at Olivier's tonight. I have a new dress. It's green and a Dior, of course. I found a little pair of gold sandals and a gold Chanel bag on markdown at the boutique. I hope JP thinks I am tres magnificent. I'm writing on the Metro, on my way home from L'Ecole. Today was a half day. I only have ballet and French literature on mercredi et vendredi.

Vadé closed her journal and returned it to her Chanel backpack. Before she closed the bag, she took a quick peek into the secret compartment where she kept her Visa and cash. She saw a few francs as she remembered the Visa was still lying on her dressing table, which meant she would have to go home and get it if she wanted to go shopping.

She dashed off the train before the doors closed at the Louvre exit and sprinted the few blocks to the town house so she could return to the station before the next train arrived.

"Bonjour, *mon ami.*"

She was surprised to find her mother sitting in the salon and dressed.

"Bonjour, Mamá." Vadé dropped her backpack on the floor by the sofa and ran toward the kitchen.

"Your father is not home. He already left for the club. Now come here." Desiree patted the spot beside her on the sofa as she looked at her daughter.

"*Oui*, Mamá."

"I want to talk to you."

Vadé sat on the sofa across from her mother.

"Over here." Desiree watched her daughter as she responded to her request. "Do you think you're too old to sit next to your mother?"

"No, Mamá." Desiree looked at Vadé's long lean legs hanging out from under the short gray and maroon school uniform. "You're getting so big and very pretty. How was school?"

"*Bien.*"

"Do you know what today is?"

"Of course I do, Mamá. Happy anniversary." She leaned over to kiss her mother's smooth, scented cheek.

"I was just so surprised to see you up that I forgot. I thought you would be asleep or having tea in your boudoir."

"I am about to have tea and I want you to join me."

"Yes, Mamá. I'll get everything ready."

"Everything's done. I just need you to help me carry some things into the bedroom."

She followed Desiree into the kitchen where several plates of food were covered on a silver serving tray.

"If you bring the champagne we can go into my room and begin the celebration."

Champagne on a school day? This is a celebration. "Is T'Giselle coming?"

"No, *mon ami.* Just you and me, if that's all right with you."

Desiree's eyes sparkled with excitement as she poured champagne into two baccarat flutes.

"No, Mamá, I don't mind. Is Lar coming?"

"No. This is a mother-daughter eighteenth wedding anniversary tea." She handed her a glass of champagne. "Do you want to make a toast?"

"Yes! To you and Papá! May your love last forever!"

"Thank you, sweetheart."

They gently clicked their glasses and drank. Desiree uncovered a plate of sliced, smoked Louisiana sausages in a pile of steaming red beans, rice, and potato salad.

"Look, Vadé. I made our favorites."

"Ooh, Mamá! This is so good." Vadé loved her mother's cooking, especially the Creole dishes she sometimes prepared, when she had the time.

The cool verdant shades of the boudoir reflected in Desiree's eyes. They also complemented the sea-foam-green skirt and silk blouse. She was wearing the emeralds her husband had purchased for her on a previous anniversary.

"I ran away from home to marry your father." Desiree stared at an invisible spot on the wall. "My father hated the band and he definitely didn't approve of your father."

"Why, Mamá?"

"He didn't want me to be in show business. He wanted me to marry some rich, boring attorney who was the son of one of his friends. I almost gave in, too, until I met your father, again."

"Again?"

"The first time I met your father I was only sixteen. I fell in love the minute I laid eyes on him. He was so fine, and that accent!"

Vadé smiled at her mother as she continued speaking.

"The first time I don't think he noticed me. He had lots of young ladies after him and most of them were older than me."

"Papá . . . girlfriends?" Vadé laughed out loud.

"Vadé, your daddy was extremely handsome and rich. He could have any girl he wanted."

"So what happened?"

"Your grandfather sent me to school in Paris several days later. I didn't see your father again until I was twenty. Giselle's parents gave us a party to let all of the eligible young men know we were back in town and ready for courting."

"Courting?"

"Dating. Big Claude was there and your daddy, too. That's when I met him the second time."

"Did he ask you out?"

"Not at first. He told Big Claude that I was too young."

"Too young?" Vadé poured a cup of tea for herself.

"Too young. But I knew he liked me . . . and he fell in love with me when he heard me sing. He said I was definitely a woman because no child could sing the way I did."

Vadé laughed as her mother continued.

"Giselle helped too. She and Big Claude were very serious. They got married later that same summer but your father had his mind on his music so we needed a little help. Giselle suggested I sing with the band. I had been singing in nightclubs in Paris for the last four years. Your daddy flipped when he heard me sing. He opened up and started telling me all of his dreams and plans for the band and how he wanted me right there beside him. The band had received an offer to tour in Europe, and Pierre wanted me to come with him but he said we had to get married first."

"You were ready to get married at twenty years old?"

"I was twenty-one. People married earlier in those days. Your daddy was the only man who ever understood me . . . my dream to sing and dance. He was so exciting. There was no way that I wasn't going to marry him. He was my best friend. Now all we had to do was tell my father."

"What did Grandpère say?"

"He didn't like the idea one bit and forbade me to go."

"What did he say?"

"He told me if I left the house to marry that man to never come back again."

"Never?"

"Never."

So that's why we've never met our grandparents. "What did you do then?"

"Well, I wasn't about to lose my dream and my man so I ran away with your father. We flew to New York and were married that same night at a club in Harlem. Your father's band used to perform there. Big Claude was the best man and Giselle was my maid of honor. A minister from a local church performed the ceremony "

"That is so romantic."

Desiree had her wedding photos out and pointed to various pictures. Vadé had seen them all before but now they took on a new meaning with her mother's narrative.

"The Temptations and Marvin Gaye sang for us."

Vadé studied each picture carefully.

"That's a beautiful dress, Mamá. Did you know you were going to be married when you bought it?"

"No. I bought that dress from a boutique for graduation but I never wore it until my wedding day."

Desiree poured the last of the champagne into her glass and stuck the empty bottle back into the silver ice bucket.

"Our honeymoon was like a never-ending fairy tale. We left for Paris the next day. We were onstage every morning until four. We'd sleep in until evening and then we were up and back onstage again. Candlelight dinners and champagne every night."

Desiree glanced over her glass at her daughter.

"It was a crazy wild life, but we all loved it. I guess that's why we stayed in Paris. It's like the honeymoon never ended. After you were born, we moved into an apartment to give you some stability. We needed more space after Laurent was born so we bought this house."

"Did you miss your parents?" Vadé spoke softly, not wanting to spoil the magical moment for her mother, but eager to learn more about the family she had never met.

"Yes . . . but not as much as I used to. Time heals all wounds. But I've never regretted it. Your father is the only man I ever loved. He was my first love and he'll be my last."

"Who's having a party without me?" Laurent interrupted their girl talk as he entered the room. "Hi, Day! Hello, Mother!" Laurent kissed Desiree on the cheek and drank the last drops of her champagne.

"Mother?" She pulled her son into her lap and kissed him. "Since when did you start calling me Mother?"

"Lar is quite the American now, Mamá. He even wants to live in New York or Los Angeles."

"Lar can live anywhere he wants."

Laurent stuck out his tongue at his sister and she laughed.

"Just as long as it's in this town house," Desiree quickly added.

Laurent inspected the remains on their plates."Ooh. You guys had red beans and rice. Is there any more?" He gave his mother his most charming smile.

"Of course there is. In the kitchen, sweetheart. I'll warm some up for you."

The two of them got up from the love seat and headed toward the kitchen, as Vadé gathered up the dirty dishes.

"Happy anniversary, Mamá!"

"Oh yes, happy anniversary, Mamá!" Laurent added.

"Thank you, *mon ami.*" Desiree smiled at her daughter with sparkling green eyes that shone with excitement from their private conversation.

Later in her boudoir, before she dressed for her parents' anniversary party, Vadé opened her journal.

Mamá and I had a wonderful time today. She prepared a special tea and she told me her secrets . . . how she met Papá and when they fell in love and married. For the first time, I felt like we were friends.

SIX

The International Music Festival held annually in July on the white sand beaches of Cannes against the azure Mediterranean was another family tradition. Every summer the entire family, Chevaliers and Oliviers, escaped to their summer home in Antibes, perfectly situated between Nice and Cannes on the French Riviera. The villa was nestled on a bluff in Cap d'Antibes overlooking the sparkling bay. The twenty-one rose-, aqua-, and peach-roomed house was more like a miniature hotel than a summer home.

The bedrooms offered their occupants breathtaking views of the private beach or exotic gardens and chiseled cobalt-blue mountains. There were freshly cut flowers everywhere. The family's suites were located on the third story of the pink-washed structure. Oliviers and Chevaliers shared a large sitting room and kitchen. There was a wonderful pool and deck, which offered a view of the grounds below. A small restaurant and the main salons were found on the first floor.

Cook, the club's best chef, was on hand to run the kitchen. Menus were posted daily. The family's meals were sent up from the kitchen. Platters of *fruits de mer*—fish fritters, warm scallop salads, and grilled salmon were family favorites.

Vadé was having breakfast alone. She sat on the deck with a plate of fresh fruit, warm muffins, and *un omelet des scallops* listening to the wild birds chirp. The boys had gone to pick up Laurent's friend

Simone. She was visiting for the weekend with her parents as guests of the family.

Vadé heard them get off the lift in the kitchen. Laurent was telling one of his favorite anecdotes and everyone was laughing. *Lar, ever the charmer.*

JP sat down across from her and quickly covered a Belgian waffle with warm syrup and stuffed a sizable portion of it into his mouth.

"You ready?"

"I just need to get my sunglasses and suntan oil."

"You should see your brother's friend, she is beautiful."

"Really?" Vadé stiffened in her seat. "What does she look like?"

"Beautiful. Here she comes."

Vadé watched her brother stroll out on the deck in white tennis shorts. The Mediterranean sun and water had deepened his bronze complexion and lightened his curly hair. The muscles in his thighs and calves gently rippled with every step.

"Day, I want you to meet my friend Simone." He smiled at an olive-skinned beauty with sparkling honey eyes and jet-black hair. Iridiscent pink lip gloss shimmered on her lips. She looked just like the fashion models in *European Vogue.*

"Hi." She kissed Vadé on both cheeks warmly. "Lar's told me all about you."

Lar? Vadé returned the greeting. "Welcome to the villa."

"Traffic in Cannes will be heavy today with Madonna performing at the music festival. We'd better get going." JP swiped a napkin across his mouth and extended a hand to Vadé. "Come on, baby, let's get the car."

Vadé smiled as she caught her slender hand in JP's strong one, admiring her summer-reddened mocha skin next to his coppery hue. This was the first summer that the children had their own car. Papá and Big Claude had leased a convertible Mercedes for them. JP, shy of nineteen by only several weeks, was the designated driver.

Laurent and Little Claude climbed in the back with Simone, as JP cranked the stereo.

"Are you wearing that gold metallic bikini?" he yelled over the music.

"Yes, but you won't be able it see until later at the pool party." She removed her sunglasses and smiled into his eyes.

"Cool." His accent had softened after a year in Paris, but it still drove her crazy.

"I know you're going to give me some of your sweet chocolate before I go back to New Orleans next month. School starts the day after Labor Day."

"Labor Day? Labor Day was in May."

"I keep forgetting you're not from America. We have a Labor Day, too. It's our last summer holiday back in the States."

"Oh . . ."

She turned to gaze out of the window. This wasn't their first discussion about sex. At L'Ecole, the sisters always told them good Catholic girls remain virgins. She stroked the back of JP's hand, allowing her fingers to caress the silky black strands of hair surrounding his watch.

"If I don't decide to become a nun, I might marry you. Then and only then will you have some of my *amour de chocolate*."

Her green eyes twinkled with mischief as she tried to keep a straight face. She had no intention of becoming a nun, nor a desire to get married. The only thing she wanted to do was decorate houses.

"Marriage? That won't be until forever, Day." JP looked hurt as he parked the Mercedes and cut off the engine. "I want to be with you now."

Vadé looked to see if the boys had heard any of their conversation as she got out of the car, but they were having their own conversation with Simone. They scrambled out of the backseat and headed toward the stage on the beach carrying lawn chairs. The boys looked a lot like brothers. Little Claude, not quite as tall, had green eyes like Vadé, and black hair.

"It won't be forever, JP. I'm only sixteen. I don't want to marry anyone yet. I have to attend design school at the university first."

"I forget you're only sixteen. You just look too good, baby. And that body is definitely not sixteen."

She was wearing a gold and white midriff top with a white sarong and gold sandals. He looked her up and down with a look that made her shiver.

"You want me." His tone was not lacking confidence. "I can see it in your eyes."

"Maybe after college."

"Maybe during college. You can go to school with me in New Orleans." He pulled her into his arms and kissed her.

"New Orleans . . . never. I'm not leaving France. So you'll just have to move back to Paris and live with me!"

"You want me to live with you? This is getting better already."

"You know what I mean. Let's go!" She jogged off in the direction of the boys.

"You know you want me, girl!" JP laughed and ran to catch her.

The boys had set up chairs near the front under a tent reserved for VIPs. They were all drinking Evian while Laurent rubbed suntan oil on Simone's back.

"You have the softest skin." Laurent place the cap on the tanning oil and gently brushed his lips across her shoulders.

"That brother is smooth," JP whispered. "Too smooth."

"Lar . . ." Vadé shook her head and smiled. "My little brother is growing up."

The sea breeze was refreshing against the hot sun.

"Yo, C-Note. Toss us a cold one." JP nodded at an Evian cooler stocked with bottles of water on ice.

Little Claude grinned and tossed his cousin two bottles of water.

"He asked me not to call him Little Claude in front of the ladies." JP twisted the cap off a bottle of water and handed it to Vadé.

"*Merci.*"

"So you're really serious about interior decorating?"

"Yes. They have a great course of study at the University of Paris. And with all the people we know here and around the world, I'll be very busy working."

"See, you're much more mature than the girls at home. You already know what you want to do."

"You mean the girls in America don't know what they want to become? I always thought people were the same everywhere. There were girls from L'Ecole from other countries, but I didn't find them much different than myself."

"I'm not saying they don't know what they want to do with their lives. But they're not like you."

"What's so different about me?" She was genuinely interested.

"The way you dress, the way you walk and talk . . . I don't know what it is exactly, but I do know I've never met anyone like you. You're special, Day."

Vadé sipped her water and stared at the tranquil electric-blue water. *He's never known anyone like me and he thinks I'm special.* She knew he meant it.

"Well, my law firm will represent your business." JP had grown uncomfortable with the silence between them.

"That might be nice, we'll keep all of the money in the family as Papá would say."

"Yeah, but technically, I'm not your family."

"I know." Jean Paul was the son of Big Claude's older brother, making him no relation to her whatsoever. "But our families are family so that makes us family, too."

"Did you see who just walked by?" Laurent ended their conversation and began another.

"Who was it, Lar?" Vadé knew her brother would not interrupt them if he didn't have something important to say.

"Stevie Wonder. He's already here for his concert tomorrow. I was just talking to him. He wants to come to the villa."

"No stuff, Lar?" JP was obviously impressed.

"No stuff, man." Laurent was really starting to speak American well.

He focused his attention back on Simone when the audience suddenly began screaming hysterically.

"Who is it? Who is it?" JP jumped on a chair as the band pumped out the music to "Holiday."

"Madonna!" Laurent and Simone sang in unison. For the next hour, everyone danced and sang.

Back at the villa, the party continued. Cook already had Louisiana sausages, shrimp, and chicken smoking on the grills. The boys and their guests from the festival gathered around the villa's largest pool and Jacuzzi on the second level to swim and dance.

"Now back to that conversation we were having earlier."

Vadé could hear faint strains of music and laughter from the villa as they watched the sunset on the beach.

"Isn't it the most beautiful thing you've ever seen?"

The sun slowly sank into the horizon until it disappeared completely and left the bay glowing like copper.

"It most certainly is." JP sprinkled powdery white sand on her thigh.

"You're not looking at the sunset." She laughed as she brushed the sand from her leg.

"Yes, I am." He looked into her eyes. "The most beautiful thing I've ever seen is right here."

She smiled and stroked his hair as she kissed him.

"I'm going to wait for you, Vadé. I don't want you going out with any of those Parisian playboys."

"Parisian playboys?" She laughed at the thought.

"Parisian playboys. You know the type . . . smooth, good looking, and rich. Like your brother."

"You think Lar's a playboy?"

"Lar is the man. Just wait until he's old enough to really date. He's going to be a real heartbreaker. If I wasn't in love with you—"

"If you weren't in love with me, what would happen, JP?" She sat up and gazed into his eyes.

"If I weren't in love with you, I'd be right there by his side living the good life with him because my man is headed straight for the top."

SEVEN

Pierre gently kissed Desiree's shoulder, inhaling and tasting the sweetness of her shower *gelle*. They had traveled to St. Tropez to spend some time alone. They always took their holiday while the children were at home preparing for the fall semester at L'Ecole during the last sultry days of summer.

In the beach house kitchen, Desiree sliced fresh plantains and dropped the pieces into sizzling-hot olive oil. She knew how her husband adored the island fruit sprinkled lightly with powdered sugar. She enjoyed making the dish for him just as much as he enjoyed eating it.

"Bonjour, *mi amour.*"

"Good morning, again, beautiful." His smooth chocolate skin and black silky hair were still glistening and damp from the shower. He pattered into the kitchen barefoot wearing white linen drawstring pants.

"You smell like de island, woman." He rubbed his beard across Desiree's cheek and she laughed. Even though Pierre had been away from his native home of Haiti for more than twenty years, his accent was still quite pronounced.

She handed him a plate of plantain, scrambled eggs, and bacon and a glass of fresh-squeezed orange juice as he gave her a kiss. "I've got to stop this or else we won't get anything done around here."

"Isn't that the point of a vacation?"

Desiree removed her favorite chef's apron to expose a football jersey gracing her generous curves. She tossed the apron across a stool as Pierre dabbed a slice of plantain in the sugar and placed it in her mouth. She stood there, slowly chewing the fruit. When she was done, she cast him a glance, and walked toward their bedroom. Pierre laughed, picked up his plate, and followed her.

Later, they sat down to a candlelit dinner of delicately chilled oysters, slivered vegetables sprinkled with caviar, grilled kid, baked apricots, and pistachio ice cream. Afterward, they held hands as they walked past local fishing boats in the harbor.

"Let's go fishing tomorrow," Desiree suggested eagerly.

"I haven't been fishing in years."

"I know. That's why we should go."

Without another word, they walked into the chateau and made arrangements to charter a small fishing boat.

As the sun pressed its way into a new day, Pierre started the motor and cruised out of the quiet fishing port. By midmorning they were anchored with fishing rods suspended in a placid abyss of radiant blue water.

"I cannot believe you got me to go fishing." He grinned and took a puff on his pipe. "That's just another reason why I love you, Dez."

Flaunting a new cerise bikini, she removed her husband's shirt and rubbed his back with sunscreen. "It's going to get hot out here."

"Not for a while and when it does, we'll just find something else to do."

She spread colorful beach towels on the lounge chairs on the deck and stretched out on one of them.

"My woman got me on a fishing boat."

"How long has it been, Pierre?"

"Too long. I haven't been on a fishing boat since that last trip to New Orleans with my father. I enjoyed those trips with him. When I was a kid I worked on the boat every summer. When I turned seventeen, my father wanted me to work full-time but my mother refused. She said no son of hers would work on a boat."

"And that's when you came to New Orleans. One of these days I must meet that mother of yours and thank her for sending you away."

"That'll be the day. The last time I spoke with her she asked me when I was going to get a real job. After all this time and all my accomplishments she still doesn't take my music seriously."

"We don't ever want to get her and Father in the same room. They'd sentence us to the guillotine for making a living as musicians."

"Among other things . . ."

They both stared in silence at the water, reliving the past.

"Do you ever want to move back to New Orleans to be closer to the family?" he asked.

"What family? You're my family now. Giselle and I have always been like sisters. I have no family in New Orleans."

He pulled her into his lap and kissed her on the top of her head.

"Big Claude and I've been talking . . ."

"This sounds serious, baby."

"Well . . . it is."

Pierre stroked Desiree's hair as he spoke.

"Business at the club has been a little slow this year."

"It'll pick up now that summer's over."

"No, Dez, business has been slow the last three years."

"Three years? Why did you wait so long to tell me?"

"Because I didn't want you to worry your pretty little head. We're not losing money yet, but we will if we don't do something about this now."

"And you feel the answer to this is what?"

"Dez, we've been thinking about selling the club and the houses and going home."

"Home?"

"New Orleans."

"And leave Paris?"

"Yes."

"Wow . . ."

"I can't make a decision like this without you."

"Leave Paris . . ."

"You don't have to give me an answer right now."

"When do you want to go?"

"We already have an offer on the club. If we leave within the next few months, we should be able to get the new business up and going by Mardis Gras."

"What kind of business are you planning to open?"

"Something similar to Olivier's would do very well in New Orleans."

"You know . . . I inherited a piece of property from the family."

"Where, Dez?"

"It was my summer home when I was a little girl. It's been in the family forever. Mother gave it to me as a peace offering when Vadé was born, hoping to lure us back to New Orleans."

"Really? Is it someplace you'd like to live?"

"Sure. It's right outside the city. The property has a splendid view of Lake Ponchartrain. We used to swim there in the summer. It could be our American villa."

"Is it that big?"

"Actually, they're probably about the same size."

"We'll have people from all over the world coming to the Chevalier Hotel. You know how the villa gets every summer."

"Pierre! That's it!"

"What?"

"The Chevalier Hotel. We could turn that place into a miniature resort."

"Dez . . . that's a great idea!"

She flashed him a radiant smile.

"We're going to have to make a lot of cutbacks."

"So what? I already have everything money can buy. And I've got you. . . ." She stroked his silky beard and smiled. "It'll be fun."

"I'll run everything by Claude and see what he says."

"I know Giselle won't mind. She won't have to carry around her own personal bottle of Louisiana hot sauce." Desiree laughed.

By noon the sun was blazing in the sky. They put away the fishing poles and dove into the sea before Pierre started up the boat and cruised back to the village. They paused to watch an artist painting the boats in the harbor.

"That was fun, Dez. We should go fishing more often."

"I know, sweetheart. Pierre, what about the children?"

"I've been thinking about them, too."

"Lar can't wait to get to America. He talks about it all the time."

"I know. I think I saw him crying when we put JP on the plane last month."

"Pierre, stop. My baby was not crying."

"Okay, he wasn't, but what about Princess?"

"She won't like it at first, but she'll be fine as long as she has you and her brother around."

EIGHT

Vadé sat down at her Louis III desk and began writing in a new
jade and rose journal.

12 Novembre

*Sunlight burst through the clouds and danced upon Papá's pearl-grey
Rolls Royce as we cruised across the Lake Ponchartrain Bridge this
morning. Papá said no other car would match Mamá's eyes so perfectly,
so it was imported to New Orleans like the rest of us. We arrived in
America yesterday. Everything seemed unusually grey . . . the sky, the
water, the car.*

*We gazed through its windows from our official seats. I always sit be-
hind Papá, who always drives, and Lar sits behind Mamá. After what
seemed like forever, Papá turned down a long road past houses with
sprawling lush green pastures. He said they were horse farms and I
could have my own horse.*

*Finally, Mamá pointed to a big, old house and we turned up a long
drive etched between a forest of pine trees. We drove for several more minutes before we reached the house. I was surprised to see it was much bigger than I thought, but it was horrible. Weather had worn away the
paint. Shutters were missing and those that were still attached hung
crooked. Weeds grew for grass. Bricks and tile lay broken in the pathways
around the house. How are we supposed to live here?*

Lar and Mamá were the first ones out of the car. They were both so excited. I guess because this old plantation house was Mamá's childhood summer home and Lar had finally made it to his beloved America. Papá just stood next to the car and puffed on a gauloises as he watched Mamá and Lar trot up the walkway to the house.

I just sat in the car and stared, and this old house just stared back. It seemed to be telling us to go away. Mamá took a key out of her bag and tried to open the door. When she couldn't, she called for Papá to come and help her. I was surprised when he threw his cigarette on the ground and came around to the back door to talk to me instead.

"Let's go see our new home, princess." I didn't want to go in, but since this was my new home, I thought I should appear to be interested. New Orleans is barren and dull compared to Paris and I don't want to be here. But I let Papá help me out of the car. He took my hand as we started walking toward the house.

He told me he knew I didn't want to come to New Orleans. I only have one last semester at L'Ecole and a job at Le Boutique, I explained for the hundredth time, hoping he would change his mind and send me back to Paris. But no one was listening to me . . . not even Papá.

"I'm sorry about school, princess. And you don't need a job. Don't your mother and I give you everything you want?"

NO . . . I wanted to shout. I turned my head and stared up at the clouds so he couldn't see I was crying, but he saw me. He pulled me in his arms, hugged me, and rubbed his beard across my cheek.

"Do this for me, princess." He was practically begging. "Just do this one thing for me and I'll send you to school in Paris next year." Papá never breaks a promise so I nodded my approval as he found a handkerchief in his pocket and wiped my eyes.

Mamá and Lar were still struggling with the double doors. There was a problem with the lock. Papá placed his weight against the door and it swung open to reveal what time had sealed shut and should have left shut forever.

We stepped into a large foyer that divided the massive downstairs area in half. A double staircase wound its way up and around, joined in the center, and branched off into the main corridor. I could see the remains of ragged, faded floral carpet. Wallpaper hung from the walls in strips. A dusty, tarnished brass chandelier was suspended from the ceiling, a story above. Everyone stood in silence and stared. I think we all were in shock.

Mamá pushed open a set of drawing doors. It was the ballroom. She smiled at Papá and kissed him. The hardwood floor spanned the width of the house. It was covered with dust but it was a magnificent room with ceiling-to-floor windows in all three walls, and a superb marble fireplace. Papá and Mamá started doing one of their silly old dances and we all laughed.

Papá said the room would be finer than any they had ever played in Paris. I could tell he was excited. I was hoping that he would hate this ugly house as much as I did, and take us back to Paris immediately. But he didn't. He loved it. He and Mamá started kissing again and that's when I knew we would never leave. Dez and Pierre were happy.

I could hear Lar running around upstairs. I found him opening and closing doors. "Isn't this great, Day? We're finally in America." He was radiantly happy so I decided to try and be happy too. Lar found the perfect rooms for our suites. We have a spectacular view of Lake Ponchartrain. The few items we had shipped were in one room. Mamá and Papá's bedroom set and my Louis III desk, which Lar and Papá moved into my room. There are some additional pieces of furniture downstairs but everything else was sold along with the house.

I didn't think Papá was serious about moving until he put the house up for sale. That's when I started going to chapel every day to light candles and to pray. I didn't want my family to move to America. When Mamá started selling the furniture I changed my prayer and asked God to allow me to remain in Paris while everyone else moved to America. I knew I would be fine on my own. And I could always go visit. That was a much nicer prayer and everyone would be happy.

But here I am. What happened, God?

I'm not going to cry anymore.

Vadé carefully wiped a teardrop from the page of her journal.

I promised Papá I would go along with this so I have to change my attitude. He and Mamá are really excited. Hotel de Chevalier is their dream. It will be nice to watch things unfold. One year is not so bad. Papá said I could go to the university next year so I will only attend school in New Orleans for one year.

JP does live here too. Lar constantly reminds me. He called yesterday shortly after we checked into the Hyatt Hotel. He said I was his amour de chocolate. I can't wait to see him. We will have our first official date on Sunday. He's taking me to Mass. Now we may go out without Lar and Little Claude.

I must find something to wear. I went shopping before we left. Papá gave me his credit card and said to buy whatever I wanted. I know he was trying to cheer me up. Of course I brought all of my old things and my armoire. I wonder where people shop here.

NINE

Jean Paul Olivier rang the doorbell at Hotel de Chevalier early Sunday morning. Pierre was waiting for him in the main salon where the walls had been stripped clean of paper and primed for painting. Vadé was still upstairs dressing when she heard the bell. She galloped down the stairs in a cool green silk suit as Pierre opened the door.

"Good morning, Papá!" She touched her cheek to each of her father's and smiled at JP. He was wearing the gray Armani suit they had shopped for in Paris.

"Bonjour, JP. I'm ready to go."

JP grinned at her as the two of them lit up like Christmas trees.

"Not so fast, Mademoiselle Chevalier. May I speak to Jean Paul too?" Her father pulled her back into the house

That's exactly what she didn't want him to do.

"Good morning, Jean Paul. Dez told me you're taking my little girl to Mass this morning?"

"Yes, sir."

"Where?"

"St. Augustine's."

"Good." Pierre finally smiled. "I like that. How's your father?"

"Fine, sir. He said to make sure I tell you that he said for you to put a decent green in this place, so he can beat you on your own golf course."

"Rene, ever the joker." Pierre laughed. "I'll speak with him later. And when will the two of you be back? I understand this is an official date?"

"We'll be back by dinnertime."

"Fine. JP, take care of Princess for me."

"I will, sir."

"Go." He kissed her on the cheek and pushed her toward the door. "Have fun and say a prayer for me."

"I will, Papá."

He closed the door behind them as they strolled into diffused sunlight.

"Look, at you, Day. You are looking too delicious. Um, um, um."

He twirled her around, noticing everything about her. The suit emphasized her lean curves ever so gently. Splashes of gold sparkled on her earrings, shoes, belt, and scarf. She had tried to put a few curls in her black straight hair and a few of the long locks were beginning to straighten out.

"You look good, too, Jean Paul."

JP, nearly six feet tall, was the color of honey with black hair, cinnamon eyes, and dimples. Vadé thought he looked cute in anything he wore, but he looked particularly handsome that morning. The suit made him look older and sophisticated. She gave him a light kiss on the cheek as he opened the car door.

"I need a real kiss, baby. What do you think that's going to do for me?"

Vadé kissed his full lips softly. "That's all you're getting until after Mass."

They walked hand in hand into the cathedral.

"This is where the family goes to Mass. That's my mom and dad right there."

As he pointed to the couple sitting together on the pew in front of them, a New Orleans brass band began playing a hymn.

"JP, I thought you said we were going to Mass. They're playing jazz."

"Would you be quiet, Day, and listen?" He covered his mouth and coughed to keep from laughing.

"Oh." She smiled sheepishly as she recognized a soulful jazzy rendition of "When the Saints Go Marching In." "This is a very unusual Mass, but I like it."

"Your father looks a lot like Big Claude, only not as big," Vadé whispered.

"That's because he doesn't have T'Giselle cooking for him. My mother can cook, but not like T."

"She really is a good cook. The family's going to her parents' house for dinner."

"I know . . . but we're not. I'm taking you to lunch in the French Quarter."

"The French Quarter?"

"That's correct, Mademoiselle Chevalier, the Vieux Carre."

There were additional selections from the band before the minister attired in an afrocentric robe took the pulpit.

"His robe is beautiful." Vadé was whispering again.

"It's Nigerian. He got it when he went to speak there."

"I'd like to come again next Sunday," Vadé declared when the service was over.

"Very well, Princess, your every wish is my command."

JP gazed into her eyes and she felt her head spin.

"You must be Day." The sound of Mrs. Olivier's voice brought her back into the present. "We've heard so much about you."

"Vadé," she corrected gently. "I am very pleased to meet you, Monsieur and Madame Olivier."

She kissed them on both cheeks, the customary greeting in France.

"Oh, Rene, isn't her accent cute? And she's so pretty."

"Her accent is not cute. It's absolutely charming." Rene's tone softened as he took her hand and gently kissed it.

"Thank you, monsieur."

"Now I understand why my son wanted to stay in Paris."

"So you two are going on your first date." Aubrey Olivier was extremely pleased.

"Yes, JP is going to show me around New Orleans."

"Good." Rene pulled out his wallet and gave his son several crisp bills.

"Thanks, Daddy." He quickly tucked the bills inside his wallet.

"Take Pierre and Dez's daughter somewhere nice to eat. I can't believe this is the first time I'm meeting my beautiful goddaughter."

Rene Olivier handled all of the band's legal affairs. He made the band's first deal with Brunswick Records and had since built a reputable practice with offices in New York as well.

"You're my godbrother?"

"Yes." JP laughed as he ushered Vadé into the courtyard of a very fine Creole restaurant in the French Quarter. Following his suggestions, they selected fried green-tomato crab cakes, jambalaya, blackened rib eye, and Vadé's favorite—red beans and rice.

"This food is so good. It seems strange to go in a restaurant and order things that Mamá and T'Giselle cook at home."

"Well, it's like that here in Nawlins, the Paris of the South."

Vadé could only laugh. She loved being with JP. New Orleans was looking better by the day. She paused to admire the intricate wrought-iron railings adorning the balconies, windows, and gates in the courtyard. It was the character behind the city's architecture. Live jazz music peppered the air.

"In some ways this place does remind me of Paris, especially when we're together like this."

"There's a lot of history behind those railings you see everywhere. They were hammered out by African slaves."

"Really?" They had touched on slavery at L'Ecole, during a brief study of American history, but that was as far as her exposure to African-American history had been.

"The music, food, art . . . all heavily influenced by African slaves."

"I never knew this. It's all very wonderful. . . . Now please explain to me how you are my godbrother."

"You're back to that?"

Vadé folded her arms and crossed them in front of her.

"Before either one of us was born, and before anyone was married, our fathers made a promise."

"What was it?"

"That your father's children could marry my father's children."

"Really? Why?"

"Families used to arrange marriages. There was so much drama back in the day with your dad being from Haiti and playing in a band

and his social and economic status that they made a promise not to let their children be brought up under those stupid old customs. So, if they had children, and if the children were so inclined . . . the children could marry."

"That is the most ridiculous thing I've ever heard. You're serious, aren't you?"

"Sure I am."

"People should get married because they're in love. . . . Do you know why my grandfather didn't want Mamá to marry Papá?"

"Not exactly. I heard he wanted her to marry some rich attorney here in town. They were about to become engaged when Dez ran off with your father."

"Wow. I didn't know she came that close to marrying someone else. Why didn't you tell me any of this before?"

"It never came up while we were in Paris. Those traditions are embedded in the South. And my dad just told me those things about your grandparents since I returned."

"Did he tell you anything else?"

"No. Only what I've told you. He didn't tell me anything until I started telling him about you."

"What did you tell him about me, JP?"

"I told him you were very beautiful and that I was in love with you."

"In love with me? You've never told *me* that you were in love with me."

"Yes, I have." He was trying really hard not to blush.

"No, you haven't."

"I have," he repeated firmly. "You just weren't listening."

He paid the check and escorted her out of the restaurant onto the narrow bricked streets of the French Quarter.

"Where are we going now?"

"You ask too many questions." He laughed and pulled her closer. "Want to ride on a streetcar?"

"As long as I'm with you."

They walked several blocks to Canal Street and waited for the trolley.

"Now you'll get to see some of the older parts of the city in the Garden District. Those historical homes are really nice. I know how you like houses."

"I don't care about the historical homes. I want to see where you live." She snuggled closer to his warm body.

"We'll go to my house next time. I promised Pierre I'd have you home by dinner."

JP stopped his mother's Jaguar in the circular drive in front of the house and got out to open her door.

"Hotel de Chevalier. This place is going to be something else."

He took Vadé's hand and led her toward the house.

"Wait." She pulled him into her arms and kissed him. "I love you too, JP, and I'm glad our fathers made the promise."

TEN

Vadé sat on the floor in her bedroom wrapping Christmas presents. She paused briefly to glance around at the peacock-green walls and smiled. She had done all the decorating herself. Pierre had given her an allowance and she had spent days combing antique and art stores in the French Quarter for the perfect furnishings.

The scavenger hunt began with an area rug she spotted while browsing with JP. She had even taken fabric swatches to the paint store for custom coloring. Yards of jade silk and satin brocade adorned the bay windows that offered a magnificent view of the lake. Laurent's painting of their Paris courtyard was framed and hanging over the fireplace where orange and blue flames sputtered and crackled.

This was the first Christmas there would be no *reveilion*. Hotel de Chevalier still needed major renovations, so there was no place to host the family's lavish annual celebration. Pierre had also curtailed their spending. The Chevaliers would be on a tight budget until the hotel's grand opening. Laurent walked into her room and stretched out on her queen-size bed.

"It looks really nice in here, Day . . . cozy and elegant. I want you to do my suite next."

"Okay. I saw the perfect things for your room while I was out shopping. I was hoping you'd ask me to decorate it for you. I'll start right after Christmas."

Vadé tied a cherry-red bow on a box with green metallic paper.

"Can you believe we're finally going to meet Grandpere and Grandmere Legrande tonight? Papá's nervous. He's been smoking cigarettes all afternoon and you know he only smokes them when he's nervous."

"Mamá's nervous too. She came in here and told me what to wear. She never tells me how to dress." Vadé smiled, shaking her head.

"This will be the first time that she's seen them in nineteen years."

"Lar, could you imagine not seeing Mamá for that long?"

"No. Nothing could make me leave my family."

"What if you were in love and Mamá and Papá didn't approve of the girl?"

"If they didn't approve, then she couldn't be the girl for me."

The Legrandes lived in a mansion on Claiburne Street. Vadé gasped when Pierre stopped the car in front of a lemon-yellow two-story house trimmed in white with miles of black wrought-iron railings framing the grounds. There was a huge weeping willow in the front yard.

"Mamá! Your house looks like a castle." Laurent was already getting out of the car.

"It was my palace when I was growing up."

Pierre slowly removed the key from the ignition and looked at his wife. They had driven past the Prideaux home on the way to her parents'. He had never told anyone, not even Desiree, about his visit there.

"Well, Dez . . . let's go in."

Mother and daughter were both wearing green, their favorite color. They got out of the Rolls and slowly walked up to the house.

"Things will be different now, Pierre. You'll see." Desiree linked her arm under Pierre's for strength.

Silently, the family drew together in a tight knot as Desiree pressed the bell. The sound of it ringing echoed their beating hearts. Pierre took one last puff on a cigarette and tossed it away as Amelia Legrande opened the door. She was a petite woman like her daughter with the trademark gray eyes, and her hair had turned the same color. Her creamy skin crinkled under her eyes as she smiled. Vadé was surprised by her extremely light complexion.

"Hello, Mamá." Desiree's voice cracked when she spoke.

"Oh, look at my baby. You're all grown up. She gave her daughter a kiss and a warm hug. "Maurice, Desiree and Pierre are here. Come in! Come in!"

The Chevaliers filed into the living room while Amelia continued to make a fuss.

"My goodness, this can't be Laurent and Vadé. You're so big. Come give your grandmother a hug."

"Hello, Grandmother, these are for you." Laurent handed her a large bouquet of fresh flowers and kissed her on both cheeks. "That's the way I kiss all the ladies in France."

"The ladies in France." She laughed and pulled him into her arms. Laurent, ever the charmer, had already stolen her heart.

"Laurent, you look just like Maurice did when he was your age."

Maurice had finally joined them. He was a stout man with a swarthy complexion and jet-black stringy, straight hair. He reminded Vadé of the old aristocratic men in France. Nothing about him resembled her brother or her mother.

"Hello, Desiree . . . Pierre."

"Hello, Papá." Desiree gave her father a light peck on the cheek and then the two men shook hands.

"And this young lady must be Vadé. You look just like your father."

"Hello, Grandpère." She touched her cheek to her grandfather's. "That's funny. Everyone always says I look like Mamá."

"Well, let's have dinner now. We don't want to be late for Mass." Amelia led the family into the dining room where a huge table was set with a white linen and lace tablecloth. Hand-painted pearl china, sparkling crystal, and gleaming silver flatware all reflected warm, glowing candlelight.

"Laurent, you and Vadé come sit by me," Amelia commanded.

As the family found their places at the table, a dark-skinned maid dressed in a uniform carried in a large tureen of gumbo. Another woman brought out a bowl of rice. She placed several spoons of rice in each soup bowl as the other maid poured ladles of the Creole stew over the rice.

"Maurice, darling, Vadé has my eyes." She buttered a hard roll and ate a dainty forkful of the cold stuffed crab that had been served to each of them.

"Vadé, you are a beautiful girl. Pierre, she has your beautiful brown skin and hair and my eyes. What a combination. I understand why JP Olivier is smitten."

Amelia smiled warmly at Pierre.

"I am so glad you all are here. It's so good to see you. This is such a wonderful Christmas present."

"It's so wonderful to meet you, too, Grandmother. It is a wonderful present."

"And that delightful accent. Vadé, you and I are going to be fine friends. And, Laurent, Stella bakes petit fours and praline sugar snaps every Saturday."

Amelia smiled at both her grandchildren before she continued speaking. "Desiree, thank you for finally bringing my grandchildren home."

The dirty dishes were removed and the main course was served. Stella set platters of black-eyed-pea fritters, roast duck, honey-orange-glazed ham, Creole potato salad, and green beans with little pearl onions. Maurice blessed the food and began serving the duck.

"Grandmother, I like the food at your house. I'm going to come over here so much, you'll get tired of me."

"That's fine with me, Laurent, you may come over as much as you like."

"Papá, you and Mamá must come to see the hotel. We're putting in a golf course, an outdoor Olympic pool, and tennis courts."

"That sounds wonderful, Desiree. My ladies' club can use it for our annual teas and luncheons."

"Pierre, do you intend for your band to provide entertainment?" Maurice, breaking his silence, sliced off a bite of ham and chewed slowly, deliberately.

"Yes. Occasionally, we'll bring in other acts and there will be one or two nights set aside for dancing. We'll see how the people respond."

"How many guest rooms will be available?"

"Twelve. The others will be reserved as living quarters for the family."

"We're adding some bathrooms too. Mamá, I can't wait for you to see everything."

As the family finished the last of dinner, a dish of bananas was brought in, sprinkled with brandy, and lit. The flambé was served over ice cream with wafer-thin sugar cookies.

"I forgot how well Leo cooked. Mother, that was a fabulous dinner."

They retired to the parlor where a roaring fire was blazing in the fireplace and Maurice poured the grown-ups glasses of Dubonnet wine.

"Laurent and Vadé, you may have a small glass of the orange cordial. I know you drink wine in Paris."

"Get me a glass, Lar," Vadé called out to her brother, who was already inspecting the crystal decanters.

Amelia and Desiree took the children on a tour of the house. Desiree sighed when they entered a pale green bedroom with teddy bears on the bed.

"You never changed a thing." She picked up a bear and hugged it.

"I kept hoping you would come home and I wanted things to be just the way you left them."

Vadé excused herself to go to the bathroom while the ladies and Laurent sat down at the piano in the music room. After checking her reflection in the mirror she decided to freshen up her hair. As she went to get her purse, she overheard the men talking in the parlor.

"Pierre, I'm very happy that you and Desiree decided to return to New Orleans. How long were you in Paris?"

"About nineteen years."

"Nineteen years."

Vadé started to go into the parlor to speak with her father and grandfather, but something wouldn't let her.

"Before you married my daughter, she was in Paris singing in nightclubs. Did you know that?"

"I know that, sir."

"She thought I didn't know, but I did."

Vadé moved closer toward the parlor as Maurice paused to light a cigar. She fought the urge to cough when she smelled the smoke.

"I'm glad my daughter's home, but I don't want her singing with that band of yours. Desiree's no bar room maid."

"I know that, sir."

"Good. I'm glad we're in agreement. Then you won't object to my request."

"Desiree loves to perform with the band, sir. I would never want to hurt her like that."

"I don't either. But you're back in America and I won't stand for my daughter singing in some nightclub. Not in this city."

"I'm afraid I can't agree to that, Mr. Legrande."

"Oh, yes, you can, Pierre. And you will . . . that is, if you want to see that hotel of yours get off the ground. People talk. I can't afford for people to speak unfavorably about my family. I have a college to run. You understand, don't you?"

Pierre stared at him in shock.

"I'm a very influential man in this town. I have friends who will do me favors. You'll need all types of various permits and licenses to operate. If you don't do as I ask, I'll make sure you never get them. Are you understanding me?"

Pierre looked sick and his voice trembled. "I understand, Mr. Legrande."

"Now there's just one other small thing I want you to do."

"And that would be?"

"That would be you not telling my daughter about this conversation. I've been the bad guy in her life too long. You're her husband. She left this house against my will to marry you, she'll forgive you for it."

Vadé couldn't believe what she was hearing. She heard the others coming and walked into the parlor before someone realized she had been outside the door listening.

"Grandfather, you have a very beautiful house. I wish you could have seen our house in Paris. We lived only blocks away from the Louvre where Lar and I took art classes on Saturdays."

"Vadé is going to be the most sought-out interior decorator in Paris, Mother." Desiree smiled at her daughter fondly.

"You can certainly help me bring some sparkle to this old place. Everything has been the same for so long. Maurice and I were just talking about remodeling the living room."

"You have some fine pieces of furniture. We can have all the wood restained and select new fabrics for the sofas and chairs and add some new window treatments and wall coverings. You'll think you're in a new house and you'll have all of the pieces you treasure. If you want a completely different look we'll have to purchase some additional items of furniture."

"I'm sold already. We'll get started right after Christmas. I'll have to show you some of the galleries too."

"Lar, you must paint a picture for Grandmother's house. My brother is a wonderful painter who doesn't take himself seriously because he wants to be onstage like Michael Jackson."

"Are you that good, Laurent? I can't wait to see you perform, but you must not neglect your painting either. You should utilize all your artistic gifts."

"He's wonderful onstage, Mother." Desiree cuddled her son and smiled proudly at her parents.

"Is this true, Laurent?" Amelia asked the question as the rest of the family looked to see his response.

"If you mean am I good and am I going to sing professionally, the answer is most definitely yes."

"Wonderful. I can't wait to see all the things my grandson has to offer the world." Amelia smiled and Desiree relaxed.

"That's just a lot of childish nonsense." Pierre interrupted. "Laurent is going to law school."

Vadé was surprised by what her father said. He knew how much his son adored singing.

"Laurent will be onstage. It's in his blood. Pierre knows Laurent has spoken of doing nothing else since he was a little boy and we took him to see Michael Jackson. And Laurent can always put together a collection of his paintings when he's famous."

She pulled her son into her arms and kissed him. "We'd better get going so we won't be late for Mass."

Vadé studied her father carefully as he helped Desiree into a gleaming sable coat. I *can't believe Papá said Lar's dream is childish nonsense. And Grandfather. I can't believe what he said to Papá. Can they really mean what they said?* She looked at her brother, who was helping their grandmother with her mink coat. *Lar in law school? That'll be the day.*

ELEVEN

M ardis Gras arrived with no celebration at Hotel de Chevalier. They were way behind schedule with the construction. There were additional changes needed that had not been planned for. A commercial kitchen had to be installed for the restaurant and club, which would open in summer with a big pool party. Golfing, tennis, basketball, jazz under the tent, and a Creole barbecue were also on the menu.

Despite setbacks at the hotel, Mardis Gras did not go unnoticed. JP hosted a party for Vadé, Laurent, and Claude at the House of Blues in the French Quarter. Specially engraved invitations were sent out to the who's who of New Orleans. The guest list included the family, friends, JP's classmates, and Rene Olivier's business clients.

Vadé sifted through her armoire of new clothes on hangers. Just about every item still had a price tag. She needed something very special for the evening. She stopped at a sea-green party dress she had purchased at the Collections. It was the perfect thing to go with her favorite metallic gold sling-backs.

She washed her hair and rolled it up on huge plastic rollers with mousse and left them in for hours, so her curls would last through the night. Later, she drove Laurent and Little Claude to the club in her mother's Mercedes coupe. Her parents had left several hours ago with Giselle and Big Claude. They were going to the party and some other clubs afterward with Rene and Aubrey. All the children were spending the night at the hotel.

"We are going to have so much fun tonight." Laurent looked extremely handsome in designer jeans, a crisp white shirt, and a black blazer. JP was right, Laurent definitely had the makings for an international playboy.

"I'm sure all of your girlfriends from the academy will be waiting for you. Especially Krista Broussard. How is it that the girls in my class always have a thing for you? You're younger than they are."

"I can't help it if women of all ages find me irresistible."

"Oh, please." Vadé laughed and made a face while Little Claude rolled around in the backseat laughing.

"You're one to talk, Day. JP is going to have a fit when all of his friends see you. They're going to be all over you and he's not going to like it one bit. This is going to be so much fun!"

"You be quiet and fasten your seat belt." She glanced at her cousin in the rearview mirror. "His friends will do no such thing."

The party was in full swing when they arrived. Vadé saw her parents sitting with the Olivier brothers and their wives at a table upstairs on the balcony, which overlooked the stage. A local band, jazz infused with funk, provided the entertainment while young people danced and conversed at the bar. JP was sitting at a table near the dance floor talking to several young ladies.

"The guests of the hour are finally here. Day, you can have my chair and we'll bring others over to the table."

"Hello, JP." Vadé kissed him on the lips and JP grinned. "This is Vadé and my boy, her brother, Laurent. You know my cousin Claude."

Chairs were found and conversation resumed.

"You look too delicious in that dress, Vadé. Look at you." He kissed her on the neck and fingered one of her long curls. "Did you do all of that for me?"

She was about to respond when she looked up to see two of the ladies giving her looks of death.

"Let's go get a Coca-Cola."

"You know I'll do anything you ask." JP squeezed her and kissed her. "Where's your daddy, beautiful? I don't want him on my behind tonight." He glanced up toward the balcony before he ordered their Cokes.

"I saw him sitting upstairs when we came in. I'm just happy that

Papá likes you. It's a good thing our fathers made that promise." Vadé smiled as she took a sip from the glass. "Who are those girls you were sitting with?"

"Friends. Gabrielle and I have gone to school together since kindergarten. Danielle is her older sister."

"Do you know that they both are in love with you?"

"Gabrielle thinks she's going to marry me. She's been saying it since junior high school. But that doesn't mean anything to me."

Vadé kissed him on the end of his nose.

"Olivier, where did you ever find such a beautiful lady? Where have you been all of my life? Can I taste you?" The young man grinned impishly as he looked Vadé up and down as if she were good enough to eat.

"This is Vadé Chevalier from Paris. And this shady character is my friend Jeffrey Washington."

"It is very nice to meet you." Vadé extended her hand to Jeffrey and the two young men accompanying him.

"Voulez vous coucher avec moi?"

Vadé blushed and laughed. She couldn't believe Jeffrey had just asked her if she would go to bed with him, and in front of JP. He was challenging JP for her attention.

"And she blushes too. I'm in love. Olivier, you'd better marry this woman or I will."

"Man, get away from my woman and stop drooling." JP stood between them and laughed.

"I'm going to be a rich man when I turn pro. He'll still be in law school and I'll buy you anything you want."

"He thinks he's going to play for the Dallas Cowboys. Man, stop trying to move in on my girl. What kind of friend are you?"

"A real one. At least I'm not behind your back trying to get your woman. I'm doing it right here in front of your face."

"You're brain-damaged, Jeffrey. You've been hit in the head too many times with the football on the playing field."

"You the man." Jeffrey laughed as he and JP shook hands and patted each other on the back. "Save me a dance, beautiful." He blew a kiss at Vadé and walked off.

"He is so fresh." Vadé laughed.

"I've never seen him act like that. I'm taking you home before I have to hurt somebody. Stepping toward my Day like that and right in front of me." He took her hand and whispered in her ear. "I'm spoiled. I'm used to having you all to myself."

Vadé took his hand and kissed it softly. "I'm your girl, JP. You never have to worry about me wanting someone else."

"You are so sweet." He gently brushed cheek. "And so beautiful."

He spoke in that tone that sent chills racing through her body.

When they returned to the table, Krista Broussard was sitting with Laurent. Even though the girls were in the same class, Krista never spoke to Vadé, but she made her affection for Laurent no secret.

"Vadé, look who's here, Krista. Gabrielle and Danielle Poirier are sisters and Krista's cousins. Krista, you know my sister Vadé."

"Hello." She spoke very coolly to Vadé and flipped her ginger hair. Krista's skin was extremely light, like her grandmother's. Her honey eyes were mean and cold.

Vadé ignored her completely and focused her attention on JP. She watched her brother take turns dancing with each one of the girls and wondered which of them, if any, he prefered. She knew he wasn't particularly fond of Krista. He still kept in touch with Simone. Several letters were delivered to the hotel every month from her.

"JP, Lar, Claude. Let's dance!" Vadé jumped up, grabbed JP and Lar by the hand. The four of them and Krista ran onto the dance floor.

"Shake that booty, JP."

JP doubled over laughing. She sounded so cute and so funny when she tried to speak American slang. He had fallen in love with her the moment he saw her. She was sexy too. Her accent drove him wild, especially when she whispered in his ear and kissed the tip of his nose. There was an innocence that glowed under the sophisticated designer clothing. She was his delicate flower that needed protecting.

They stood together at the buffet creating personal samplers of barbecued ribs, seafood, salads, and the ever-present gumbo.

"I got your favorite. Caramel corn and Coke for the movie tonight. I can't wait." She smiled happily.

"What movie did you get?"

"*Purple Rain*. You know Lar picked it out."

"That boy loves himself some Prince."

"And MJ, and Marvin Gaye and someone new . . . Babyface."

"Well, none of them have movies yet." JP laughed. "But, we'll have fun anyway."

"Always, as long as I'm with you."

When they returned to their seats, the ladies were sitting alone. The conversation ceased the moment they walked up to the table.

"Hello, JP." Gabrielle smiled warmly at him. "I'm still waiting for that dance."

"The food looks very good, ladies. Would you like for me to get you something?"

"Laurent and Jeffrey went to get us some." Krista lit a cigarette and looked at Vadé.

"Good, because it's a very good buffet."

The guys returned with plates for everyone and soon Laurent and Jeffrey had all the girls in stitches.

"Those two should never have hooked up." JP glanced at Laurent and Jeffrey. "They're exactly alike."

"Lar's not like Jeffrey." Vadé laughed.

"Yes, he is. Lar just has more finesse. He's smoother than Jeffrey. The ladies know Jeffrey's a fool. But Lar will have them all eating out of his hand."

"I can't see him like that. But girls do love him. They always have. Older ones, too, drooling over him."

"Of course you don't see him that way. He's your brother."

Vadé nodded in agreement. "You're right, JP. Lar is a Parisian play-boy."

They laughed together as they watched all the ladies hang on to his every word.

The girls excused themselves and headed for the powder room, while JP and Jeffrey began a conversation about the Super Bowl and Jeffrey's quarterback position on the Grambling football team. Vadé found her gold bag and went to the ladies' bathroom. When she walked into the persimmon and silver lounge, she saw Gabrielle and her cousins standing in front of the gleaming mirror, applying makeup.

"Can you believe *she's* his sister?" Krista laughed as she dusted her face with blush.

"I know. If Laurent is her brother, then her mother was definitely carrying on with the mailman or somebody."

Their laughter wasn't kind.

"Excuse me?" Vadé heard herself say. Before she realized it, she was standing beside them in the mirror. "If there's something you'd like to know about my family, feel free to ask."

She glared at each of them. "Krista, don't waste your time thinking you'll ever get your hands on my brother. He would never bother with trash like you." She took a comb out of her bag and ran it through her waist-length hair.

"You stuck-up black bitch. How dare you speak to me that way?"

Black . . . bitch. The words cut her like a knife. She wanted to slap Krista's face but she restrained herself from doing so. And w*hy did she say Mamá must have had an affair?*

She cursed them politely in French and went into the washroom. The entire confrontation with the girls left her feeling uncomfortable. She was ready to go home. Vadé washed her hands and reapplied her lipstick. *Black bitch.* The words haunted her as they echoed over and over in her head.

"JP, I'm ready to go home," she announced the moment she returned to the table.

"Don't you want to . . ." He couldn't finish the sentence when he looked into her eyes and saw her pain. He had never seen pain in her sparkling green eyes and he never wanted to see it there again.

"All right," he agreed quickly. "Lar, Little Claude. We're going home now. Vadé isn't feeling well."

"What's wrong, Day?" A look of concern clouded Laurent's handsome face as he rushed to her side. The boys ignored the ladies completely as they all fussed over Vadé.

"I'll be fine. Something upset my stomach." She found her gold jacket and tucked an arm under JP's. *"Au revoir,"* she called coolly.

"Good night." Laurent remembered to speak to the ladies as they headed for the door.

She had won. A lady's best weapon at times was being a bitch and Vadé knew how to play the role well, if necessary. She was taking every last male that one of those man-hungry cousins wanted to get her hands on. They were all hers and the cousins knew it.

"What's wrong?" JP inquired just loudly enough for her to hear once they were in Desiree's car.

He pulled the car into traffic and turned up the volume of the tape.

"Nothing."

"What happened in the rest room? You've been acting strange ever since you went to the bathroom."

His tenderness and concern brought tears to her eyes that spilled down her cheeks. She reached into her bag for a tissue.

"You guys get the movie started and we'll be there in a minute," JP called after the boys.

"Now tell me what happened." JP pulled her into his arms where she cried like a baby.

"I'll be fine now." She dried her eyes and managed a hint of a smile. "Krista called me a black bitch."

"That high-yellow bitch." JP was furious.

"I'm okay now." She thought about the looks on all of the girls' faces when she left with the guys and smiled. "It just hurt me terribly when she said it. She was so nasty and mean. Why would she call me something like that? I overheard her saying if Lar was my brother, Mamá had to have an affair with the postman. I wanted to slap her face."

"She deserved to be slapped her for saying something so ignorant."

"Why did she say that?"

"Because she thinks she's better than you."

"Why?"

"Because her parents raised her to think like that."

"Why?"

JP looked at Vadé and wondered how to explain the racism that existed between people of color in America.

"It began during slavery when the lighter offspring of African slaves worked in the house and those with darker skin worked in the fields. The lighter-skinned slaves began to feel they were better because they were more like white people than those with darker skin, so a major rivalry developed between them."

"But that's so stupid. Everyone in Paris wanted suntans. If white is better, why does everyone want to be darker?"

JP stroked her smooth cocoa skin as he spoke.

"It's a lot of stupidness that's been passed down between generations of families and it's wrong because it hurts." He stroked her face gently. "But the real reason Krista calls you names is that despite everything she's been taught, she's jealous of you."

"Why?"

"Because you're beautiful and they were intimidated by you."

"But why? Things in America sure don't make a lot of sense."

"No, they don't. Now don't give it another thought."

They changed clothes and lay together on Vadé's bed watching shadows from the fireplace dance on the ceiling. Noel Pointer played softly in the background while dozens of thought occupied Vadé's mind.

Africans have dark skin and Papá has dark skin, which means he's African, too. Only Papá isn't from Africa, he's from Haiti. And if Papá is African, that means Lar and I are African, too. But Lar doesn't have dark skin. She sometimes wondered why Lar's skin was light and hers dark.

Even Mamá refers to her African blood. But she never made it sound like it was anything bad. Maybe because she's light, which means she's more like white. Grandmother and Grandfather Legrande don't look like they have any African blood.

She looked at JP, who was sleeping soundly next to her. He looked so peaceful she hated to wake him, but if Pierre found him in her bed, he wouldn't wait for an explanation. He would kill them both. She shook him gently and watched him stumble down the hall toward Lar's room where he would sleep.

JP's constantly talking about African-Americans. He likes his African blood. Maybe this has something to do with why our fathers made a promise . . . because Papá was darker. But Mamá loves Papá, she left her family to be with him. And now I know why she likes Lar more than me. I always thought it was because Lar sang, and painted, like her, and he was her baby boy . . . but it's because he's more white, like her, and Grandmère and Grandpère Legrande. . . . That's what she and T would never discuss in front of me. . . . That's why Grandpère sent her to Paris . . . . because Papá has dark skin.

TWELVE

The Independence Day jazz festival at Hotel de Chevalier was the social event of the summer. With golf on the sprawling eighteen-hole green, swimming in the Olympic pool, a wonderful barbecue, and great jazz, it was a pleasurable day with something on the menu for everyone.

Vadé had the best time monopolizing all of the guys' attention. JP and Jeffrey were putty in her hands. She also managed to keep Laurent and Little Claude occupied and out of the hands of the cousins. Now that she knew they hated her, she enjoyed twisting the knife. She smiled as she rehashed the day in her mind.

Vadé tightened the cap on a tube of sunscreen and returned it to her apple-green straw bag that also contained a bottle of Evian. She had just taken a dip in the pool and her sun-reddened skin made a striking combination with her shiny black hair. She pulled on a vibrant cover-up and focused on the clear aquamarine water in the swimming pool. It was hot and it was still early.

"Hello, Princess."

Vadé was surprised to hear her father's voice.

"Hello, Papá." She stood and kissed him on the cheek. "What are you doing out here?"

"Is there something wrong with me joining my beautiful daughter for a swim?"

"No. It's just that your beautiful daughter isn't used to such an honor. Are you really going swimming, Papá?"

"Sure, it's nice out here."

He removed his sweats to expose green swim shorts. She watched him swim the length of the pool, barely splashing the sparkling water, climb out of the pool, and stretch out on the lawn chair beside her.

"Everything looks so beautiful, Papá. Hotel de Chevalier is a success."

"We still have a long way to go in order to have all the guest rooms completed in time for Mardis Gras."

"I know, Papá. Is there anything I can do to help?"

"Yes . . . there is. I've been meaning to have this conversation with you for some time."

Vadé felt the smooth silky hair on her arms and the back of her neck bristle.

"What is it, Papá? What's wrong?"

"I'm sorry, Princess, I . . ."

"Just tell me, Papá."

"I'm not going to be able to send you to school in Paris this fall. We just can't afford it right now. I thought I was going to be able to until we had to step up construction to have things ready in time for Independence Day."

Vadé stared at an invisible spot in the pool. "I won't be able to attend the University of Paris?"

"No, sweetheart. Not this year."

"I can't take another year of this awful place, Papá."

She was unable to hold the tears back any longer.

"I know, sweetheart, and I'm sorry. But there's nothing I can do about it. But you can go to school here and JP . . ."

Go to school here? In this god-awful place in the country, where everyone is so stupid and slow, and people dislike you because your skin is darker . . . What did I ever do to deserve such punishment?

"I will not attend school here."

He was surprised by her angry tone.

"Vadé, this isn't at all like you."

She crossed her legs and gave her father much attitude. She wanted to scream, shout, and cry but she knew it wouldn't do any good. Still, she had to do something to ease the painful disappointment raging through her body.

"I will not attend school. If I can't go to school in Paris, I will not attend school here either."

Pierre stared at the beautiful child who had suddenly turned into a gorgeous young woman, looking at him through his wife's gray eyes.

"If you only knew how much this hurts my heart, Princess."

Vadé felt something melt inside her.

"I know, Papá." She kissed him on the cheek.

"Ahh, sugar smacks. There's my girl."

"But now I want you to do something for me in return."

"And what is that, Princess?"

"I want a job."

"A job?"

"A job here at the hotel. I want to work for you."

"You're serious, aren't you?"

"Yes, Father—"

"Father? What happened to Papá? I don't know if I'm going to like this."

"We're in America now, Father."

"All right."

"And you're going to pay me a lot of money." She laughed.

"I am? And what are you going to do for all of this money?"

"I'm going to be your executive assistant. You have a lot of things to do around here and you can't personally attend to everything. So I will. I'll make sure that things get done and Hotel de Chevalier runs smoothly."

Pierre looked impressed. "I'm beginning to like this idea of yours."

"I'll also be working for the family business."

"I like this very much, Princess. Write out your ideas and your salary requirements and give them to my secretary."

"I will, Papá. You'll find my proposal on your desk when you get to work on Monday."

"But, Princess, what about school?"

"I thought we were done with that little conversation, Father."

The beautiful young woman with Desiree's eyes met his eye, and he knew not to press the issue. She had won . . . but so had he because they were both happy.

"You're right, Princess, we are done with that conversation."

She smiled and the storm was over.

"I was bored in class and we weren't learning anything new. There's a time for school and there's a time to work."

"Good. I'm glad we worked that out. Welcome to the family business, Vadé Chevalier."

"*Merci*, Papá."

"By the way, when I came down, your mother was on the phone with your grandmother. She was telling Dez how much better she enjoys the house since the two of you decorated."

"Oh, Grandmother is so much fun. We go shopping and she loves to eat."

"That's wonderful, Vadé."

"And you should see her and Lar together. They are so cute. He flirts with her and she's just as bad as the girls at the academy. She has Stella prepare all of his favorite meals whenever he goes to her house."

"That's my boy."

"JP calls him the international playboy."

"That's my boy."

"I know. He gets it from you. Just like I have Mamá's eyes, he has your smile."

"That's my boy. How's your grandfather?"

"He's fine. He doesn't talk much."

"What does he say when he does talk?"

"Not much. We just talk about school and Paris."

She looked at her father and wondered if she should tell him about the conversation she had overheard between them earlier that year.

"Papá, Grandpère doesn't like us, me and you, very much, does he?"

"What would ever make you say a thing like that?"

"It's okay, Papá. I know he doesn't like us because our skin is darker than his."

Pierre's face clouded over like a thunderstorm.

"Did he say something to you?"

"No. But I heard him tell you not to let Mamá sing."

"You did?"

"Yes, I was out in the hallway. That's why you and Mamá moved to Paris and why we never visited here."

Pierre let out a long sigh.

"I never wanted you to feel that pain."

"I didn't, Papá . . . not until we came to America."

"From your grandfather?"

"No."

"Then where?"

"A girl from school called me a black bitch."

"When? Why?"

"The night of JP's Mardis Gras party. She's in love with JP. The girl and her cousins were in the powder room saying mean things about the family, so I cursed them in French."

"Vadé!" Pierre tried not to laugh.

"I wanted to slap her. JP said she deserved it."

"He wasn't in the powder room too, was he?"

"Of course not, Papá. I told him everything afterward."

"Good. . . . You're still my beautiful girl, no matter what anyone ever says. Don't ever let anyone make you feel that they're better than you because their skin is lighter."

"Even Mamá?"

"Your mother doesn't feel that way. She loves you very much."

"But she likes Lar more than me. I always thought it was because he was her baby boy, but now I know it's because he's light . . . like her and—"

"Your mother thinks no such thing. And she would be heartbroken if she knew you felt this way, Vadé . . ."

They both gazed at the aquamarine water.

"My mother . . . your Grandmother Jacqueline is light like your mother."

"Was she beautiful like her, too?"

"Yes. My father was brown like me. Her family disowned her for marrying him. They live on the same street as the Legrandes."

"Really?"

"When I first came to New Orleans, my mamá drew me a map. I knew exactly where to go. When I arrived at the house, Marie Prideaux allowed me to come in her kitchen for five minutes while she called me all sorts of names before sending me back into the street. I had no place to stay. She could have cared less about me being her sister's son, she just didn't want anyone thinking she was black."

"Papá . . . that's horrible. What did you do?"

"I went back into town. It was Mardis Gras, my first in New Orleans, like you. I got a job as a busboy, and I eventually became a waiter. I met your Uncle Claude a few months later . . . you know the rest."

"Papá, why are people so unkind in America?"

"I don't know, Vadé, but your mother . . . don't ever think she doesn't love you . . . especially because you're darker. My God, how could you?" He looked at her with the saddest eyes she had ever seen. His voice cracked, and for a minute, she thought he was going to cry.

"I'm sorry, Papá."

She was even sorrier that she had told him. Tears spilled out of her eyes and down her cheeks.

"See how painful this color thing is? I wish we had never come back."

"I'm so sorry, Papá. I would never want to say or do anything to hurt Mamá."

"No, Princess. I'm sorry. Your mother and I should have explained these things to you when you were younger."

"How do you explain something like this? I don't think it would have helped. You can't understand what it's like until someone makes you feel it."

Vadé sniffed and focused on the water again.

"When you were born, your mother was so proud. She thought you were the most beautiful child in the world, a reflection of our love. She said God took the best from us and made you. That best included my brown skin. She would dress you up so pretty in green, her favorite color. You were her baby doll."

"Really, Papá?"

"Really. Your mother thinks I spoil you."

"You do, but she does the same thing with Lar."

Vadé laughed because she and her brother knew whom to go to, for what.

"She spoils him and I spoil you, because we love you both. We adore you. So your original thoughts were right. It has nothing to do with color. People have different ways of demonstrating love. Love is a gift and we must receive it however and whenever it's given. Do you understand?"

"Yes, Papá."

"Nor do we ever take it for granted."

"*Oui*, Papá."

"Good. We'll keep this conversation just between us. I never told your mother about my experience at the Prideauxs."

"Why? Don't you tell Mamá everything?"

"Yes, but I didn't have anyone to talk to during those days. When I met your mother, it was at a different time in my life and I didn't want to go back. And there was no reason to, until today."

"I understand, Papá. I'm glad I have JP to talk to."

"So am I. Want some lunch, baby girl?"

"Sure, Papá. Can we have it out here by the pool?"

"Certainly, beautiful daughter." He picked up the phone and dialed the kitchen. "What would you like to eat?"

"Fried chicken and Creole potato salad."

"Sounds like the perfect thing to me." He rattled off their order and added a pitcher of sangria and several bottles of Coke.

"So how are you and JP doing?"

"We're fine."

"His father told me that he had more B's than A's last semester."

"He thought he was going to get a C in statistics."

"Rene thinks you're distracting JP."

"I'm not a distraction, Papá." She smiled sweetly.

"I know you're a distraction. I don't want any little JPs running around here."

"Papá!"

"I was good looking and young once. I know what runs through a man's mind."

"Papá!"

"Don't Papá me. I've seen how you look at him. I'm jealous. You used to only look at me that way. That's why I'm worried."

Vadé stared at her father in disbelief.

"I don't know why you're staring at me like that. I'm your father and I will always know what's going on. You may not be sleeping together yet—"

"We're not, Papá." She picked at a cube of potato on her plate.

"Just make sure it stays that way. Because once you do it, you'll want to do it again and I'm not having any of that. When the two of you decide you're going to have sex, you'd better be married."

Vadé watched her father polish off the rest of the fried chicken.

She had never felt so embarrassed. She knew she wanted to go all the way with JP, but so far she had resisted the urge. JP wasn't putting her under any pressure either. Just being around him drove her crazy, but she had no intention of giving in. She wasn't getting married either. Vadé had a hotel to run, and eventually, college in Paris.

THIRTEEN

The day just didn't get started right. He nicked himself with the razor, had a flat tire on the way to work, and burned the stuffed quail with oyster and scallop dressing all before noon. But those things always happened whenever he stayed out all night gambling and drinking. It was Mardis Gras and time to party, and a few minor casualties were part of the course.

Black eyes in a face of smooth dark chocolate looked back at him in the bathroom mirror. Nothing he did ever affected his looks. He pulled a pale gray silk undershirt over well-defined pecs and abs and slipped on the trousers to his rented tuxedo. The older he got, the better he looked. Women loved him and he loved women.

Vicenté Francois pulled into Hotel de Chevalier's tiled circular drive and prayed his car wouldn't do anything stupid like cut off in the middle of the driveway. He needed a new car, but he couldn't afford to buy one. He was a professional chef, and if his cooking show got the green light, he'd be able to get something really nice.

A doorman dressed in an olive-green and black designer uniform stood waiting to open the car door when Vicenté brought the Corolla to a stop.

"Happy Mardis Gras. Welcome to the grand opening of Hotel de Chevalier, monsieur."

He opened the door for Vicenté as another doorman held out a gloved hand to his date, Martine Bárres, a fiery number, the color of caramel.

Vicenté watched her get out of the car. Martine had the sweetest lips and loving. She was the bookkeeper at Copelands, the classiest soul food restaurant in New Orleans, where they both worked.

Together they walked up a royal red carpet into the foyer of the hotel. Right Bank, a restaurant offering the finest in French and Creole cuisine, was on the right. Left Bank, a Parisian-style bar and jazz club, overflowed with patrons on the left.

"This place is fabulous, V." Martine's red dress, red lipstick, and red nails were the same color as Vicenté's cummerbund and bow tie.

"I see it is." He excused his way through the crowd of mingling people with cigarettes and drinks to order a double of Courvoisier at the bar. "You want a drink, baby?"

"I'll have what you're having." Martine's full red lips turned up into a smile when he handed her the glass. She gazed at him with velvety brown doe eyes, watching him gulp the amber liquid and order another.

"Slow down, V. The night is young, baby."

She nibbled on his ear just long enough to get his manhood at attention. The alcohol burned like fire as it flowed into his system. He lit in to Martine's luscious lips with hunger. She gave him strength.

"I'm straight."

"Let's walk around, V. I want to see everything."

Vicenté swallowed hard as he placed his empty glass on the counter. He wanted another but Martine had already clocked him.

"Yeah, let's check out the House of Chevalier."

He placed a hand around her waist as they followed a group of people outside to a casino set up in a big white tent. A crowd was gathered around the baccarat table.

"Ooh, look, V." Martine immediately took out her wallet, pulled out some cash, and got into the game.

"I'm going to get another drink, baby. I'll be right back."

The casino bar was crowded so he decided to walk back to the hotel to relieve himself. The men's rest room was by the kitchen. In the elegant brown and gold lavatory, he splashed cold water on his velvety skin and ran a comb through black silky hair cut close to the scalp. Clatter from the restaurant's kitchen beckoned for his attention.

"Not bad. Not bad at all."

He quickly scanned the latest and the best in kitchen hardware. A variety of brass, copper, and aluminum pots and pans dangled from racks in the ceiling. A gleaming commercial stove and a grill with smoldering mesquite chips were silent. Trays of blackened chicken, fish, and shrimp were carried out by waiters to the buffet set up in the restaurant.

I could work out in there. . . .

"I hope everything is just as you requested, mademoiselle."

Vicenté was just about to leave when he heard a female voice speak rapidly in perfect French. It was rare to hear someone of color actually speak French in the Little Paris of the South. He looked back into the kitchen to see a young woman with the most beautiful brown skin and long black hair he had ever seen. The forest-green taffeta dress came to life on her cute little body. Before he realized it, he was staring.

"Everything looks absolutely wonderful. My father will be pleased."

My father . . . *That means she's Pierre Chevalier's daughter. Oh my God.*

He turned to leave but she had already seen him.

"Hello. Is there something I can assist you with?"

Vicenté looked into piercing green-gray eyes and felt his heart beating in his ears.

"No, thanks," he managed to whisper and jetted for the bar.

The alcohol flowed ever so smoothly over ice cubes and down his throat. He felt his body relax again and found his way back to the tent where Martine had turned her five dollars into five hundred.

"Oh, no. Here's my boo. Martine's gotta go now. Bye, bye."

She smiled and smooched kisses against a din of protests from her male admirers.

"I can't leave you alone for five minutes."

"Look, baby. We have money." She waved the wad of cash in his face like a child.

"You put that away and buy yourself something pretty." He folded the money back into her hand and kissed her. "I don't want that."

Women had been trying to give him money since he was a teenager. They bought him clothes, let him drive their cars, cooked for him, and made love to him. But that was before Martine. Now there was only after Martine. She had changed all of that. She had changed him.

"Let's go inside and find a seat before the band comes on." Vicenté led her back inside the hotel. "They were setting up a nice spread for dinner."

There was a line for the buffet. Laurent and Little Claude discussed the contents of the table as they deliberated over each platter of food.

"This looks good." Laurent pointed to a tray of crab-deviled eggs.

"There's gumbo too, man."

"Man, do you ever eat anything besides gumbo?" Laurent laughed as he teased his friend. "I'm changing your name to Gumbo."

Laurent smiled as he looked at Martine, who was standing behind them. He looked her up and down with a casual glance. She was a beautiful woman.

"Mademoiselle, I want you to meet my friend, Gumbo."

"Hey, Gumbo. What's happening?" Martine said to Little Claude.

"Lar, see, man, you're wrong."

Laurent doubled over laughing. "I'm sorry."

Something about his laughter was infectious and Martine smiled.

"I apologize, *mon ami.* Mademoiselle, this is my friend Claude. I'm Laurent."

He smiled warmly at Martine. Her red dress said fun and her sparkling brown eyes spelled mischief. She was older, in her twenties, but that didn't bother him.

"And I'm Vicenté." He couldn't believe the young brother was flirting with *his* woman and she was enjoying it.

"Excuse me, mademoiselle. . . ." Laurent stopped to smile ever so sweetly at Martine.

"Martine." She smiled back at Laurent. He was young, but awfully cute.

"Martine is exceptionally beautiful." He smiled at her again.

"You are smooth, too smooth." Vicenté laughed. "You the man." He shook his head in amazement. "I can't even touch that, and this is my woman."

"He's just too cute. And that accent and those eyes and that cute little smile . . ." Martine closed her eyes and sighed.

"See, man, like I said. You the man."

The guys shook hands and laughed.

"Is this your first time at Hotel de Chevalier?" Laurent placed a seafood kabob on his plate.

"Yes. This place is really nice."

"Thank you. My parents are the owners."

Vicenté almost choked on the piece of blackened steak he was chewing.

"Your parents *own* this hotel?" Martine was obviously impressed.

"Yes. Would you two like to have drinks with Claude and me at our table?" Laurent was smiling at Martine again.

"Of course," she replied before Vicenté could utter a word.

Laurent and Little Claude led them to a table near the front with an excellent view of the stage. Ever since Vadé and JP had started dating, the children had their own reserved table for guests. Giselle and Desiree were just a table away.

Laurent signaled for a waitress as everyone was seated. "What would you like, Mademoiselle Martine?"

He was smiling and charming again. He didn't even have to think about what he said or the way he said it. His charm was as natural as breathing.

"A glass of champagne." She smiled back at Laurent. "If I was five years younger and single, I'd give you a chance."

"I know you would." There wasn't a hint of a smile on his face.

"What?"

"And then you'd probably break my heart. And you, my friend?" Laurent nodded at Vicenté. "What will you have?" His smile was sincere.

"I cannot believe this young brother is putting the moves on my woman and I'm sitting here watching him do it, and I'm not mad about it. You are smooth, little brother, too smooth."

"He's definitely a charmer." Martine smiled.

For the moment Vicenté had forgotten whom he was talking to and why he was there. The club filled up as everyone waited with anticipation for Pierre Chevalier and Amour. The lights in the ballroom dimmed as Laurent watched the group take the stage. He saw his father and Big Claude take their positions, but grew concerned when he didn't see his mother. He glanced at her table. Giselle was sitting alone.

He excused himself and rushed to the back of the stage. She wasn't in the dressing room. As he headed for his favorite position, an equipment trunk right on the side of the stage, he found her in the wings crying.

"What's wrong, Mamá?" Fear raced through his heart.

"Nothing, sweetheart. Nothing for you to worry about. Go back out front with Little Claude."

"How can you say nothing's wrong when you're back here crying?"

"I'm fine, sweetie. Really I am."

"Mamá, why aren't you out there singing?"

"I'm not going to sing with the group anymore and I'm a little sad about it, that's all."

"Not going to sing anymore? Why not? Mamá, you love singing."

"Laurent, I told you to go back out front with Little Claude. I'm fine. This is nothing for you to worry about."

She had never spoken to him in that tone. *Something is definitely wrong.*

He went back outside to the table. He wasn't in the mood for music anymore. He was glad to find Martine and Vicenté engrossed with the band. He wasn't in the mood for company either.

The group finished the set and disappeared. Laurent and Little Claude left the table also. Vicenté patted the envelope in the breast pocket of his tuxedo jacket for an extra boost of confidence as he watched Martine head back out to the casino. It was now or never. He felt his legs take him toward the back of the stage.

"I'd like to see Monsieur Chevalier." He tried to be extra polite.

"Is Monsieur expecting you?" An older man's eyes met his.

"Huh? Yeah," he blurted out. He could feel himself sweating in the air-conditioned hallway.

"What's your name?"

"Francois. Vicenté Francois."

The backstage attendant quickly checked a list. "No Francois here." He looked up in time to see Vadé approaching her father's dressing room.

"Mademoiselle, there's a gentleman here to see your father whose name is not on the guest list."

"I'll handle this." Vadé smiled at the doorman as he walked away. "The gentleman from the kitchen. You're here to see my father?"

"Yes." Her gray-green eyes made him shiver.

"About what? Are you a friend of his?"

"Yes."

"And your name?"

"Francois. Vicenté Francois. The gentleman here before you said he couldn't find me on the list."

"That's right, Mr. Francois. I give the doorman my father's guest list every evening and he didn't mention your name to me. Your name wasn't on my master list for the party either. He can't be disturbed right now. Is there something I can assist you with?"

"Yes, I need to speak with your father." *I wish she would just go get him.*

"I'm afraid that won't be possible now. Perhaps you can catch him in the casino later."

"I need to speak with him privately." Vicenté was seconds away from turning and running as fast as he could out of Hotel de Chevalier, but he had come too close to turn around now. He had promised her he would do it.

"If you call my office tomorrow, I'll be more than happy to set something up."

"No, that won't be necessary." His speech was cool and even, as if the weight of the world had been lifted off of his shoulders.

"You tell him his son, Vicenté Francois Chevalier, is here to see him."

FOURTEEN

A shiny black-and-white-tiled floor covered Pierre's art deco dressing room. Vadé had supervised every single detail of the decor. Pierre sat on a director's chair and poured himself a drink to help him face Desiree's livid gray eyes.

"Pierre, did my father say something to you? That's all I want to know." She folded her arms over her chest and gave her husband a look that said *you're giving me answers.*

Vadé opened the door, walked into Pierre's dressing room, and focused gray-green eyes on her father.

"Papá, this man, Vicenté Francois, says you're his father."

Pierre looked into Vicenté's eyes and immediately knew. They were Felicite's eyes in his face, on his body, years ago.

"Oh my God." Desiree dropped the glass of wine she was holding and watched it shatter into pieces.

"Mamá! Are you okay?" Laurent walked in and rushed to his mother as she dashed out of the room brushing past Little Claude.

"Dez . . ."

"Mamá?" He turned to look in the direction his mother had gone. "What's going on here?" He looked to his father for an explanation as JP tiptoed in and stood against a wall.

"This man just said Papá is his father!" Vadé informed her brother.

"What's your name again?" Pierre walked over to Vicenté for a closer look as everyone waited for his response. There was no way he could deny it. The man looked just like him.

"Vicenté. My mother's name is—"

"I know who your mother is. How is she?"

"She died almost eight years ago."

"Felicite is dead? Oh, no." His handsome face clouded with pain. "I'm sorry to hear that."

Laurent and Little Claude went to stand by Vadé. JP joined them as well. They couldn't believe what they were hearing or seeing.

"She gave this to me before she died." He handed Pierre an envelope with a pink satin ribbon tied around it.

"Papá?" Vadé was waiting for some sort of explanation that would make Vicenté magically disappear.

Pierre carefully untied the ribbon and read the envelope addressed to him care of the Prideauxes where he had never spent a single night. It was marked *return to sender.*

> *My dearest Pierre,*
> *I can barely wait until I join you in New Orleans. Everything is so boring since you are gone. There is nothing here for me. Pierre, I just found out I am pregnant. We are going to have a child.*
> *All my love,*
> *Felicite Francois.*

Pierre closed the note and returned it to the envelope and carefully tucked it away in his pocket.

"Papá, what does that letter say?" Vadé's eyes bored a hole to the core of his soul.

"Nothing for you, Princess."

JP gently folded his arms around Vadé as he stood behind her, as if he were shielding her from the world.

"She gave me these too." Vicenté handed Pierre a stack of assorted newspaper clippings. "She said you were my father. She talked about you all the time, but she didn't show me these until she gave me that letter."

"How old are you, Vicenté?"

"Twenty-eight."

Everyone in the room subtracted twenty-eight from forty-five, which meant Pierre was seventeen when he first became a father.

"Is he really your son, Papá?" Laurent finally asked the question that everyone was dying to know.

"Yes. Yes, he is. Vicenté, this is my son Laurent." He tried to pull him by his side, but Laurent was hesitant.

"Vicenté and I already met."

"And, Princess . . . my daughter, her name is Vadé. This is JP and that's Little Claude. This is my family. Now I've got to go talk to Dez. Princess, make sure Vicenté has whatever he needs."

"I will do no such thing." She glared at Vicenté as Pierre left the room. "I don't care what my father says, you will never be my brother." She turned and ran out of the room.

"Day! Sorry, man. She's just upset." JP gave Vicenté an apologetic glance.

"Did you know who I was before I introduced myself to you at the buffet?" Laurent demanded.

"Yeah, I'd like to know the answer to that question as well." Little Claude stood beside his cousin.

"No. Not until you introduced yourself to my woman. If you re-member, you were the one hitting on my woman."

Laurent and Little Claude laughed as the others joined in.

"Sounds like Lar to me. The brother is smooth." JP laughed.

"I'm just glad to know he's my brother. Now I don't feel so bad. No one's ever tried to pull my woman with me right there and be suc-cessful at it. Little brother, you are the man."

The young men all howled with laughter.

"At least I know my woman is safe now."

"I don't know about that," Little Claude warned.

Vadé heard voices the moment she stepped out of the old-fashioned elevator that had been installed in the hotel for the family and their guests. She tiptoed down the hall to her parents' door.

"Why didn't you ever tell me about her, Pierre?"

"Tell you what, Dez?"

"About her."

"She was someone I knew when I was a teenager in Haiti."

"You left that island with her thinking you were going to send for her?"

"Dez, we were just kids."

"Why didn't you send for her?"

"I don't know. I got busy. The time was never right. We lost contact. I didn't know she was pregnant. This was over long before I met you."

Vadé knelt by the door and continued listening.

"Dez!" Pierre's voice pleaded. "Say something."

"For all these years I thought I was the only girl who was special to you."

"Dez, you were. You are. Help me out here."

"But that's not true. She was first. And your black bastard son."

Black . . . There was that horrible word again. Only this time it wasn't Krista from school. It was Mamá saying it to Papá about Vicenté, the mysterious stranger who was ruining all of their lives and changing everything again, this time forever.

Vadé dragged herself down the hall to her room. She felt as if she had just been stabbed with a knife. She lay on her bed and sobbed as her lifeblood flowed from an invisible wound. The elevator doors opened and JP walked swiftly down the quiet hall to Vadé's room and tapped on the door.

"It's me, Day, let me in."

He jiggled the doorknob slightly as she got up and went to open the door. Her face was still wet with tears. The taffeta party dress was crumpled and wrinkled. Half of her hair was still pulled up into a bun while the other was hanging down in her face.

"Are you okay?"

"Yes."

"No, you're not. Come here." He brushed the hair from her eyes and pulled her into his arms.

"Mamá called Papá a black bastard. It was just like the time Krista and her cousins called me a black bitch."

"No, it's not. Your mother's upset. She didn't mean what she said."

"She sure sounded like it to me. And that horrible man who says he's my father's son . . ."

He had to stop her from saying something awful about the man downstairs who was indeed her brother. The only thing he could think of was to kiss her, long and hard and with passion. To his surprise she didn't say another word. She reached up and unzipped her dress, stepped out of it, and threw it on a chair. She stood there looking at him dressed only in her panties, brassiere, and garter belt.

"Day, what are you doing?"

"I want to be with you, JP."

He allowed her to remove his tuxedo jacket, shirt, and bow tie before he realized what was happening. He watched as she unbuckled his pants.

"Are you sure, Day?"

"I'm very sure."

She had never been more sure of anything in her life. Nothing was the same anymore except JP. He was always there for her and tonight she needed and wanted all of him.

For a moment, they stood there as if they were seeing each other for the first time. Vadé took off her stockings one by one and unpinned the rest of her hair as he took her in his arms.

In the club, Vicenté found Martine at the bar having another glass of champagne.

"You ready to go?" She took a puff on her cigarette and watched the smoke ascend in a cloud.

"Yeah, let's get out of here, baby."

She finished the last of her champagne and stamped out the lipstick-covered butt in an ashtray.

"You'll never believe what just happened." Vicenté handed the valet a dollar as they got into the Corolla.

"What?"

"I just met my father and his family for the first time."

"Really? Your father was at the hotel? Why didn't you introduce me?"

"I will at the right time."

"Who was he?"

"Pierre Chevalier."

"Pierre Chevalier? He's your father? Why haven't you ever mentioned this before?"

"Because I wasn't sure if he'd own up to me, but he did."

"Did he give you a hard time?"

"Not at all."

"So what did he say?"

"Nothing too much. Asked me my name. I think he knew as soon as he saw me. My mother always said I looked just like him."

"So tonight, just now, was the first time he found out about you?"

"Yes."

"He's married, isn't he?"

"Yes."

"I wonder what his wife will say."

"She was there. Everybody was there. His entire family. His wife didn't say anything. She just screamed and broke a glass when she saw me."

"That's because you look just like your daddy, and he's your daddy, and she's not the mother. If it was me, I'd be kickin' Pierre's behind right now."

"Why? It's not like he played around on her or anything."

"It's the principle of the matter." Martine pushed some buttons on the radio. "It's a woman thang."

"Well, she'll just have to get over it. She's got more than my mother ever had."

"That's true. I'm sorry about your mother, V, but just imagine being Mrs. Pierre Chevalier."

Vicenté made a face. "Little sister acts like she's his wife."

"Little sister? You have a little sister? Where was she?"

"Baby girl has some kind of position. I saw her in the kitchen but I didn't know who she was. Everyone was calling her mademoiselle and practically bowing at her feet. She acts like she thinks she's better than everyone."

"Hmm. People probably wouldn't be able to stand me either if my father was rich. What does she look like?"

"She's gorgeous. She looks like she should be my sister. She's a little lighter than me and my father. She got the cream from her mother, but she has the same black hair. It's down to her waist and these grayish green eyes."

"Green eyes. She is beautiful. She's a Princess Sister."

"Princess Sister . . . You know, my father was calling her Princess, but her name is Vadé. What's a Princess Sister?"

"A Miss Thing. You know . . . a girl who's got it goin' on. Rich, powerful, beautiful, in control . . . There's just something about her . . ."

"Like you?" Vicenté smiled at Martine.

"Yeah . . . like me." She paused to smile. "But your sister's got the money. And she was working? You go, girlfriend!"

Martine snapped her fingers and they both laughed.

"Remember the young brother who put the moves on you?"

"Laurent?" She had to laugh.

"He's my—"

"Your brother," Martine finished for him. "What a trip. . . ."

The family's suites were quiet now. Vadé and JP snuggled closer together under the covers as they slept peacefully in her darkened bedroom.

Downstairs in the club, Amour began their last set. Laurent and Little Claude sat with Giselle at the family table. Laurent, uninterested in the band, tapped nervously on the side of his glass.

"Baby, what is it?" Giselle placed her hand over his.

"Nothing, T. I'm fine." After he smiled and kissed her hand, he whispered in Little Claude's ear. They left the club and headed for the dressing room.

"You all right, man? That was deep what Pierre laid on us about his son, but don't let it get you down."

"No, *mon ami*, I'm cool with all of that. Things happened. . . . I have an older brother. Welcome to the family."

"He seems pretty cool. Especially when you were trying to pull his woman. A brother can get shot for something like that in America, Lar."

"I know." Laurent's dazzling smile lightened his face as he laughed. "But she was much too pretty for me to ignore."

"She was fine. I can dream about Martine."

"It might be nice having an older brother. You've always been my brother, but Vicenté is older than us all, including JP. He's twenty-eight and he can take us youngsters places."

"I know, Lar. I see a lot of potential there, so what's bothering you?"

"I saw Mamá backstage crying when she should have been singing. I asked her what was wrong and she told me nothing."

"Well?"

"She wasn't crying over nothing."

"Lar, that's between her and Pierre. Whatever it is, I'm sure everything's fine. You know how they're always somewhere kissing and holding hands. They're worse than my father and mother."

"I know, Claude. You are right. I wonder how she's handling this situation with our new brother."

"She seemed a little upset when she left the room."

"A little? She only broke a glass and screamed."

"Lar, you know she can be very emotional at times. Especially when it comes to Uncle Pierre."

"I know but even that seemed a little extreme for Mamá. That's why I am so concerned."

"I wouldn't be because Uncle Pierre can't live without Dez, and T can't live without him."

"They do share a very special love for each other."

Upstairs in the master suite, Desiree quickly sifted through dresser drawers and tossed articles of clothing in an open suitcase. She removed a photo of the children from her dressing table and tucked it in the suitcase as well. Finally, she snapped the suitcase closed and sat at the desk in her sitting room. In the desk drawer, she found a piece of stationery engraved with the letters DC and opened a fountain pen.

> *Pierre,*
> *I need some time to think. Don't try and find me. I'll find you when I'm ready.*
> *Dez*

She tucked the note into an envelope, sealed it, and placed it on Pierre's pillow. She picked up her suitcase as she closed the door to her room. Down the hall, she tiptoed past her daughter's room where Vadé and JP still lay intertwined.

Down the elevator, Desiree eased out the back door by the side of the stage where the band was about to complete its last session. Outside, she got into a waiting taxi and disappeared into the dark night, unaware of the eyes that had watched her.

FIFTEEN

Vadé smiled at her reflection in the bathroom mirror as she played with her hair, finally sweeping it up into an updo. She glanced at the steam shower where she and JP had concluded their night of lovemaking. *Papa was right. I do want to do it again . . . and again and again.*

She closed the door to her suite and went downstairs to open up the hotel's corporate office. It was a small suite of offices including space for her secretary, Jewel, and Mrs. Lipscomb, who handled all of her father's personal business.

She pushed the button for the CD player. Noel Pointer's sweet strings were soothing. She sat down at her desk and opened her "to do" folder and sighed. She couldn't think or concentrate on anything but JP and their incredible night as she floated off into Loveland.

"Good morning, mademoiselle."

Vadé jumped at the sound of Camille Lipscomb's voice.

"Good morning, Mrs. Lipscomb. I didn't hear you come in."

Vadé looked at her watch. It was almost nine-thirty.

"I've got to change that music or I'll never make it," she whispered to herself.

She yanked open a drawer in her Louis III desk, which she had moved into her office, and flipped through the extra CDs and pushed it shut. Everything was too mellow. She needed something from her brother's eclectic collection to keep her from daydreaming.

"I'll be right back, Mrs. Lipscomb. I've got to go upstairs and get something."

Vadé sprinted up the stairs in the front of the hotel rather than taking the elevator. She was surprised to see the door open and light streaming out of her parents' suite. She paused by the door of the silent room and noticed their bed had not been slept in. She poked her head in and saw her father sitting in a chair, staring out the window. An ashtray overflowed with half-smoked *gauloises*.

"Papá? What's wrong?"

He looked at his daughter to make eye contact and looked away. *Those eyes.*

"Where's Mamá?"

"I don't know, Princess. She's gone."

"Gone?"

"Yes, sweetheart."

"Where?"

"I don't know."

"When is she coming back?"

"I don't know, Princess, soon. Now be a good girl and plan a dinner for me, tonight, in the suite. We're having a family meeting. Call Big Claude and T, JP, and your brother. . . . I'll call Vicenté."

"Vicenté? He is not part of our family. That horrible black man is the reason why our mother's gone." Her eyes sparkled like a cat's.

"Vadé! Do not ever speak that way about your brother again."

He had never used that tone of voice with her, nor had she ever seen him that angry.

"Never." He turned back to gaze out of the window.

She wanted to die from the hurt. She had to get out of there before she started crying.

"Is there anything in particular you'd like served?"

"No. Just make sure it's very nice and get several bottles of champagne for the bar."

"*Oui,* Papá." She closed her father's door and ran down the hall to her room. *Champagne . . . my mother's gone and he wants to have a party for that . . . man.*

Vadé was on the telephone when Laurent walked into her office around four o'clock. He picked up her phone and ordered a steak sandwich to be brought up with their tea.

"Day? Have you seen Mamá?" He tossed his book bag on the floor and stretched his long legs.

Lar doesn't know Mamá is gone.

She stared at her brother with a funny look on her face.

"What's wrong?" He looked up from a music magazine he was reading when she failed to answer. "Why do you have that look on your face?"

"She's gone, Lar."

"Where?" He frowned.

"Nobody knows although Papá said T and Grandmother know. But I don't think so. T was surprised when I told her and she said not to tell Grandmother."

"She left because he wouldn't let her sing. That bastard."

"Lar, don't say that about Papá! She left because of that horrible man."

"Horrible man? Who are you talking about, Vadé?"

"That man who showed up yesterday and said he was Papá's son."

"Vicenté? He is, Day, Papá said so."

"I don't care what Papá says, he'll never be my brother."

"Day, he seems nice. Give him a chance."

"Never. Do you know Papá is having a dinner for him?"

"When?"

"Tonight, around seven. I had to call everyone."

"Do you think Mamá and Papá will get a divorce?"

"Papá said not to worry. Mamá will be home soon. They love each other."

Vicenté and Martine arrived at the hotel around seven wearing red. They were two beautiful people out to have a beautiful time. A doorman escorted them to the family elevator.

"Can you believe this?" Martine squealed once they were inside the elevator alone.

"Papá's got it going on." Vicenté ran his fingers over the jade marble covering the inside walls and floor.

When the doors opened, forest-green carpeting covering the corridor sprawled before them like the Yellow Brick Road. Mrs. Lipscomb stepped into the hall and beckoned for them. She led them into a sitting room with a view of the lake. A waiter made them doubles of Courvoisier.

Lar came out of his room first wearing a mint-green sweater and khaki Dockers.

"What's happening, big brother?" They patted each other on the back as if they had been *boys* for a while.

"How are you, gorgeous?" Laurent allowed his eyes to inhale Martine's beauty and smiled.

"V, you better come get him. He is such a flirt."

"She certainly is gorgeous. I must agree with my sons." Pierre walked into the room and gave his glass of Chevis Regal to the waiter for freshening.

"Good evening, Papá. How was your day?"

"Fine, son. Hello, Vicenté." He extended a hand toward his eldest son. "And who might this beautiful lady be?" He took Martine's hand and kissed it.

"Oh my God! Are you all this way?"

Laurent and Vicenté looked at each other and laughed.

"Yes," the brothers chorused.

"I'm Martine and it's a pleasure to meet you, sir."

"Good evening, Papá. Hello, Lar."

"Everyone looked at Vadé, who had just made her grand entrance wearing a black St. John that hugged her gentle curves. The one-karat diamond earrings sparkled at her ears and a hammered gold choker and bracelet seemed to glow against her cocoa skin. Her presence commanded their attention.

Vadé's gray eyes converged on Martine's brown ones until Laurent interrupted the silent duel.

"Hey, Day. Vicenté's here with his girl, Martine."

Vadé's and Martine's eyes locked in battle.

"Is that supposed to be French?"

"What?"

"Your name."

"No, it's Span—"

"Whatever . . . Are the two of you supposed to be dressed alike or something?" Vadé focused her eyes on Martine's red dress and Vicenté's red shirt.

"No, we—"

"Thank goodness."

"Day, can I get you something to drink? Martine, would you like another glass of whatever it is you were drinking?"

"Thanks, Laurent."

Vadé's eyes followed Martine as she got up to give her brother the glass. *I bet she has the hots for Lar. They always do.*

"She is such a bitch," Martine whispered just loud enough for Vicenté to hear.

"I told you," he whispered back.

Giselle, Big Claude, and Little Claude walked in laughing. Pierre introduced everyone to Vicenté and Martine. JP arrived several minutes later.

"Hello, beautiful," he whispered in Vadé's ear with a kiss. "I haven't been able to think about anything but you, and what we did last night."

She blushed at his remark. "I know." She smiled. "I feel the same way."

"Let's get out of here." He took her hand and tried to lead her toward the door.

"No, we can't leave right now. We have to stay for Papá's precious little dinner for Vicenté. Besides, we can't do that with everyone up here."

JP suddenly noticed the group of family members who had gathered.

"Maybe you're right. Do you have any vacancies downstairs?"

"JP, you are terrible . . . but I think we do." She smiled.

They joined the rest of the family in the dining room at the Louis III table for twelve. Pierre sat at the head of the table and Big Claude at the other end. Laurent sat on one side of Pierre, who invited Vicenté to sit on the other. Vadé and JP sat in the middle.

"Thank you, Lord, for bringing my entire family together, again. Amen."

Pierre blessed the food and nodded for the waiters to serve the family. The kitchen had prepared a dinner of fried chicken, shrimp, and oysters, Creole potato salad, grilled vegetables, steak, salmon, gumbo, and dirty rice.

"Before everyone eats up all my food and drinks all my alcohol, I just want to make an announcement." Pierre grinned from the head of the table.

"He's lit," JP whispered to Vadé.

"He's been drinking all day. Mamá is gone."

"What?"

"This is Vicenté's official welcome to the family," Pierre continued. "Welcome home, son." Pierre lifted his glass and toasted his firstborn.

"Where did Dez go?" JP and Vadé were whispering again.

"We don't know."

"Deep."

"That's why I can't understand my father. He's throwing champagne dinners and my mother is God knows where."

JP kissed her with a little more passion than he normally did in front of the family.

"JP, stop. Not in front of Papá."

"He's too ripped to notice us and I had to do something to get your mind off of the family and back on me."

Martine finished her drink as she watched Vadé and JP.

"This is my son, Vicenté Francois Chevalier, and he is part of this family. And anyone who doesn't like it will have to deal with me. Now eat."

He glanced at his daughter, who was occupied with JP.

"Let's go," Vadé whispered to JP. "I've had enough of this charade."

They eased out of the kitchen and downstairs to a bedroom below.

"Let's play the rich young lawyer seduces his fine, sweet secretary who can't speak any English, only French," JP suggested as she opened the door.

"That sounds wonderful, Monsieur Olivier. I am ready for dictation."

Laurent joined his father and Big Claude, who were talking with Vicenté while Martine sat down with Giselle and Little Claude on the sofa in front of the big-screen television.

"Vicenté, what do you do for a living? I have so many things to learn about you." Pierre nursed a fresh drink and a cigarette.

"I'm a chef."

"Really?" Laurent was impressed. "What type of food do you prepare?"

"Haitian, Creole, southern, some French, and Jamaican. Several desserts."

"All that?" Pierre was equally fascinated. "We could use someone like you in the kitchen. Give the menu a nice Third World flavor."

"Yeah, Papá, that sounds great." Laurent was already licking his chops.

"You interested in coming to work with your old man? We like to keep all of our business in the family."

"I could be interested in doing something like that . . ."

"If the money is right?" Laurent finished with a smile.

"I love this little brother," Vicenté offered sincerely. "I really do."

Pierre rubbed his hand across Laurent's hair. Now that he was in America, he and Little Claude both wore their hair cut short and close to the scalp.

"Call the office and arrange an appointment with my secretary. I'll talk with Vadé. We'll work out something for you. I already know you can cook, son, because you're a Chevalier. And whatever we do, we do well."

"My mother taught me how to cook when I was very young. She was the cook for a missionary and I used to help her. The older I got, the more she let me cook."

"Tell them about the show, V." Martine smiled proudly at Vicenté.

"I'm working on an idea for a show for the cooking channel on cable."

"So what's stopping you?" Pierre finished his scotch and set the glass on the table.

"I need the experience of cooking some various cuisines. I want to cook Creole and Caribbean dishes, and Copelands just wants me to prepare southern."

"It's settled then. You will cook here at Right Bank."

"My brother, Vicenté Chevalier, the world-famous master chef, who thinks he's a player, cooking right here at Hotel de Chevalier," Laurent teased.

Vicenté smiled as Pierre made a champagne toast. As hard as he tried to fight it, he was enjoying his new family. He had come for revenge but Laurent was making things difficult.

Pierre was pleased to see his sons conversing with Big Claude. He politely excused himself, avoiding eye contact with either of them, went to the bar, and poured himself another double of Chevis Regal, and tried to stop the gnawing ache in his heart spreading through his body like wildfire.

SIXTEEN

The academy's high school graduation fell on a lovely morning in June. Bouquets of magnolias, azaleas, and camellias added splashes of color around the podium and platform that had been set out on the lawn. The family stood and cheered as Laurent Chevalier and Claude Olivier's names were called and the cousins received their diplomas with honors. Martine watched Laurent stroll cross the stage in a cream designer suit.

"He is so fine."

"He's a Chevalier. He can't help it," Vicenté reminded Martine.

"When Juliet turns sixteen, I'm going to introduce them."

"Your sister Juliet? That tall, skinny little girl?"

"Yes."

"Martine, baby, my brother likes women. Don't forget he was looking at you when we met him."

"My point exactly. Give my princess sister a minute. She'll have Laurent all deep off in love just like you."

She closed her eyes to kiss him as Vadé walked up.

"My men are the most handsome around. Just look at them."

Vadé kissed Laurent and Pierre on the cheek as she locked each of her arms through one of theirs, and posed while Giselle clicked away with several cameras. The family was stunning in the custom suits Vadé had made in Paris.

"Where's your suit?" Martine asked under breath. "You're part of the family."

"I know." He looked at the family laughing and talking and wanted very much to belong. "This is another one of princess sister's attempts to keep me out. Those suits came from Paris."

"Oh."

Martine glanced in Vadé's direction. "Where's pretty boy?"

"JP has final exams."

"Isn't he going to be a lawyer or something?"

"Yeah. He's going into law school at Grambling. He's a real good brother."

"Princess sister snatched herself a good one."

"JP said their fathers planned for their children to marry before they had any. If he's not around to keep Miss Thing occupied, you can't get near Laurent or Pierre."

"She acts like they're her men. Look at her." Martine nodded at the Chevaliers in front of the camera.

"Come, Vicenté and Martine. You're part of this family, too." Laurent called them over for more pictures. He stood between the two of them and smiled. "T, take one of me and Vicenté, me and my big brother."

They stood together, Laurent slightly taller than Vicenté, with their arms bent around each other's shoulders, and smiled.

"Thank you, *mon ami*. Thank you for coming to my graduation." Laurent's words and smile were sincere.

Vicenté felt himself choke with emotion.

"Excuse me, I'd like to speak with my brother." Vadé turned eyes cold and hard as cat-eyed marbles on Vicenté as she spoke to Laurent privately.

"So how shall we celebrate your graduation?" Now she focused mischievous green eyes on Laurent.

"I wish Mamá was here."

"She would be if it wasn't for him. . . . It's all his fault."

"Day—"

"Okay. I made plans for you, Little Claude, and me to meet JP for lunch."

"Day, I told you I'm having lunch with the fellas and JP's coming too. Vicenté already made plans."

"I thought I had talked you out of that silly idea. I can set something up for us in the restaurant. Play some music—"

"No, Day." He spoke firmly but gently. "You just want to find some way to exclude Vicenté. If you don't come to the restaurant with us, you'll have lunch by yourself."

"I'd rather die first."

She stormed off toward her mother's Mercedes coupe and left. She had plans of her own. When JP returned from lunch with the guys, she had reserved a room for them to play in. She was the doctor, and he was the very willing patient. She smiled and stepped on the gas. *Let them have lunch with Vicenté. I have better things to do.*

At a soul food restaurant on the other side of town, Vicenté ordered fried chicken, barbecued ribs, potato salad, yams, and collards. A pretty waitress passed out jelly jars of lemonade spiked with Jack Daniel's and plates of green-tomato crab cakes while they waited for the food.

"Congratulations, son."

Pierre smiled warmly at Laurent as the family extended fresh jars of lemonade and toasted the cousins.

"May your journey to happiness always be filled with prosperity."

They clicked their glasses and dug into the platters of food being placed on the table.

"This is the best fried chicken I ever had."

Laurent bit into a crisp wing while Vicenté pulled apart another one and sprinkled it with hot sauce.

"What are your plans for the future, Laurent?"

"I'm going to sing—"

"Laurent is going to college to begin his studies in law and oversee the legal matters of the family businesses," Pierre, who had overheard the question, answered for him.

"Papá, you know JP's going to do that. I'm going to sing."

It tore him to pieces when his father contradicted him like that. Laurent looked at his father and wondered why he was so against him becoming a singer. *He knows this is something I've talked about forever. I wish Mamá was here.*

It had been several months since Desiree's disappearance. With the exception of a ten-second message on the service, telling the children she was fine, no one had heard another word from her since. She had even called during the day when no one was around.

Laurent dropped his fork into his plate. He was no longer hungry. He asked for a refill on his lemonade and was silent.

"What's wrong, Laurent?" Vicenté was genuinely concerned.

Laurent looked into Vicenté's eyes and recalled his sister's words, blaming Vicenté for their mother's departure.

"Nothing." He grinned at his handsome brother. "Martine, you don't mind staying alone while V takes me out on the town? I'm all graduated now."

"I guess he can go." She looked at them both skeptically. "The two of you together might be lethal."

"Might?" Laurent laughed.

"Most definitely." The brothers slapped a high five.

"Martine, have I told you how beautiful you are looking today? If I didn't, please forgive me."

Laurent poured on the sweetness for Martine, who did look very pretty in a black and white sundress, red straw hat, and red sandals. He bowed his head and kissed her hand.

"Go away," she gasped. "Both of you."

Outside the restaurant, Martine gave Vicenté a long kiss and took their shiny black BMW. With Vicenté's position at the hotel, the couple had purchased the car, new. She blew a kiss at the brothers as she sped off with hip-hop music blaring out the windows. Laurent and Vicenté waved and fastened seat belts in Laurent's classic red Mustang convertible, a graduation present from Pierre.

Vicenté paused to admire the rich butterscotch leather seats in the automobile.

"This is sweet!"

"She sure is. So that's what I call her, Sweet."

Vicenté doubled over laughing. Laurent could be such a kid.

"You know Papá calls his Rolls She?"

"Get out of here. I thought he was just referring to the car as *she* as most men do."

"No. He calls her She because the color of the car is the same as my mother's eyes."

"Your sister has those eyes, too."

"Yes. The *shes* of the family. The ladies."

"I'm sorry about your mother taking off and all. Wherever she is I hope she is well."

"She's fine. Thanks, V, I know she is. I just miss her. I pray for her every day."

"I still miss my mother, too."

"Your mother was a missionary?"

"No. She was the cook at the mission."

"That's really great. That's why God's always been watching you, my friend."

"I never really looked at it that way. I guess He has."

"No doubt. That was great the way you used to cook with her. Now you always have a part of her."

"You're right. I do. Sometimes when I taste certain foods I can go right back to the time I first tasted it and what we were doing then."

"That's the way it is for me with my music."

"Music does take you places. I can hear a song and remember what I was doing when I heard it. Who's that playing now?"

"It's some German dance music I purchased in Paris."

"It's got a nice beat. Are you really into music like Pierre?"

"Most definitely. My mother has a beautiful voice. I grew up with the band, listening to jazz. I love all kinds of music, but I want to perform American pop music."

"Cool. I'll take you to take you to a reggae festival when we get back from the track."

"Reggae? I love reggae. This is going to be great."

At the racetrack Vicenté bought a newspaper and explained his personal betting system to Laurent. They chose several horses and placed bets using Vicenté's method and won five hundred dollars each.

"Can you believe this, V? We won five hundred dollars! This is so much fun."

Vicenté rolled up his wad of bills and placed it in his pocket.

"Lar, that's no money for you."

"Oh, yes, it is. Papá has money. This is mine."

He yelled with excitement and ran to the window and plopped down all five hundred dollars on a horse named Sweet while Vicenté tried to talk him out of it.

"I can't lose, V, that's my girl."

They returned to the stands with large plastic cups of Long Island iced tea with crushed ice. Laurent was thirsty and he took several gulps of the drink.

"Man, don't be getting drunk. I don't want Pierre getting on my case about you."

"V, I'm not drunk. Remember, I'm from Paris where we drink wine all the time."

"All right, Lar. Just be cool."

Laurent grinned and jumped up and started shouting.

"Come on, Sweet. Come on, baby. Run for Daddy."

Vicenté jumped up and followed the horses through binoculars. "Run, girl, run."

The brothers watched as the horses thundered across the finish line.

"Dang. Sweet missed it by a second!"

"A second too late." He looked sad as he thought about the five hundred he had won and lost so quickly. *I could have bought something nice for Mamá.* Then he remembered he couldn't have anyway.

"I've lost thousands, man. But I don't take as many chances since I got with Martine. Don't waste your life being a loser like me. Here . . . take half of mine." He handed Laurent two hundred and fifty dollars.

"No, V. That's yours. I lost mine."

"I insist." He pressed the bills into Laurent's hand. "A graduation present from your big brother, because you're a winner."

"All right. Thank you, *mon ami.* And you're a winner, too. We're Chevaliers."

He placed a hand on Vicenté's shoulder as they headed toward the car.

"I'm ready for de reggae, mon." Laurent feigned the island accent very well.

They finished their iced teas and drove across town to a park overflowing with people, vendors, and stalls of Caribbean art and food. They left the car parked on a street several blocks away. The infectious reggae rhythms filled their souls and bodies as they were automatically drawn toward the pulsating beats.

"This is great, V."

Laurent danced around eating a Jamaican meat patty and fried plantain.

"You look right at home here," Vicenté hollered over the music.

"I am. Mamá always makes fried plantain for Papá."

They stayed until Ziggy Marley performed. Then they sat down to plates of rice'n'peas, jerk chicken, and curried goat.

"You can really cook all of this stuff, V?" Laurent shoveled rice and peas into a pile with his fork.

"I sure can. I'm going to feature a Caribbean dish each night as a special at Right Bank. I'm also going to add some items to the new menu like fried plantain." Vicenté smiled as his brother wolfed down the last piece.

"When does the cooking show start?"

"I'm going to submit everything once we get some reviews in newspapers and magazines."

"We'll have to plan a party for you at the hotel."

"Slow down, Lar. We haven't had any reviewers come in yet."

"You will. You'll be world famous, you'll see."

The brothers ended their celebration with more Long Island iced tea as they watched fireworks on the upper deck of a juke joint overlooking the Mississippi River.

"Lar, do you really want to be a professional singer?" Vicenté focused his eyes on his brother.

"More than anything in my life."

"Are you any good?"

"Am I a Chevalier?"

The brothers grinned at each other in response.

"All right. Come with me, little brother."

He led Laurent back inside the club and across the floor where a local band plucked out dance tunes.

"What do you want to sing?"

"You're kidding? You want me to sing here? Now?"

"You're not for real, man."

"I am so for real."

"Then stop talking about singing and get up there and sing. Show me what you can do. These guys are buddies of mine. All I have to do is give the word."

Vicenté had called Laurent on the carpet. Singing around the family was one thing, but to sing in front of these American strangers . . . Yet, it really wasn't that different from singing at one of his parents' soirees, but there he always had Mamá with him.

"Can they play 'My Cherie Amour'?"

"They can play anything you want."

"Fine, that's what I'll sing then, some Stevie Wonder."

Vicenté whispered with several of the guys during their next break.

"You're the first thing on the next set."

Laurent gulped and swallowed hard. He had never been nervous before. He looked around at the room of people drinking, smoking, and talking. *What if they hate me?*

Vicenté handed him a real drink, a double of Courvoisier, as he took the stage.

"Just take a gulp of that to help the jitters and get on out there. You're a Chevalier. You're going to blow them away, little brother."

"Are they going to introduce me?"

"Sure. Is there some special name or something you want them to say?"

"Lar . . . Lar Legrande."

Laurent walked onto the small stage as the lights went down. He was wearing a pair of his favorite jeans and a new reggae T-shirt he had purchased from a vendor at the festival. Laurent was extremely handsome no matter what he had on. His bronze hair had deepened and his butterscotch skin was extremely tanned. A few women screamed when they turned blue and white spotlights on him.

As the music to Stevie Wonder's classic thumped through the speakers in the joint, Laurent began to cast his spell. He sang and danced, with an intensity he had never experienced before. He could feel every single person and connected with their souls, mesmerizing them with his Chevalier charm and music. When he sang the last note, the women screamed and everyone applauded. Their eyes tried to follow him as he left the stage.

"That was the best feeling in the world."

"You were all right, Lar Legrande. I'm impressed."

"Thanks, V, and thanks for setting that up for me. That was the best graduation present I received."

Vicenté smiled knowingly. "My little brother is going to be a star."

Laurent, who had been walking a few steps ahead, turned around and walked back to meet his brother.

"Speaking of graduation presents, didn't we park the car here?"

"I thought we did. I remember that pink house was right across the street."

"I remember the pink house, too. So where's my car?"

"I think somebody got you, little brother."

They walked back to the club and phoned the police.

"I hope they find Sweet. I really liked my car."

"I hope they find her too, man. I'm sorry."

Laurent was glad to have Vicenté there to talk to the police. He had never had a car stolen and he found it a relief to have his brother there with him.

"We'll take a cab to the restaurant and I'll get the BMW and take you home."

"No, V. You don't have to take me back to the hotel. I can take a cab home."

"A cab? You live way on the other side of town. You are not taking a cab because I'm taking you home."

"But—"

"Don't say another word."

They listened to rap music all the way to the hotel. It was the only tape Martine had in the car. Vicenté pulled the car into the circular drive and gave it to the valet.

"Good evening, Monsieurs Chevalier."

The brothers nodded at the parking attendants and took the elevator to the third floor. They were both surprised when Pierre met them in the living room.

"Laurent, where is your car?"

Laurent looked at Vicenté and wondered how he knew.

"The police already found it. Your stereo and rims were stolen. They were just about to take the seats out when the police caught the thieves."

"Thank God." Laurent sighed with relief.

"The car was impounded. You can pick it up tomorrow."

Pierre lit a cigarette and faced his other son.

"Vicenté, what were the two of you doing in that part of town? You had no business taking Laurent there. Anything could have happened to him."

"But nothing did," Laurent added softly, attempting to pacify his father's rage.

"You may want to wallow on that side of town but don't you ever take my son there again. You two smell like a still."

He glared at Vicenté through alcohol-hazed eyes, then poured himself another drink and tried to rid himself of the memory of the girl he never returned for. A woman who died of a broken heart while she waited for him to return. He looked at Laurent and looked away. His sons and their mothers had brought him too much pain.

"Laurent is my son, and don't you ever let anything like this happen again."

"Why? Because he's *her* son?"

Some of the spite and hatred he had nursed in his own heart for his father and his other family suddenly surfaced.

"No. Because you're the eldest and you should know better."

Pierre's words cut his own heart and he was immediately ashamed. He would never let anything happen to Laurent or Princess Sister. There was a grueling battle raging inside him, holding on to his hatred or letting it go so he could belong.

Laurent watched his brother as he walked away.

"See you, V. I had a great day."

The elevator opened and whisked Vicenté out of sight. Laurent looked at his father as he downed yet another drink. Suddenly he felt lonely as he walked down the hall toward his room and tried to overlook the emptiness that had haunted him every night since he had watched his mother disappear in a taxi.

SEVENTEEN

Vadé fastened a black silk stocking to her red garter belt and adjusted the tight French maid's uniform over her boobs. She brushed her hair up into a ponytail, which she never wore, and secured it with a black rubber band. In the mirror of her sea-foam-green marble bath, she carefully applied fire-engine-red lipstick to her lips. Finally she tied a white apron over the sheer black dress she had her seamstress make for the game.

She opened the bathroom door and stepped into her bedroom where JP was stretched out on her bed in black silk pajama pants. Vadé walked into the room and opened a bottle of champagne.

"Bonjour, monsieur. I am Fifi, the chambermaid. Is there anything I can do for you?" She smiled and winked while JP sat straight up in bed.

"Dang, Day, you look fine."

He took the glass of champagne and set it on the table and pulled Vadé down on the bed and kissed her.

"But, Monsieur Olivier, I cannot do this."

She stood up and straightened the uniform. Now she was going to play hard to get.

JP sat back and grinned. He loved this part of the game. It would make it even better at the end.

"Fifi, I'll have that massage now." He turned over on his back and she began to rub in almond cream. Her hands felt so good.

This was the hardest thing for her, not giving in before the skit was over, but JP loved it no matter what she did.

"Monsieur Olivier." She stood up and pulled the apron off her see-through uniform and allowed the dress to drop to the floor. "I'm ready now."

JP was all over her in a matter of seconds and she heard herself screaming.

"Vadé, are you in there? Is everything all right?" Someone was knocking on her bedroom door.

"Don't answer it," JP whispered.

"It's only Lar."

"Still, don't answer it."

"Lar's cool. I want to know if he heard me screaming."

"I'm sure everyone in the hotel heard you screaming."

They both laughed as Vadé found her robe and opened the door to her sitting room.

"Day, do you want the whole world to know what you and JP are up here doing?"

She saw Vicenté standing in the hall behind Laurent laughing.

"You go, little sister. Must be those Chevalier genes getting off up in there."

"What is *he* doing up here?"

Vadé slammed the door shut and went back into the bedroom.

"That wasn't Pierre, was it?"

"No."

JP sighed with relief. "Who was it? Lar?"

"And Vicenté." She had never called him by his name.

"Day, did they hear us?"

"Yes. Vicenté made some disgusting comment about my Chevalier genes. I don't know why Lar hangs out with him."

"Come here, Fifi Chevalier. Put that dress back on and stuff one of these in your mouth."

He handed her a black silk stocking and they both laughed.

She showered after JP left and put back on the green silk Chanel suit she had worn to work. She pinned her hair back up and applied an earth-tone lipstick.

"Hello, Mrs. Lipscomb. Did you enjoy your lunch? Mine was delightful."

She breezed into her office and sifted through the messages that had accumulated while she was at lunch.

"Mademoiselle, your brother is here to see you." The receptionist buzzed through on the intercom.

"Oh, send him right in."

She looked up, expecting to see Laurent, and was surprised to see Vicenté walk into her office.

"What do you want?"

"I just wanted to speak with my beautiful sister for a moment."

"So what do you want?" She sighed with impatience but Vicenté would not be moved. He did indeed bear a strong resemblance to her father and she hated to admit it.

Vicenté couldn't believe he had gotten this far with his princess sister. All he had to do was to stand his ground and stop being intimidated by her. She was just a kid.

"Mademoiselle, I have some new dishes I'd like for you to sample."

He couldn't believe how much older and sophisticated she appeared in her suit and chignon. Nothing like the girl he had witnessed earlier, standing in the doorway with her hair in a ponytail, wearing red lipstick. He covered his mouth and coughed to keep from laughing.

"When would you like for me to try them?"

Her green eyes were sparkling for once, instead of mean and cold. He could tell she was still jazzed from her rendezvous upstairs. She looked like a woman who had just had some really good loving.

"Shall I send them upstairs to your room around noon tomorrow?"

She looked at Vicenté and tried to muster up an ounce of hate, but couldn't. He knew what she had been doing and now he was part of her secret.

"Can you send them up at eleven-thirty?"

"*Oui*, mademoiselle. At eleven-thirty."

"Vicenté! Wait!" Something had been bothering her since noon and she didn't know whom to ask.

"What is it, mademoiselle?"

"Is it bad to scream?" She was a little girl and he had never seen her so vulnerable.

"Are you in love with him?"

"Yes."

"Good. Then it is not bad for you to scream, but a good thing."

"Really? Why?"

"Because when a man makes a woman scream like that, she'll never let him get away."

Vadé blushed as she tried to suppress a smile. She couldn't believe she was discussing her sex life with, of all people, Vicenté, but there was no one else to ask. She could never ask Laurent or, God forbid, Papá. Vicenté was her last resort and she was relieved to have an answer to her question.

"Next time, just turn on some music or something to cover up the noise."

Vadé sat daydreaming and thinking about JP. Playing Fifi had been fun. She picked up the phone and dialed Olivier's law offices and asked for Jean Paul.

"Jean Paul, it is me, Fifi. How are you this afternoon?"

"Day, I can't think of anything but you and that sexy French maid's uniform."

"But of course," she giggled.

"I want to see you now."

"I want to see you too, Jean Paul."

"When?"

"I'll have dinner waiting for you in my chambers at seven, monsieur."

"Day, I'm going to be all over you," he breathed into the phone.

Vadé hung up the phone laughing and dialed the kitchen. "Vicenté, can you prepare those dishes for seven tonight?"

Six o'clock finally arrived and Vadé had the corporate offices locked by five after. She rushed upstairs, showered, covered her body with almond cream, and slipped into the tight little dress. She threw on her robe and opened the door as one of the room service girls wheeled in her dinner.

"Just leave the tray by my bed." She spoke in a feeble voice. "I feel like I'm coming down with something."

"*Oui*, mademoiselle. I hope you feel better." She removed the dishes of food from the tray and left.

Vadé threw the robe back on the chair and ran back into the bath to comb her hair and apply the red lipstick. On second thought she removed the black dress, put on a red bustier and garter, and put the dress back on. She slipped on heels and stockings as her doorbell rang.

"Hello, beautiful."

JP walked in and handed her a bouquet of long-stem roses, a box of chocolate-covered strawberries, and a bottle of champagne.

"Hello, baby."

She allowed herself to be pulled into his arms and kissed.

"We've got the entire night."

Downstairs, the band had completed its first set. Pierre, not up for company, decided to spend the hour break in his room. He grabbed a bottle of scotch and headed for the elevator.

In her room, Vadé, dressed only in the bustier, stockings, and garter, began to massage JP's shoulders and back.

"That feels good, Day. But I don't know how much more of this I can take."

"Oh, but it will be so much better, Jean Paul." She purred in his ear in French as she stroked a rose across his back.

"That did it, Day."

He threw her down on the bed and climbed on top of her.

"Jean Paul." She moaned as he began to kiss her body all over. Minutes later she was screaming.

JP looked for a stocking to stuff in her mouth but she was still wearing them. Pierre, who was just about to enter his room, ran down the hall to his daughter's room when he heard her scream.

"Princess!"

He burst in through the small corridor that led through the living room. Vadé and JP tried to get under the covers but Pierre had already seen and heard.

"Vadé!"

She shivered under the covers at the sound of his voice. He stood there, angry beyond his wits, as he looked at the two of them, together, in bed.

"I want to see you both, in my room, in thirty minutes . . . with your clothes on."

He stormed off toward his room while Vadé and JP trembled with fright.

"What do you think he's going to do to us?" JP whispered.

"I don't know," Vadé replied thoughtfully. "Me first in the shower."

Thirty minutes later Vadé and JP walked into her father's suite. She was so embarrassed she couldn't even look in his direction.

"Have a drink, son." He handed JP a glass of scotch and ice.

JP stared at the glass, and Vadé stared at JP.

"Drink it."

JP took a big swallow and coughed.

"That's good for you. You're a real man now."

"Sir—"

"Shut up. I'm not ready to talk to you yet. I want to have a word with your woman."

"Here, you have a drink, too. You look like you can use one."

He poured a shot of vodka in a glass, added a twist of lime and a cube of ice, and handed the drink to Vadé. She took the drink and gulped half of it down.

"Good, huh, Miss Like-to-Scream-in-my-House? Now you can scream louder."

Vadé could tell he was one step away from losing it. She had never seen him this angry in her life. She gulped the rest of the drink and wanted another.

"You want another one, don't you?" He smiled like a crazy man as he poured more vodka in a glass. "Here."

He extended the drink. As she reached for it, he slapped it from her hand. She watched the glass and ice cubes sail across the hardwood floor in the family room.

"I will not have my daughter behaving like a common whore."

"Papá!" she yelped and JP jumped to her side.

"Sit down! She is not your responsibility yet. She is still my daughter."

Vadé began crying and his heart melted. But she was his baby girl and now she had to receive the consequences for her actions.

"Sit down and stop crying."

He poured himself another drink as Rene and Aubrey Olivier entered the suite.

"What's going on, Pierre? You said there was a family emergency. Is something wrong?"

Rene looked at his son, who was comforting Vadé.

"No, just that we're having a wedding."

Pierre calmly sipped a fresh scotch as he looked at his daughter.

"Well, I've always known that we would, Pierre, the minute I laid eyes on Vadé. JP knows what he wants and I agree."

"Good. Because the wedding is tomorrow."

"Tomorrow? What's the rush?"

"Rene, the kids were just telling me how much they want to be together."

"But what's the hurry, Pierre? I thought they would at least wait a few more years so JP can finish law school first."

"JP is going to finish law school. There's no question about that. But the kids can live here in Vadé's suite until JP finishes."

Pierre looked at Vadé and JP, who were totally surprised by every word coming out of his mouth.

"But I still don't understand the rush. I thought we would plan a big wedding for them here at the hotel." Aubrey looked at her son and back at Pierre.

"Aubrey, I feel the same way." Pierre walked over to the bar for ice. "But Vadé and JP are determined so I've given them my blessing, so let's have a drink and toast the newlyweds-to-be. Vadé, there's more ice in the kitchen."

JP started to follow her but Vadé signaled with her eyes that she wanted him to remain with their parents.

"JP, tell your parents what you were just telling me about my daughter."

Vadé had returned with the ice and placed it on the bar.

"Dad, I'm in love with Day. I'm crazy about her and I can't stand to be without her. She's in love with me and we want to be together . . . all the time."

JP looked at Vadé and smiled.

Vadé smiled back at JP. She loved making love with him but marriage . . . even if she did want to object, there was no way out. They had to get married now. Papá was serious.

"We're going to be married tomorrow at City Hall with a big party tomorrow evening, here at the hotel," Vadé offered.

"Pierre, it seems like the three of you have really thought this out." Aubrey was still somewhat skeptical.

"Yes, we have, Mother." JP took another swallow from his drink and smiled at her.

The following day, Thanksgiving eve, Jean Paul Olivier and Vadé

Michel Chevalier were married. All of the family attended and Vicenté prepared a wonderful buffet for the reception. He walked over to her while no one was looking and whispered just loudly enough for her to hear.

"Did Pierre catch you?"

"Yes, last night," she whispered back.

"You just couldn't get enough. I know he heard you screaming." He started laughing hard.

She was still embarrassed by the thought of her father finding them in bed.

"Princess Sister, it's those Chevalier genes. You can't help it. That's why he made you get married. He knows what it's like."

Vadé had to smile as she watched her father converse with Big Claude and Rene . . . the Olivier Brothers. Now they were all family by marriage and blood, and Vicenté was part of it.

"Everything will be beautiful, Princess Sister, just like you. JP is a good man and he loves you. A good man needs a good woman," Vicenté whispered and was gone.

How does he know? Is this a brother thing or what?

She watched him as he walked away and recalled a similar conversation she had had with Laurent several years ago in France.

EIGHTEEN

Martine opened the door to the town house in the French Quarter. She got excited every time she came home to the condo that she and Vicenté had purchased together. She dropped a huge set of keys into a good copy of a Lilique bowl that her mother had found on sale in a crystal shop. The town house, which was one month new, was three stories. It sat on a narrow cobblestoned street in a seventeenth-century facade.

Martine cut on the stereo and dashed up several stairs to the dining room where she dropped her accounting books on the table. There was a huge kitchen on the other side of the dining room and two additional bedrooms up another level. There was another bedroom and bath on the bottom level that the couple utilized as an office. It was noisy at times because they were right in the heart of the Vieux Carre, but Martine loved it. There was always something going on. Police sirens, music, and laughter were constant intrusions and the neighborhood tingled with excitement.

Vicenté had wanted them to move into the hotel with the family, but she had finally talked him out of that whacked idea. Mainly because Pierre said there would be no shacking up in his hotel. She dashed up the stairs to the master suite she shared with Vicenté. A king-size black wrought-iron bed, an armoire, and a chaise lounge were the only furnishings. A comforter and drapes in forest green complemented the deep mauve walls. She had an endless list of other things she wanted to buy for the house.

Martine kicked off her shoes and stretched out on the bed. She had just taken a calculus final. She had put off taking the requisite course for her business management degree as long as she could. If she went to summer school she would graduate from Dilliard next January. She went into the bathroom and turned on the shower. As she stood there drying off, Vicenté walked into the room.

"I see I'm just in time."

Martine tucked the huge green towel under her arm, pulled the shower cap from her head, and shook it in Vicenté's direction.

"No way. You're not getting anything right now. Did you bring some food home? I'm hungry."

"I know you are." He stepped toward her and smiled.

"V."

"*Oui*, mademoiselle."

"And don't start that Chevalier French charm. You know I can't resist that stuff."

"I am aware of this, mademoiselle." He kissed a droplet of water from her neck.

"V."

Martine tried to protest as he removed the towel, but the Chevalier charm had caused its victim to succumb once again.

They sat in the living room in pajamas, on a huge stuffed sofa made out of fabric the color of gingersnaps, eating pasta, curried chicken, and grilled vegetables.

"It's nice to come home and find my woman waiting for me wrapped up in a towel."

"Baby, as long as you cook, you can come home and find me wrapped up in a towel every day. It's so wonderful having a man who cooks."

She laughed and stretched her legs so that her feet were in Vicenté's lap.

"Especially when you can't." He smiled as he massaged her feet.

"Yes." She laughed. "Guilty as charged. I hate cooking."

He took out a bottle of gold fingernail polish and handed it to Martine.

"Look, baby. I got you a new color."

She shook the bottle and handed it back to him.

"This is real pretty, V." She watched him thread toilet paper through her toes.

"My princess sister was wearing this color and I thought it would look nice on you, too."

"Thanks, baby. That was so sweet of you."

She watched him carefully apply polish to the big toe of her pretty, slender foot.

"I love your feet." He kissed her toe after he finished polishing it.

"All right, V. Don't start that."

He laughed as he added a second coat of polish. "We're not doing anything now. I'm not messing up my handiwork and you're not getting polish on this sofa."

She laughed and threw a pillow. "We'll see."

She watched him finish the job with clear polish. Vicenté screwed the top on the bottle and set it on the glass coffee table in front of him.

"I miss you, baby. The only time I'll get to see you is tonight, 'cause you're usually studying all day Saturday and Sunday."

"I know, V. But I've just got one more year until I graduate."

"And then what? More work?"

"At least I'll only work during the day."

"Yeah, and at night when you come home, too, Miss Executive. I know you intend to pull a major power play."

"Ah, V. It won't be like that. Your sister works and she doesn't have to. She can just spend her daddy's money."

"Yes, but she goes home to her man, too."

"Yeah, Miss Thing did up and get married. Her and pretty boy must be getting crazy busy." Martine started laughing. "And they're living in that hotel. Ugh."

They both laughed for their own reasons. Martine because she couldn't imagine being married and living in the same house with your parents. Vicenté could still see his sister's face when Laurent knocked on the door to tell her to shut up because everyone could hear her screaming. He had never laughed so hard, nor had he ever told anyone about their subsequent conversation.

"Marry me, Martine, so we can make lots of beautiful babies. I'll take care of you. I'll cook, polish your toenails, make love to you."

Martine, who was lying with her head in Vicenté's lap, sat up.

"V . . . you're serious, aren't you?"

"Woman, you know you had me hooked lock, stock, and barrel the day you walked into Copelands looking for a job. I told Copeland he had to give you that job or else I was going to quit."

"You really said that? I can't believe you did that."

"Oh, yeah. I had to make sure I saw you and your fine self again."

"I'm so glad you did. We were going through some rough times. Daddy had just passed and I needed money for college. Daddy always wanted me to go school. So, see, I have to finish, Vicenté."

"I'll make sure you finish school. If you want to quit Copelands and just go to school, I'll take care of you."

"Quit Copelands? But, V, if I keep working, we can use the money to buy some furniture for the condo."

"Martine, will you let me be your man? I want to take care of you."

She looked at Vicenté and thought about what he had just said.

"It would be nice to just go to school. Can we afford it?"

"Let me be the man. Besides, you keep all the money, so you should know if we can afford it."

Martine pulled several checkbooks out of her bag. She looked at the balances in all their accounts and closed the books.

"We can afford it. We'll have to stick to our budget."

"And . . ."

"All right, I'll do it. I'll give my two-weeks notice on Monday."

"Wonderful." Vicenté smiled, exposing perfect white teeth. "Now what about the rest of my question?"

"What?"

"I asked you to marry me."

"Oh. That's right, you did."

"Well?"

"All right, let's do it." Martine was excited.

"When?"

"One year from now. That will give us time to save for our wedding and me finish school."

"All right, Madame Chevalier."

"Chevalier. I'm going to be Martine Bárres Chevalier."

"Sounds like one of those corporate power players to me." Vicenté stroked her hair. He loved seeing her that excited.

"It does, doesn't it? V, can we go pick out a ring tonight?"

"Tonight? I thought you were tired."

"That was before we were shopping for engagement rings."

"Martine, it's the middle of the night. I don't think we're going to find any jewelry stores open now."

"Oh. Then I guess we'll have to go first thing in the morning."

It was an extremely warm Saturday morning in February. It felt like summer. Vicenté dropped the top on the couple's convertible as Martine locked the condo and ran down the stairs to the car. She popped a Luther Van Dross cassette in the player as Vicenté jumped in and pulled off.

"It is such a nice day." She put on a pair of sunglasses and stretched her arms to the sky.

"Do you know what today is?" Vicenté grinned at her from behind a pair of dark shades.

"No." She gave him a quizzical look.

"It's Laurent's birthday. We have to get him a gift. Vadé is setting him up with food from the restaurant at his own table in the club. I think they said Babyface was performing tonight at the club."

"Babyface? You're kidding. I think he is so fine."

"So that's why you're always playing his tape."

"V, you're crazy. Why didn't you tell me all of this was going on tonight?"

"I told you Lar was having something at the hotel for his birthday."

"Yeah, but you didn't say it was going to be all this."

"Baby, with my family, everything is always all this."

All of the store windows in Riverwalk were garnished with red, pink, and gold hearts of all shapes and sizes. Vicenté and Martine walked hand in hand through the mall.

"V, baby, I've been so busy I forgot it was Valentine's Day."

"All day long."

"This is so romantic, us looking for an engagement ring on Valentine's Day."

"That's because I'm romantic."

"You sure are, baby. You're the most romantic man I know."

"What other men do you know? Are you talking about that clown I took you from when I first met you?"

"Alphonzo?"

"Yeah, that fool."

Martine threw her head back and laughed. "You're still jealous."

"Of that fool? Please . . ."

Alphonzo was a chemical engineer. They had begun dating while she was in high school and Alphonzo a student at Dilliard. He had asked her to marry him, but she had said no.

"He was probably boring."

Martine squealed to keep from laughing harder because Vicenté was right. Alphonzo was sweet, but he bored her to tears.

They stopped in front of the first jewelry store they came to and paused to look at the diamond engagement rings.

"Not." She smiled and the couple moved on to the next jewelry store.

"These are nice, V."

He followed her inside the store. A saleslady seated them in front of a glass counter where Martine described the ring they had seen in the window.

"I can't believe we're doing this," she whispered while the woman arranged the rings in a black velvet box and placed it in front of them. Martine picked up the marquise-shaped three-carat diamond surrounded by several carats of smaller diamonds and tried it on her ring finger.

"This is fabulous, V." She extended her hand for Vicenté to see.

"That's real fine, Martine. How much is this one?" He looked at the saleslady.

"Fifteen thousand dollars."

"Fifteen thousand dollars?" Martine carefully removed the ring and placed it back in the velvet box. "That's me and my champagne taste on a beer budget."

Martine . . . not letting me be the man.

"There are several other rings here at various prices. Why don't you look through these?"

The saleslady took the marquise so she could return it to the window.

"I know you want to buy me that ring but you can always get it for me on one of our future anniversaries."

"That's right, baby."

He watched her examine rings and look at the prices. But that was just another one of the reasons why he loved her. She was strong and willing to do things for herself like his mother, Felicite.

None of the other rings excited her especially for the price. They were all around five thousand. Martine picked up the last ring and immediately fell in love with the brilliant cut stone in a baguette. She was equally pleased when she saw the ring was only thirty-five hundred dollars.

"V, this is the one I want." She extended her hand so he could see.

"The stone is one carat and the stones in the baguette are half a carat. That's a very pretty ring and it's nicely priced."

"Are you sure that's the ring you want?"

"Yes, V. It's absolutely perfect. I won't even need to have it sized."

Martine thought she would explode while Vicenté counted out the price of the ring in cash.

"Where did you get all of that money?"

"From a stash I've been saving for the Martine Ring Fund."

"You've been planning this for a while . . ."

"From the day I first saw you. Now come with your man to buy a birthday present for his brother."

"Lead the way, Big Daddy."

Vicenté smiled to himself. He had been saving all his winnings from the track to buy her a nice ring. He had been prepared to buy the first ring, but that was Martine, forever running the show.

"It figures that Laurent would be born on Valentine's Day."

The designer jeans and pink polo shirt for Laurent sat on the back-seat of the Beemer, appropriately wrapped in shiny white paper covered with red hearts. They had changed and were on the way to the party. Martine, in her trademark red, couldn't help admiring her ring. She held her hand up to the window watching the light reflect in the stones.

"Are you going to tell your family we're engaged?"

"I'm going to tell the whole wide world." He smiled happily.

They walked into the club where Laurent was dancing with a beautiful blonde.

"Happy birthday, little brother!" Vicenté greeted him with a hug.

"Hello, beautiful." Laurent was already flirting.

"See this, man?" Vicenté held out Martine's hand. "See that ring?"

"Yes. It's very nice."

"I'm serving notice on all you dogs, keep your hands off my woman."

Laurent carefully examined the ring.

"You two are engaged?" He flashed a brilliant smile at his brother and then Martine.

"Yes." They were unable to contain their smiles.

"Congratulations, V and Martine. Did you tell Papá?"

"We haven't told anyone yet but you."

"Happy birthday, Laurent." Martine kissed him and handed him the gift.

"Do you think this gift is supposed to make up for you breaking my heart like this?"

"Laurent, stop."

Martine and Vicenté laughed as he continued his act.

"I'll never fall in love again." He broke into laughter.

"We have something bigger to celebrate than me turning eighteen."

He led them over to the table where his father and Big Claude were sitting.

"Papá, Vicenté and Martine just got engaged. Show him the ring."

Martine extended her hand so they all could see.

"Congratulations, son."

That was the first time Pierre had ever called him son.

"Thank you, Pierre." For the first time he wanted to say Papá like Laurent, but the word just didn't feel right yet.

"This calls for a toast." Pierre called a waiter and instructed him to bring champagne and glasses.

"To my son, Vicenté, and his lovely fiancée, Martine. May you give me lots of beautiful grandchildren."

Martine looked around and suddenly realized what her liaison with Vicenté meant. She was actually going to be a member of this family.

Vadé walked up to the table in a red minidress. She looked like a different person with her hair done up in a ponytail and bright red lipstick. She was so beautiful Martine had to gasp. Martine could see the huge diamond rock and wedding band on her finger as she took the glass of champagne her husband poured for her.

Vadé took a sip of the bubbly as she stood next to Martine and smiled.

"Congratulations."

"Thanks, Vadé."

Martine really hoped the two of them could become friends since they were going to be sisters-in-law.

"You didn't stop until you got your hand on one of them. Unfortunately Vicenté is the poorer one, but nevertheless a Chevalier."

Martine was so surprised her mouth dropped open as Vadé continued.

"Sweetheart, I hate to inform you that this hotel and everything in it belongs to my mother, so don't waste your time thinking you will ever get a penny."

NINETEEN

It was Christmas Eve in Nawlins once again. The second without Pierre's beloved Dez. It would be two years in February since he saw her last. He poured himself a shot of Chevis Regal and drank it straight. It was noon and he hadn't bought a single gift for the family.

Pierre ran his hands through his hair as he stepped into a chocolate marble shower. He propped his head on the wall and stood there allowing the water to massage his back and soothe his soul.

Where are you, Dez, and when are you coming home? I miss you and I need you.

He mindlessly soaped his body. At forty-seven, he still didn't have a stomach with everything he loved to eat. But he knew he needed to get back to the gym. He hadn't gone in months.

Dez has to be missing me as much as I miss her.

They had never been apart for more than a couple of days. That was while she was pregnant with Laurent and Pierre was in New York handling business. They were in Paris the entire time while she carried Vadé.

I miss you, Dez. I miss your face, your voice, and your body . . . Oh, God, could You please send her home tonight?

He took the stairs and stopped on the second floor to make some phone calls to order gifts for the children and to speak with Mrs. Lipscomb. Vadé had taken care of the other presents.

Hotel de Chevalier's corporate offices were beautifully decorated with garland and artificial shiny red candy apples that looked good enough to eat. There was a Christmas tree in the lobby by the registration desk. Vadé had decorated the hotel before he even thought about Christmas. He ran smack into the tree on his way to his office on the first of December. That's when he realized it was Christmas.

He glanced at Vadé as he sat down at his desk and picked up the phone. She was on the telephone, and hadn't seen him come in. Things had been extremely cool between the two of them since her wedding a year ago. Vadé was still embarrassed and Pierre couldn't handle looking into Dez's gray eyes in his daughter's face. Desiree's eyes were always gray when she was upset or not smiling. Just like his daughter's. He couldn't handle those eyes. Now it was one year later and they still hadn't spoken about anything except work, and that was only when Vadé found it absolutely necessary.

Pierre missed his daughter. She had always been his baby girl, his little princess from the moment she opened her eyes and smiled at him the first time he held her in his arms. He had been her favorite guy until JP entered her world. With Desiree gone things were already bad enough. Now he had to endure a cold war with the only other woman in his life, his daughter. When it rains, it pours.

He went out the lobby door and down another flight of stairs. The hotel had never looked more beautiful. Vadé had really outdone herself with the decorations. There were beautiful vibrant poinsettias everywhere. Miniature white lights were strung through ropes of garland in the restaurant and club. Nat King Cole crooned softly in the background.

Pierre winced and ducked into the empty club. "Have Yourself a Merry Little Christmas" was Dez's favorite song. As he went to the bar, he saw Big Claude going into the dressing room.

"Don't tell me you're coming to work, Chevalier." Claude laughed when Pierre walked in behind him.

"No, man. I'm not playing tonight. I just came in here to talk to you."

"You've haven't played since we broke for Labor Day. You don't want to play your music anymore?"

"I'm not in the mood to play." He looked behind the bar for some scotch, but there was none so he picked up the phone and ordered a bottle of Chevis Regal and a bucket of ice.

"How are you, Pierre?"

"Terrible." He took out a box of *gauloises* and lit one.

"I've noticed the way you've been lighting into that scotch and those cigarettes."

"This is the second Christmas Dez hasn't been here. I don't know how much more of this I can take."

"As much as it takes. You know Dez is fine wherever she is."

"Why do you say that?"

"Don't forget that Dez's mother, Amelia, is Giselle's aunt. None of them seem overly concerned."

"Has Giselle ever mentioned anything?"

"She told me she hasn't spoken with her, but Amelia has."

"I know that much. I was hoping you might have heard that she was coming home for Christmas."

"No."

Pierre poured himself another drink to help numb the pain that never went away.

"What if she never comes back?"

Pierre nearly dropped the glass. Someone had finally voiced his greatest fear.

"Dez will be back."

"How do you know?"

"She said she would."

"But that was almost two years ago."

"Don't remind me."

"Have you considered seeing someone?"

"I haven't been with another woman since I met Desiree and I don't want another woman."

"That's why you need to focus on something else."

"Like my music?"

"Or your kids."

Pierre poured himself another drink. Big Claude was going for broke today.

"What about them?"

"How's Vadé?"

"Still not talking to me."

"I wouldn't talk to you either."

"I had to do something or kill her."

The men finally laughed.

"I can hear her screaming now and me running down that hall to save the day. I had no idea anything like that was going on."

"Something was definitely going on. JP is an Olivier."

"I know she thinks I saw them. But I didn't see anything but my baby under the covers with JP."

"That was enough. Did you tell her?"

"No."

There was a brief knock on the door and Vicenté walked in.

"Good afternoon, Pierre, Mr. Olivier."

"Vicenté, how many times have I told you to call me Big Claude. Mr. Olivier is my father."

"All right, Big Claude."

"Vicenté, is there something you needed, son?"

"Just to confirm tonight's menu."

"Didn't you take care of that with Vadé?" Pierre lit another cigarette.

"Yes, but she told me to double-check everything with you."

"Make whatever you like, Vicenté. It's your dinner too. You and Martine will be joining the family for Mass?"

"Yes."

"Good. I will see you at St. Augustine's."

Vicenté closed the door and left as Pierre made himself another double of Chevis Regal.

"It's Christmas, Claude. Have a drink with me." He splashed scotch and ice into another glass.

"You treat him like a servant." Claude took the drink from his friend.

"I don't intend to. He's my son. He looks like I spit him out."

"You ain't never lied."

Big Claude had him laughing. Maybe things weren't as bad as they seemed. But who was he trying to fool? His woman was gone and it would be awfully nice to get laid. He took a sip of his drink. He used to hate scotch. He once said anyone who drank it wanted to get drunk . . . real bad.

"I don't know what else to say to Vicenté."

"Have you ever just taken him out for a burger, just you and him?"

"No, but he spends a lot of time with Laurent."

"That's Laurent, not you. Do you know what his favorite color is? The date of his birthday?"

"No."

"Chevalier, get to know your son. You've got a lot of catching up to do."

"I don't want to deal with that yet."

"Why?"

"Because I know he and Laurent want to ask me questions that I don't want to answer."

"What questions?"

"About their mothers. I know Vicenté wants to give me the third degree about Felicite, and Laurent has questions that I don't have answers to."

"So you're avoiding both of them?"

"Yes. I'm a punk with a broken heart."

They both laughed.

"I'm sure that has something to do with why they're always together."

"I couldn't keep those two apart if I wanted. I know Vicenté takes him out to clubs. They go to the racetrack too."

"Little Claude thought I was going to let him club-hop on school nights. He's running around here talking about how he's Lar's manager and he's going to sign him to a record deal."

Pierre almost choked on his drink. "Not if I have anything to do with it."

"Chevalier, you are not going to stop Laurent from going onstage. It's in his blood. He grew up around the group and music. There is no way you're going to stop that boy. He's a man now and it's his life."

"Claude, I had to become a musician like Vicenté had to become a cook. We found something we were good at and learned to do it well enough to make money."

"You talk like there's something's wrong with being a musician or a cook. Both of you are masters of your crafts and make good money."

"I've recorded over a dozen albums that sold well and traveled around the world living out of a suitcase. Since Vicenté took over, the restaurant is always overbooked. He's going to teach Creole and Caribbean cooking classes in January."

"And something's wrong with all that?"

"Nothing is wrong with all that, but it was our only option. It's not socially correct to be just a cook or a musician in New Orleans."

"Chevalier, don't tell me you're going to let a bunch of snobs dictate your family's lives."

"When we first got back in the States, Dez's father told me not to let her go onstage."

"What? Maurice Legrande is a fool. And you're one too for letting him interfere with your family."

"I had no choice. He told me he'd never let the hotel open if I allowed Dez to perform. He has friends in high places."

"So that's what that whole Dez not singing thing was about. Giselle and I never understood it. He really stuck a knife in your back."

"Did you tell her what he said?"

"No . . . he threatened me about that, too. I wanted to tell her but you know Dez would have told him off and we'd have no family business."

"But you'd still have Dez. . . . Talk about a rock and a hard place."

Pierre sighed and poured more alcohol in his glass.

"But the hotel is up and running now and no one can stop it. So there's no reason for you not to support Laurent."

"I support Laurent, but he has numerous options. I had none."

"You did have a choice. You could be in Richoux's right now waiting tables, or maybe you could just own a restaurant, like you do. Or you could be a successful musician, which you are. Now if you had to pick one, which one would it be?"

"My music."

"Your music. Chevalier, you are such a hypocrite."

"I just want something more for Laurent."

"Like what?"

"I'd like to see him solve a major world problem or come up with a cure for some disease. I want him to do something great, something important."

"Music is the universal language of the world, and your son has a tremendous gift. He's going to do something great."

"Maybe you're right. But I still want Laurent to finish school first. If he has his degree he'll always have something to fall back on."

"That's true, but you and I both know Laurent won't need anything to fall back on. The boy is magic."

Vadé opened the door and poked her head into the dressing room.

"There you are. We've been looking for you everywhere."

She came into the room with JP and closed the door.

"Thank you for our Christmas present, Papá. It's beautiful!"

"Yes, thank you very much, Pierre."

JP was equally excited and Vadé's eyes were green and sparkling. Pierre relaxed for the moment and smiled.

"You're welcome, Princess." He took her in his arms and hugged her. "And I never saw a thing," he whispered so only she could hear.

"I love you, Papá!"

She was his little girl again.

"Do you know what Papá bought me for Christmas, Big Claude?"

"Us," JP gently reminded her.

"What did you do now, Chevalier?"

"Come outside and see!"

Vadé took both of the men by the hand and led them outside to the front of the hotel where a fire-engine-red Targa with a huge gold bow was parked in the circular drive.

"That is one sweet car, Chevalier. Can you get me one of those, too?"

Laurent pulled into the drive while they continued to fuss over the Porsche.

"Merry Christmas, son." He gave Laurent an envelope as he walked over to get a closer look at the new sports car.

"You're letting me go skiing in Switzerland with Simone's family?" Thanks, Papá!"

Laurent gave his father a hug as Vicenté walked out of the hotel to wait for Martine to pick him up from work.

"You need a ride home, V?" Laurent called out to his brother.

"Sure, little brother. I have to whip up some eggnog to go with the beignet for dinner after Mass. We can sample it to make sure it's right."

"Then why don't I get my things and go to Mass from your house?"

"Cool."

"Papá gave me a trip to Switzerland. I'm leaving the day after Christmas to spend the rest of the holiday with Simone's family."

"That's great, Lar."

They watched JP get behind the wheel of the Targa while Vadé squeezed into the backseat. Big Claude sat in the passenger seat.

Now all of his children have red convertibles but me. Vicente wrestled with his thoughts.

"You see what Day and JP got for Christmas? It's for their anniversary, too."

"That car is beautiful. I sure hope I'll be able to afford one of those one day."

"You will, V, or either I'll buy you one." Laurent promised his brother.

They watched a flatbed truck drive up hauling a cherry-red Jeep Wrangler and stop in front of the hotel.

"I wonder who that's for." Laurent smiled at Vicenté.

They watched Pierre sign the paperwork, take the key, and walk over to them.

"Merry Christmas, son."

Pierre placed the shiny key in Vicenté's hand.

"Now all of my children have red convertibles."

Vicenté fought back the emotions swirling like a hurricane through his mind and body as he mindlessly followed Laurent over to the vehicle that had just been presented to him by his father. *I really am his son.* He handed Laurent the key and motioned for him to drive.

Pierre stood in the entrance of the hotel watching all of them drive away in their red toys. For a moment he forgot his sorrows and felt like Santa Claus.

TWENTY

"**A**re we gonna throw down with this music like our daddies did or what?"

"We sure are, gumbohead."

It was Saturday afternoon and Laurent and Little Claude were having lunch at a jazz buffet in the French Quarter. Little Claude had just come back to the table with his second bowl of the steaming seafood soup.

"Don't start what you can't finish."

Laurent laughed while Little Claude fished out a slice of spicy Louisiana sausage from the bowl.

"Claude, we are doing the music thing like our daddies. We just finished our first recording session. Tracks for my first tune are on the demo."

Laurent rearranged the rice and shrimp Creole on his plate. He was too excited to eat.

"Olivier and Chevalier, Part Two."

The boys slapped a high five and grinned.

"When we get three nice tunes, I mean really good ones, that's when I'll start shopping a deal and not one minute before."

"Cool. You just tell me how to do what I do."

"We're not in a hurry so we can take our time and make a serious demo."

"That gives me time to write, too. Let's go pick up some equipment so I can put together a lightweight studio in my bedroom."

"Cool. But I think we might want to put the studio in my house and you just camp out there next semester."

"That's fine with me, but why?"

"To keep Pierre off the trail."

"You're right. I don't know why my father trips so hard about me being in the music business when he's a musician. He didn't go to college. He's beginning to get on my nerves."

"He's just missing T."

"I know, but he needs to get a life and stay out of mine. If Mamá was here she'd chill him right on out."

"And you know this."

"He barely says anything to me, but let me take a keyboard home and he'd have a whole lot to say."

"That's why you need to chill out at the house. We can go to school, hit the library and the studio as much as we like. Dad won't say anything. He knows everything we're doing. He's my consultant."

"Keep it in the family, right?"

The boys slapped five again in their own special way.

"That's the only way . . . because blood is thicker than water. And when Day and JP got married, the Chevaliers and the Oliviers became blood forever."

"Good, because my father couldn't take another relationship like that."

"Why? What happened?"

"I think he caught Day and JP in her bedroom doing the wild thang before they were married."

Little Claude spat out the sip of iced tea he tried to swallow and Laurent was practically on the floor laughing.

"Tell me you lie? Day and JP getting busy in her room?"

"Yes. Vicenté and I came upstairs to have lunch and we heard her screaming her head off."

The boys laughed so hard they were crying.

"Don't you ever tell her I told you."

"You know I won't say anything. Olivier was getting off."

"Man, they are so sickening."

"Worse than they were in Paris?"

"Yes. They hug and kiss all the time. But that's when I see them. Usually they're always locked up in her room."

"And JP is cool, right?"

"Oh yes. . . . If I ever thought JP would do something to hurt Day, he wouldn't have lasted this long. I just miss my sister. She's one of my best friends. We used to hang out and do stuff. We haven't done anything together forever."

"I miss Day, too. I used to love going to the Latin Quarter with you guys, it was always an adventure."

"She's in love, *mon ami.*"

"JP too. Man, he's just as bad."

"I never see him. The minute he gets to the hotel, they are in her bedroom."

"JP's never had any and he doesn't know how to act. He's ruining the Olivier reputation. Day blew his mind."

"She is a Chevalier, but she had never any either. That's what makes it so funny."

The cousins were laughing again as they gossiped about Vadé and JP.

"Lar, it's all those artsy French movies we used to see in the Latin Quarter."

"JP never had a chance."

The cousins continued laughing.

"We all learned quite a bit about sex at those movies."

"To my brother-in-law, JP."

They clicked two bottles of Coke together in a toast.

"Now that's something I definitely miss about Paris."

"French girls," they sang together.

"I still dream about Suzette."

"I've had a few about Simone. We had a great time in Switzerland."

"I'm sure you did. What's up with her? She is so beautiful."

"She's cool. She graduated from college. She may seek employment in the States."

"What are you going to do, lease her a room in the hotel and have Pierre kicking your behind too when she starts screaming?"

"Stop making me laugh, Claude. Heck no, but we can get an apartment together in LA."

"Interesting idea. You want to live in LA?"

"That's where the music biz is."

"I want us to move back to Paris."

"Paris?"

"Yes. I miss Paris."

"I do too, *mon ami*. We used to have the best fun in Paris." Laurent looked thoughtful as he reflected. It was more than the fun he longed for, but a time when his parents were together and his mother was home.

"So we kick it for a few years in LA; then we can kick it back in Paris. Then it'll really be Olivier and Chevalier, Part Two."

"Sounds like a plan, *mon ami*. Let's do it."

A waiter removed the dirty dishes and placed ingredients on the table for bananas flambé. Laurent and Claude watched him pour rum over the bananas and light the copper pan.

Claude dug into a dish of warm bananas and cream.

"We'll meet lots of women once you start singing. They'll be all over us."

"Listen to you."

"You know women love musicians."

"I'm starting to see your motivation here . . . women."

"And money. Lar, I'm never getting married. There are too many fine women out there."

"I'm not getting married either. Not unless it's special like my parents."

"That's why Pierre's been hitting the Chevis Regal so hard. He really misses T. He's got it bad."

"You're right. Papá never used to drink."

"Can you imagine a woman who could hurt your heart like that?"

"No, but I suppose if the love was not so strong, it would not hurt so bad."

"You're right. That's that intense hurt-your-heart, 'shoot me, I wanna die' love."

"When I meet the woman who makes me feel like that, I will marry her."

"I don't know if I want to give a woman that much control over me. That's scary."

"No, it's not. That's what makes it so special when people with those kinds of feelings hook up. Look at the family."

"That's true."

"There's a lot of love and the married people are in crazy love."

"Yeah . . . my parents are as bad as yours. My father was just like JP. He's an Olivier. When he saw my mother, he said it was all over."

"See, that's exactly how it is. Once you meet the right girl, it's over. Vicenté said it was just like that with Martine. He said he was going to stay single forever and then he met Martine. They're getting married in February. You won't be afraid when you meet the right girl."

"The right girl . . . I thought they were supposed to get married during Mardis Gras."

"They are. Martine graduates from business school in January. We'll start the Mardis Gras festivities with the wedding."

"Was it like that for you and Simone?"

"Like what for me and Simone?"

"I know you had to feel something for that beauty."

"I felt something, but it wasn't in my heart."

Little Claude was laughing again. "You are such a dog. I can't discuss anything with you except sex and business."

"What else is there to talk about?"

"I give up."

Laurent closed his eyes and shook his head. When he opened them, he saw Vicenté and Martine strolling across the courtyard toward their table. Martine's curves were tucked in baggy overalls, under a red tube top. Vicenté stretched lean brown legs out in front of him as he sat down next to Laurent.

"How are you, little brothers? What are you two into this lovely afternoon?"

"Hi, guys." Martine blew them both a kiss from her luscious red lips.

Laurent kissed the air in the spot where the imaginary kiss landed.

"V, he's starting."

Little Claude started to laugh in anticipation over the scene that would be played yet again over Martine.

"V, Martine is so beautiful that I can't help the way I act when I see her."

"I know how it is, *mon ami*. But you must learn to control yourself."

"You are so right, big brother. I believe a Long Island iced tea could get me started on the road to recovery immediately."

"I bet it would."

Laurent, Little Claude, and Martine laughed as Vicenté signaled the waiter and ordered a round of iced teas for all of them.

"You only want me for my woman and to buy you and your cousin alcohol."

"V, you know it's nothing like that. But you can leave now and send a date over for Little Claude."

The cousins laughed and Vicenté and Martine joined in.

"Y'all stop doggin' my baby." Martine kissed Vicenté on the lips and cuddled up next to him. "Y'all doing all that talking and Vicenté's the one getting the loving."

"Who's the man?"

Laurent and Little Claude looked at each other and smiled.

"You are, V."

"Now you two make sure you remember that."

The young men laughed while Martine spooned ice out of her glass.

"Laurent, you're the best man and Juliet is my maid of honor. You guys will finally get to meet. She's in Europe modeling. I'm sure you two will have lots to talk about."

"I didn't know your sister was a model, Martine." Little Claude collected his notes from the meeting with Laurent.

"She was doing a lot of little things around here. She was Miss Junior New Orleans, you know, that kind of stuff. A friend of the family has a sister who works for some big modeling agency in New York. We sent her Juliet's pictures and they flew her in for an interview. Next thing she's in Europe. She's been over there doing runway and print. My mother's with her."

"Really?" Now Laurent was interested too.

"I haven't seen the kid since she left after Christmas."

"You mean she hasn't been home once?" Vicenté looked surprised.

"No. When she comes for the wedding that will be the first time she'll have a chance to come home. She's been so busy. But I made her promise to come home. She's been gone over six months already."

"Baby, how old is Juliet now?"

"She'll be eighteen the sixth of February."

"The sixth of February is Vadé's birthday, too."

"Oh, and we finally have an official wedding date. We're getting married the first of February. We've only got six more months."

"We'll be twenty in February, too, *mon ami.*"

"That's right, Claude. Soon, we'll be able to purchase our own drinks."

Laurent put his hand in his pocket to give Vicenté money for the drinks. He pulled out a twenty from his Chanel money clip and tossed it on the table.

"V, that clip is going to be full of Benjamins when we get our record deal. We laid down the tracks for our first tune. Olivier and Chevalier are officially in business."

"That's great, Claude. I've been telling Lar he needed to do that. Now what we have to do is book him in some places around town."

"No. It's too soon. We're not ready yet. We're not letting anyone see or hear anything until it's time."

"And when will that be?" Martine crunched the last of her ice.

"We don't know yet, but everything we just talked about is a secret between the four of us."

"Cool, little brothers. I'm down."

"And no one tells Day. We want to surprise her."

TWENTY-ONE

"**H**appy two-year anniversary, baby."

Vadé and JP interlocked their arms and drank champagne from each other's glasses.

"I can't believe we've been married for two years."

"And you're in your second year of law school."

Vadé poured them each another glass from the bottle of Cristal.

"It's time to start decorating the hotel for the holidays. Christmas always used to be my favorite time of year. Mamá used to let me have a little glass of champagne. I loved our annual *reveilion* after Mass. We never have them anymore. I miss Paris and I miss Mamá."

"Baby, you've never said anything about missing your mother."

"I know. But I miss her. I heard her and Papá having a fight the night before she left. I know how I feel when we have a disagreement, so I was going to make her tea. I wanted to cheer her up, only I never had a chance because she left. We had tea together for her anniversary one year and she told me all about when she and Papá were married. We had the best time."

JP smoothed her hair while she talked.

"Jean Paul Olivier, in case I never said it, I never regret the day I married you. Even though it was not our idea at the time, I always knew I was going to marry you and spend my life with someone who made me feel the way I felt when I first laid eyes on you."

"Day, you are messing with me."

She smiled and blew him a kiss. "I love you, baby."

"I love you too." Within seconds, he was all over her.

"JP, I want to go back to Paris."

"I know, baby. We'll go for a visit real soon."

He spoke while he continued to kiss his way down her body.

"Not for a visit, I want to go home."

"Home? You want to talk, don't you?" JP lay down beside her and gazed into her eyes.

"I want to move back to Paris and begin my interior decorating business. You can finish law school there."

He noticed how her eyes were sparkling with excitement.

"You're serious, aren't you?"

"Yes. You know I've always wanted to have an interior decorating business."

"Yes, but can't you do that here?"

"In New Orleans? Ha . . . you know I hate it here."

"I thought you liked living here."

"I love being with you. And you're here, and now I want to go home," she finished softly.

"But I want to finish school here and work with my dad."

"JP, you can do all of that in Paris."

She gazed back into his honey eyes and kissed him.

"Hold it, Day. Now I want to talk."

He sat up and she climbed into his lap and kissed the tip of his nose.

"What's the matter, JP?"

"Stop it, Day. Just hold up."

He rolled over and moved away from her.

"You know I can't think straight when you do that. You're talking about something serious here."

"JP, this is nothing new. I told you when we were in Paris, I never wanted to leave. You can't think I've changed my mind and want to live here."

"Okay, I'll tell you what. Wait until I finish law school and then we can talk about it again."

"JP, I want to go now." She was practically pouting.

"It's less than a year, Day. Don't turn into the drama queen."

"I am tired of this hotel. I am tired of you stuffing socks in my mouth. I want us to have our own house where we can make as much noise as we want. And I'm so tired of working for Papá. My job is so boring."

"Day, it's just another few months until I finish school. Then I can get a job and support us."

"You're not supporting us now. You're living in my father's hotel where I work."

"And that's only because your father made us get married before we were ready."

He had her there. She dropped her head and refused to meet his eye.

"Come on, babe. I don't want to fight. Don't be the spoiled brat that you are."

He walked his fingers up her back and she melted.

How could I ever live anywhere without JP?

"Day, this has been the best time of my life, coming home to you every day. Living the way we do in the hotel with me in school. It's been a fairy tale. All I do is go to school and make love to you. Let's make the magic last just a little longer."

"I agree. . . ."

He kissed her as he gently laid her on the floor.

"JP, wait. You didn't let me finish what I was saying."

She sat up and poured herself another glass of champagne.

"I always tell you that you talk too much. We're done talking."

She smiled as he took the glass from her and finished the champagne. He stroked the long mocha legs in red pumps stretched out across his lap until his hand rested on her thigh, just below the lace on her red negligee. They were sitting on the jade carpeted floor of Vadé's office. Red candles provided soft candlelight.

"You haven't done anything like this for me in quite a while."

"I know, but when I do, you get hotter; then I get hotter, and I'm the one screaming my head off."

JP tried not to laugh, but he wasn't successful.

"I'm glad you think it's funny." She took off her shoe and slapped him on the behind.

"Now she's getting really bad. Where are your handcuffs?"

She pulled out a pair from under a pillow.

"I was just teasing and you're serious. Who are those for, you or me?"

"You." She wrestled him down to the floor and snapped them on. "Now it's your turn to scream."

The following afternoon at Christmas dinner in the family's suite, Vadé got the giggles. Vicenté prepared a huge smoked turkey stuffed with scallop and crab dressing. There was also mashed sweet potatoes, collards, macaroni and cheese, gumbo and rice. Everyone heard her laughing. The room was completely silent because they were all eating.

"What's so funny, Day?" JP was whispering.

"You . . . screaming." She giggled again.

"Don't go there now or I'll have to take you outside in the garage."

Vadé burst into laughter and excused herself from the table. She went into the kitchen where she heard the doorbell ring, and moments later, the elevator doors open. Then there was a strong scent of women's perfume, Opium, and an unfamiliar female voice. When she heard her father laugh in a strange way, she felt herself bristle as she pushed open the kitchen door.

She gasped when she saw Fleur La Tiff, a jazz and blues singer whom her father had booked at the hotel for a previous New Year's Eve engagement. Vadé hated her because she constantly flirted with her father and even Laurent. Fleur looked to be about thirty-five, maybe even forty. She was a café au lait woman with big boobs and big teeth. Most men found her attractive. Vadé found her cheap and hated everything about her from her long, fake, acrylic nails to her long, fake weave.

"What is she doing here now? She's not supposed to be here yet, and on Christmas Day?"

Martine walked into the kitchen with a stack of empty plates.

"Who's that heifer out there drooling over Pierre?"

"Fleur La Tiff."

"So, who is she?"

"A singer my father booked for the hotel. She's not supposed to be here until New Year's. Look at her rubbing her boobs all up against my father while she smiles at Lar."

Vadé and Martine watched Fleur take a seat at the table next to Vicenté and smile at him with her big teeth.

"What the—"

"She'll be all over Vicenté next. Watch."

The girls stood in the kitchen peeking out of the door while Vicenté served her plate. As she took the food from Vicenté, she rubbed up against him and batted her eyes.

"Oh, no, she didn't."

"Boo!" JP sneaked up behind the girls from the other side of the kitchen. They jumped and he started laughing.

"JP!" Vadé gently cuffed his head. "You scared us."

"Sorry, Martine. I didn't know you were in here. What are you doing, girl?"

"Shhh!" She went back to the door next to Martine.

"I'm going out there."

Martine headed for the door and Vadé pulled her back.

"What are you going to do while he's at work? She's going to be here all week."

"Let's get rid of the bitch." Martine's eyes sparkled with fire.

Vadé had never seen her look so determined.

"Okay." Vadé spoke slowly as she thought. "I have an idea."

"Vadé, what are you getting ready to do?"

JP seldom if ever called her Vadé.

"We've got to get Papá to make her leave and never invite her back again."

"Vadé, stay out of it." JP looked like he meant business.

"No, you be quiet, Jean Paul Olivier, or you'll get no dessert if you know what I mean."

"Cool. So what's the plan?"

"Go on, girlfriend. You've got him trained."

She looked at Martine and smiled. She had never had a girlfriend before. It had always been her and the boys. Maybe she and Martine could be friends. She was about to marry her brother and become part of the family whether Vadé liked it or not, and if she could help her get rid of Fleur, they could be friends forever. She thought about the unkind things she had said to Martine and was immediately sorry. *I can really be a bitch sometimes.*

"JP's just looking out for his interest. Aren't you, baby?" She blew him a kiss.

"Don't get fresh. So what are Thelma and Louise about to get into?"

"You're cute, JP." Martine laughed. "Pretty with a sense of humor. I'm impressed."

"I know." Vadé kissed JP on the lips. "He's mine, forever."

"Hey . . . I've got an idea. . . ." An impish grin lit up Martine's face.

"What?" The Oliviers ceased kissing.

"I have a friend who works at a radio station. We can get some letter-head from her and send Fleur a letter inviting her to perform for some kind of special concert at the Apollo for New Year's Eve. Tell her she has to come to New York immediately for press and promotion. Offer her a lot of money and . . . is money an object here?"

"How much are you talking about?"

"A plane ticket to New York."

"If we can get rid of Fleur forever, it'll be worth it."

"Cool. I'll get the stationery from her tomorrow and bring it to you."

"Wonderful. Martine, you're a genius. JP can write the letter. He's almost a lawyer. He can make it sound real official."

"Don't put me in this."

"*Excusez moi.*" Vadé turned and spoke to JP in rapid French. Although he wasn't fluent, he understood every word she said.

"That's blackmail, Day. But I do love it when you talk dirty. Okay, I'll write the letter."

"Martine, can you drop it off at the messenger's office first thing the following morning?"

"Sure."

"I'll get her a one-way first-class ticket to New York City. The letter will say that once she arrives in New York, she'll receive her performance fee and accommodations at the Plaza. She won't realize she's been scammed until she gets to the hotel."

"You should order a limo for her, too. She looks greedy." Martine peeked out the kitchen door.

"Y'all are vicious women." JP shook his head.

"Just looking out for our men," Martine explained.

The following evening when Martine delivered the radio stationery, Vadé was waiting for her in the office.

"I've never been in here before, this is nice."

"Thank you. Let me have the paper."

Martine sat there gawking at the antiques and admiring the chaise covered in a rich jade brocade while Vadé slipped several pages of the white paper with the vibrant radio station logo into the laser printer.

"It's really nice in here. You have some beautiful pieces of furniture."

"Thank you. I did everything myself." She picked up the sheet of paper that slid out of the printer and placed it on the desk. "This is going to be great."

Martine quickly read over the letter.

"Who's Jason Love?"

"I don't know, but JP said the name sounded like someone who works in radio."

"It does." Martine imitated a disc jockey talking cool, smooth trash and they laughed.

"Are you hungry? I can order some food."

"Food sounds great."

"What would you like?"

"Just get me some of what you're having."

Vadé picked up the phone and ordered her favorite fried chicken, Creole potato salad, and red beans and rice. She picked up the letter, quickly signed it, and folded it into the envelope before she cut off the lights.

"We'll eat upstairs in my sitting room. It's more comfortable up there."

Martine followed Vadé out of the office and up the stairs. They heard Pierre's voice and Fleur laughing just as the elevator took them downstairs.

"Oh, no, he didn't entertain that heifer in my mother's room."

Vadé stopped in the family room and spotted her father and Fleur's empty glasses in the kitchen sink, and pink lipstick on cigarette butts in the trash. She surveyed her territory, looking for further signs of the unwanted intruder before she led Martine into her sitting room. It contained more antiques, a huge comfortable sofa, a big-screen television, JP's computer, and his law school books.

"Make yourself at home. I'm going to jump in the shower. If the food comes, start eating if you like. JP has class tonight."

Martine watched her disappear into the bedroom.

She is most definitely a princess sister.

She wandered around the sitting room admiring the furniture, drapes, and wallpaper that decorated the sitting room. There were also books, paintings, family photographs, and objets d'art for her to inspect.

Vadé has wonderful taste and so many nice things. Girlfriend and her fine husband are livin' seriously.

A knock at the door was room service with dinner. Martine watched the attendant wheel in the cart.

"Is there anything else you'd like, mademoiselle?"

"No, thank you."

The woman left as quickly as she had come.

Martine walked over to Vadé's door and listened. The sound of running water had stopped several minutes ago.

"Vadé." She tapped on the door. "Food's here."

"You may come in. I am only dressing."

Her accent made her cute and her nude brown body made her beautiful. Martine was surprised to see her standing there without a stitch of clothing on, smiling and talking.

"You have a beautiful suite."

Martine stood in front of the crackling fireplace letting the warmth of the fire envelop her.

"And I love this painting."

"Lar did that."

"Really? He's good."

"I know. That's the courtyard of the house we owned in Paris."

"Wow. What was it like living in Paris?"

"Fabulous."

Vadé walked out of the bathroom and pulled on a Dallas Cowboys T-shirt.

"Let's eat. I'm hungry."

They ate by candlelight.

"Merry Christmas." Vadé toasted Martine with a glass of champagne. "Welcome to the family."

"Thanks."

"Thank you again for helping me get rid of Fleur."

"You're welcome."

"I've always wondered what it was like to have a sister."

"It's great, especially if you're friends. I have a sister, Juliet. She'll be eighteen in February."

"Eighteen. I remember when I was eighteen."

"You talk like it was years ago. How old are you?"

"I'll be twenty-one in February."

"That's all? You're so mature. You have the same birthday as my sister."

"Oh. So how old are you?" Vadé poured them each another glass of champagne.

"Twenty-five. I'm trying to decide if I'm going for my master's."

"In what?"

"Finance."

"Do it."

"I should, huh?"

"Why not? You need a master's to be taken seriously in America or anywhere."

"That's true. Didn't you want to go to college? Everyone else is in school."

"I was supposed to attend the University of Paris but my father couldn't afford to send me because of the hotel. I hate New Orleans and I refuse to go to school in America when I intend to become a Parisian decorator. So I worked for my father and decorated the hotel. JP and I are moving back to Paris when he completes law school."

"You did all this?"

"Yes."

"Wow! Can you help me with my little two-bedroom condo?"

"Sure. You have your own house?"

"Yeah. Me and V bought a town house in the French Quarter."

"You are so lucky. I can't wait until JP and I have our own house and I can get out of this hotel. I love my father but I'm married now."

"Mind if I smoke?"

"Go ahead. My father smokes, too."

Martine lit the cigarette and blew out the match. "You are not at all the way I thought you'd be."

"Really? What did you think I'd be like?"

Martine noticed Vadé's eyes were green and sparkling.

"Boring and stuck-up."

"Me, boring?" Vadé laughed.

Martine began giggling too.

"It is so funny to picture Laurent with a girlfriend and now Vicenté's getting married. Girls are crazy about Lar. I guess you felt that way about Vicenté?"

"Are you crazy? Your brothers are fine and sweet, girlfriend. I'm glad I got me one."

"I'm sorry about what I said to you about this being my mother's hotel. I can be a real bitch sometimes. I'm used to being the only girl around here, so if I behave strangely, you must forgive me."

Vadé watched the messenger deliver the phony letter to the hotel around eleven. She saw Fleur come down the stairs an hour later with her suitcase. Fifteen minutes later, Vadé observed a black stretch limousine leaving Hotel de Chevalier.

Fleur La Tiff was history. She had left Left Bank at the last minute, without a special guest performer for New Year's Eve, only days away. Pierre would never allow her to set foot on his property again.

Thanks, Martine.

TWENTY-TWO

Martine stopped the red Jeep Wrangler in the circular drive in front of Hotel de Chevalier. She barely glanced at the fountain spurting water in the small garden in the heart of the circle as she jumped out of the seat and closed the door. She would marry Vicenté Francois Chevalier this afternoon.

Juliet had phoned a week before the wedding, unable to break an important modeling assignment. Vadé was now her matron of honor and she was hosting a breakfast for the bridal party at the hotel where they would also dress for the wedding. Three other doors closed as Martine's first cousins from Puerto Rico followed her inside. All the ladies chatted excitedly in Spanish.

Vadé released the elevator so her guests could come up. Martine's first cousins, Tia, Tatiana, and Toña Bárres, were gorgeous ladies, all sisters. Caramel, honey, and vanilla. They strolled down the hall making comments about the hotel in Spanish. Vadé, also fluent in Spanish, decided to keep her language capabilities a secret, so the girls would feel free to speak what was really on their minds.

"Vadé, thanks again for being my matron of honor and having this breakfast for me."

"It is my pleasure, Martine."

Vadé led the girls into her suite where they left purses, and overnight bags, and then into the family room to the buffet spread out on the dining room table. There were scrambled eggs with cheese, creamy grits running with melted butter, crispy bacon, and a tray of freshly baked breads and pastries. Carafes of fresh-squeezed orange and grapefruit juices were in a tub of ice on the bar.

"Let's eat."

She heard the girls commenting on the food and how pretty Vicenté's little sister was, and smiled.

"Help yourself to anything you like from my father's bar."

"I know I'm having a drink."

Martine and Tatiana tossed ice cubes into glasses and returned with doubles of Chevis Regal. Vadé was surprised to see them drinking scotch so early in the morning.

"I've been up all night and I'm starting to get the jitters." Martine was looking a little pale.

"So how does it feel to be rich?" Toña, the eldest of the sisters, looked directly at Vadé.

"I'm not rich. My father works very hard and this is my mother's home. I go to work every day."

"Really? What do you do?"

"Tia, doesn't she look just like Lala?"

"Oh, *sí. Ella esta muy bonita tambien.*"

Who is Lala and what sort of name is that? Vadé had stopped listening to Toña and tuned in on what her younger sisters were saying in Spanish. Tia was the youngest and the prettiest. She had an exotic look, thick, bushy eyebrows and black hair.

"Did you see the photographs of her husband and brother?"

"Yes, they are both gorgeous."

"I'm giving both of them some."

Vadé covered her mouth to keep herself from speaking out. She did not want them to know she understood Spanish. She had to restrain herself from slapping Tia's face.

How dare she come in my home and say she is going to make a play for my husband and brother! I knew there was a reason why I never liked women.

"She runs this hotel." She heard Martine brag. "This is my princess sister and she's bad."

That comment and the doorbell ended the questions from the cousins about Vadé. The ladies began discussing the wedding while Vadé went to answer the door. She was relieved to see Emilienne and Monnet, the manicurist and masseuse from the hotel's spa.

"Mademoiselles, I have a surprise. These ladies are here to do your nails. Martine, you're getting the works, Emilenne is giving you a massage."

"Vadé, this is wonderful. We were going to let Tia do our nails. She's a manicurist, too."

"I'll help." Tia got up and pulled a foot spa out of a large bag. "I can do everyone's toes."

While everyone shuffled around to get in whatever position to do whatever task, Vadé went to her father's bar and poured herself a double vodka. She added a twist of lime and several ice cubes. For the first time in her life she had an urge for a cigarette. She went into her father's bedroom to find one. He was playing golf with Big Claude and the boys. They weren't due back until two. Vadé sat on her mother and father's bed and rambled in his nightstand for his box of cigarettes.

"Vadé?" It was Martine's voice.

"I'm in here, Martine." She found a lighter and lit the cigarette.

"I didn't know you smoked."

"I don't." She coughed and handed her the cigarette. "You can have it."

Martine took the cigarette and inhaled. "Is that your mother?"

She pointed to a picture of Desiree and Pierre on her mother's dressing table.

"Yes."

"She's beautiful."

"Thank you."

Martine gave her the cigarette and this time she inhaled without coughing.

"You smoke pretty good for someone who doesn't smoke."

"I used to hang out with a couple of girls in the washroom at L'Ecole and puff away until one of the sisters caught us."

"You went to Catholic school too? No wonder we have so much in common."

"But you're getting married in a Baptist church."

"My father was Catholic. He insisted we go to Catholic school since my mother is Baptist."

Martine took one last puff on the cigarette and smashed the stub in the ashtray. "I wish I had something else to smoke besides a cigarette."

"I'll order you a cup of herbal tea. That will calm your nerves. What

are you so nervous about anyway? You and Vicenté have lived together for the last few years."

"Living together is not the same as being married."

"That is true."

"It's the finality of it. The big commitment."

"You are sure about Vicenté? You two seem to be so in love."

"I'm sure about the love I feel for Vicenté, but I wasn't always so
sure about Vicenté. Since he became a part of your family, he's
changed."

"For the better, I hope?"

"Oh, yes. He's a lot happier, and he doesn't seem so insecure."

"How was he insecure?"

"He used to get jealous if another guy just looked at me. And when
I started college, he had a fit. He said I was going to leave him once I
had my degree and got a better job. He said I wouldn't have time for
him anymore."

"You won't do that, will you?"

"Of course not. No way. I love him. Girl, he is so sweet. He polishes
my toenails and he cooks for me."

"Really? JP is sweet like that too and he is such an incredible lover."

"Vicenté is the bomb. Ooh, I don't even want to talk about that. He
just thinks he's not good enough for me because he's a cook."

"Men . . . they can be so stupid at times."

"But ever since V met your dad he's changed. Especially after he
put him in charge of the kitchen. He feels much better about himself."

"He should be ecstatic. The restaurant's business has tripled since
he came and we're beginning to get all sorts of reviews in travel and
cooking magazines."

"He told me about the story for *American Express*. I am so proud of
him."

"Good . . . you should be. . . . Did he ever talk about my father before he met us?"

"He used to say he hated his father and he was going to find him
and make him pay for not coming back for his mother. But after he
met Pierre, he couldn't hate him. He said it was easy to hate him before he knew him. He adores your father and Laurent . . . He is so
wonderful to V and V talks about him all the time."

"And he hates me."

"Oh, no. He adores you too. He's so proud of you, but he didn't like you at first because he thought you were stuck-up and you were so mean."

"I was mean and I'm sorry for that. I didn't handle that situation very well. When he showed up at the hotel and said Papá was his father . . . no one can ever imagine how I felt."

"Finding out I had a brother I never knew about would throw me for a loop, too."

"But I'm not stuck-up. . . . Why do people always say that about me? I'm not that way at all."

"You're not . . . once you give people a chance to get to know you."

Out on the green, the men completed the last hole of the First Annual Chevalier-Olivier Golf Classic, which the Oliviers won. They jumped in an assortment of vehicles and headed to Vicenté's favorite soul food restaurant where they ordered glasses of lemonade spiked with Jack Daniel and fried chicken wings. They were all drunk and laughing.

"Chevalier, what are you going to do when Vadé and JP have a child? Will it be on our side or your side?" Big Claude demanded.

"Mine of course."

"But if you win, it'll only be because you had an Olivier on your team."

The men continued laughing and drinking.

"So, V, how you feeling, man?" JP bit into a slice of lemon.

"I feel good, Olivier. I'm about to marry a beautiful woman who loves me, like you did."

"I'm with you on that. I love being married, especially to a woman like Day. But then maybe that's why I love being married."

"You talk like the honeymoon is not over, young brother." Vicenté was impressed.

"Over? Not as long as there's blood flowing through my veins."

The men all laughed at JP's honesty.

"I'm an Olivier."

Big Claude and Little Claude nodded in agreement.

"Dang. I forget all of y'all are related in so many different ways. Y'all ain't into incest or something like that?"

JP's college buddy, Jeffrey, now a pro football player, had joined them for Vicenté's bachelor bash. His Louisiana drawl and the Jack Daniel's made a hilarious combination and the men were laughing again.

"Yo, Jeff. Man, you go back to college. Try a few speech classes." JP laughed.

Vicenté signaled the waiter for another round of drinks and more chicken wings.

"What time is it anyway? You'd better not make me late for my own wedding."

Laurent quickly glanced at his watch. "One. We'd better go before we are late."

Pierre threw some money on the table and they headed out to the cars.

"V, you're coming back to the hotel with us, right?" Laurent stood next to his brother.

"No. I'm going back to the condo. I don't want to run the risk of seeing Martine before the wedding."

"Cool, big brother. Then we will meet you at the church."

Vicenté got in the Beemer and sped off with screeching tires. As he approached the French Quarter, there was heavy traffic.

"What is it with all this traffic?" he yelled. He laid his head on the steering wheel as he brought the car to a stop in bumper-to-bumper traffic. "Mardis Gras," he answered himself. "How could I forget? Why does everyone have to come to this city today for freaking Mardis Gras?" He looked at the clock in the dashboard. "It's already two and I have to be at the church by three."

He swerved off to a side street and sped down it. He was going much too fast when he saw the children playing in the street. He turned the wheel sharply to the right and crashed into a wall of stone. He heard the sound of glass shattering as his head hit the wheel.

At Hotel de Chevalier, Monnet put finishing touches on Martine's makeup. She was radiant in soft red lipstick. Her black bushy eyebrows had been tamed and highlighted in soft smoky tones. A blowdryer and light straightening comb made her jet-black hair smooth and silky. The strapless short white dress she would be married in was sexy but tasteful.

"You are beautiful, Martine."

Vadé stood beside her in front of the mirror in a short black dress. All the girls were wearing them. Vadé's was trimmed in tiny rhinestones. She looked at her own reflection and was pleased with the way Monnet had done her makeup. She had arched her own wild eyebrows when she was thirteen. A team of hair stylists did all of the girls' hair. Her silky hair was curled and sprayed to stay in place.

"We'd better get going." Martine stood up and looked for her shoes. "I can't believe I'm actually getting married."

"You're not . . . not until I give you this. Here's something old." Vadé took a lace handkerchief with a V embroidered on it in satin from a drawer in the armoire and gave it to Martine.

"This is so beautiful."

"It's from my first communion. That was a special day for me and I want you to have it on your special day."

"I'm going to cry. Thank you."

"You can't. You'll ruin your makeup. Something new. You have on your something new."

She had ordered a white satin brassiere and bikini panties from a lingerie shop in Paris. She had given them to Martine before she bathed.

"Now for something borrowed." She pulled the diamond studs out of her ears. "Take good care of these. They were a gift from my papá."

Martine watched in shock as Vadé put the rocks in her ears.

"And something blue." She handed her a lace garter.

"Vadé, we've only been friends for a month or so. How would I ever have done this without you?"

They met up with the guys down in the foyer as they were getting into the limos.

"There you are, beautiful wife." JP leaned over and kissed her.

"You're drunk, JP." Vadé laughed.

"That's not all I am."

Vadé saw Tia stroll by out of the corner of her eye. She was made like a Coca-Cola bottle, petite with a tiny waistline. She was smoking a cigarette and had darkened the pink lipstick Monnet had applied when she did her makeup. She flipped her hair over her shoulder and strutted by the other men.

"Where's Vicenté?" Vadé noticed JP giving Tia a second look.

"He went back to the condo. He's meeting us at the church."

Vadé headed for the bride's limo as her assistant, Jewel, ran out of the hotel. She started to go back, but JP motioned he'd take care of it. She leaned back and relaxed as the limo drove away. She had finally gotten those women out of her house.

"We've got to go to the hospital. Vicenté totaled the Beemer," JP informed the men.

"Is he okay?" Laurent demanded once they were inside the limousine.

"They said he's fine. He's got a bad cut on his head that needed stitches."

"He totaled the car?" Pierre looked concerned.

"Yes."

"My son is blessed to be alive. We should never have left him by himself."

The men rode the rest of the way in silence. They rushed into the emergency room where Vicenté was sitting in a chair smoking a cigarette. There was a Band-Aid on his forehead.

"V, are you okay?" Laurent hurried to his side with the others right behind him.

"I'm fine. Can we get out of here? This place makes me nervous."

JP instructed the limo driver to take them to Vicenté's house.

"V, I'm glad you're okay. I wouldn't know what to do if something happened to you." Laurent leaned forward to make eye contact with him.

"Man . . . see . . . there you go again . . . saying all that stuff." He covered his face and cried like a baby.

"Son, are you okay?" Pierre grasped him about the shoulders as he cried.

"I'm fine. Damn, Lar. You got me bawlin' like a baby." He brushed away the tears and tried to smile. I'm straight."

"Is there anything you want to talk about, son?" Pierre rested his hand on top of Laurent's copper hand, which was on top of Vicenté's brown one.

"I . . . I am just so happy to have all of you as my family." He was crying again as they pulled up in front of the condo.

"We're happy to have you too. Come on, V. You've got to get dressed." Laurent helped him out of the car and into the house.

"It's four. I know Martine is having a fit right about now. I'll call the girls while you all get him ready."

JP dialed Vadé's cell phone number while Laurent and Pierre took Vicenté upstairs.

At the church, Martine was on the verge of tears. Vicenté should have been there an hour ago.

"He stood me up, Vadé. I know he did."

Martine paced back and forth in the bridal room like a madwoman.

"No, he didn't."

"Then where is he?"

At that moment her cell phone rang. The girls looked at each other as Vadé answered.

"Oh my God, is Vicenté okay?"

"What happened? What happened? I knew something happened."

"He had an accident."

She listened to JP while Martine wailed and fell into a chair.

"But he's fine. My father's with him. And all of them will be here shortly."

She clicked off the phone and looked at Martine, who was crying.

"Martine, you cannot cry. He's coming. Monnet, touch up her makeup, please."

"I don't care about my makeup, I want V."

She ran out of the dressing room into the parking lot and paced while she waited for the limo.

"Martine, Vicenté is not supposed to see you before the wedding."

"Later for that bull. I'm gonna see my man."

Martine paced until she saw the white stretch limo pull into the parking lot. She ran to the car, yanked open the door, and practically fell inside the car.

"V, are you okay, baby?"

"I'm fine, baby."

"You hurt your head." She started crying as the other men got of the car and headed for the church.

"He's fine, sweetheart. Just a little cut on the head." Pierre patted Martine on the back as he got out of the car last.

JP, Vadé, and Laurent stood outside waiting for their brother. Inside the limousine, Martine gently kissed Vicenté's bandaged head.

"V, you hurt yourself."

"No, I'm all right. I didn't want to be late for the wedding and I cracked up the Beemer."

"V, you could have killed yourself."

"Baby, I just can't believe you want to marry me and my family loves me. I love everybody." He was crying again.

"Of course they love you and I want to marry you, baby. I thought you didn't want to marry me." Martine cried with him.

"I've done some dumb things in my life, but that would be by far the dumbest."

"I love you, V."

"I love you, too, baby."

They sat in the limo and kissed.

"Isn't it supposed to be bad luck or something for the groom to see the bride before the wedding?" Laurent looked to his sister and brother-in-law for an answer while they all watched Vicenté and his future wife get out of the limo.

"See, Day? Aren't you glad we didn't go through all that drama?"

"Actually, I think it would have been fun for us to have a big church wedding."

Vadé listened to the organ music and felt the tears begin to flow as she watched Martine float down the aisle. She had had some great times with Martine and enjoyed every second of the drama leading up to her wedding. There was something incredibly special about making a vow to God, to be one, in front of your family. Now she longed for more than her quickie ceremony with the justice of the peace. There was absolutely nothing special about it, nor had JP asked her to marry him. *Papá made him marry me.*

TWENTY-THREE

Laurent watched the spinning wheels of the dubbing recorder click to a stop in studio A at Future Stars Recording Studios and looked at Little Claude as a slow smile spread itself across his handsome face.

"It's finally done."

"Hallelujah!"

The business partners, cousins, and best friends shook hands as the engineer removed two cassettes, labeled the plastic cases, and handed one to each of them. They had just finished mixing the last song on Laurent's demo tape.

"I am so glad we got this done." Laurent sighed with relief.

"And just in time too. Day's party is tonight."

"Between finals and being in the studio, I haven't seen very much of her lately."

"That's good, because you would have told her."

"I almost did so many times. I'm glad I was staying at your house."

"You're going to throw down on them, Lar. When you sing that old school tune, 'My Cherie Amour,' and rap in French, man, those girls are going to scream their heads off."

"There you go."

"I want to see lots of ladies screaming tonight. When girls scream, that is a good indication that they are pleased."

Laurent fell out of the chair onto the floor laughing. "Did you hear what you just said?"

"What?"

Laurent continued laughing as Little Claude covered his mouth with his hand.

"Day." He sat down in his chair and laughed. "Man, you are wrong laughing at your sister like that."

Laurent was still on the floor laughing. "You're crazy, man."

"Speaking of girls screaming, are Martine's cousins still in town? Those are some fine sisters."

"They are very pretty girls."

"I want to get with Tia. She's hot."

"She is beautiful."

"I saw her throwing you action at the reception. Why didn't you give her any?"

"I was too busy tripping on Martine and Vicenté. That was one crazy wedding."

"I couldn't believe Martine was out there in the parking lot in her wedding dress and veil on running after the limousine."

"The best part was when she opened the door and dove over Papá to get to Vicenté."

"I know."

They were laughing again.

"I sure hope I find a woman that loves me enough to do something crazy like that."

"That was pretty crazy." Little Claude took the CDs from the engineer and placed them in his bag.

"They have that serious, deep love like our parents and JP and Day."

"Keep it in the family. Madame Olivier and her corporate attorney husband-in-training."

"I want to have that same kind of crazy love. It's a family tradition."

"That's true, Mr. Romance. . . . Speaking of which, we need to do a show on your birthday, Valentine's Day, too. The women will be all over you."

"Martine's little sister is flying in from Milan today. She's bringing her and their cousins to Day's party."

"Cool, 'cause I like me some Tia. That is so nice that Martine and Day became friends. My mother always said that Day needed a girl in the family to hang out with."

"JP told me Martine was the mastermind behind Fleur's sudden departure to New York and they've been buddies ever since."

"Day got rid of Fleur? If she doesn't like you she sure can be nasty."

"I know. She wasn't like that when we were little."

"It must be PMS. Thank goodness for JP."

Laurent smiled and shook his head while Little Claude continued talking.

"I invited a lot of ladies from the college, too. I want Left Bank overflowing with people, especially women."

They got into Laurent's red pony and blasted the demo as the grandfather clock in the lobby of Hotel de Chevalier sounded the last gong announcing the five o'clock hour.

Vadé slammed down the phone in her office and tossed a stack of file folders in the "to be filed" tray on her desk. She had been on the phone most of the day negotiating with contractors for the hotel's new gift shop.

"What a way to spend a birthday. I hate this job."

Her feet barely touched the plush jade carpeting on the stairs. She walked into her sitting room, and was surprised to see JP's books stashed neatly on his desk. He was home from school but nowhere to be found in the suite.

Maybe he's out planning a surprise for my birthday.

Vadé hung up the wool skirt and silk blouse in the closet, started her bath, and wondered why she had allowed Laurent and Little Claude to talk her into having a birthday party at the club. She hadn't made friends with anyone outside of the family except Martine and she was family now. But it would be fun to have the family get together for drinks and dancing. It was always a party whenever they gathered.

She removed a bottle of chilled champagne from the mini refrigerator, and watched the sparkling wine rise to the top of a goblet. She took a healthy sip as she walked into her bath, climbed into the seafoam whirlpool tub, and sighed contentedly.

Where is my husband? I wanted him to join me in the tub for a little fun before dinner.

The water was turning cool and she had finished her champagne when she finally heard the sitting room door close.

"JP, is that you?"

"Yes, baby."

She waited for him to come into the bathroom but he never did.

"JP, what are you doing?"

She could hear his laughter over the television set.

"Watching *Martin*."

"Watching *Martin*? That stupid show? Come in here."

"Okay, as soon as the commercial comes on."

"You're going to wait for a commercial?"

She hopped out of the tub, wrapped herself in a huge bath towel, and stomped into the sitting room.

"Hey."

"Hey?" You could at least wish me a happy birthday."

"I would if you would be quiet and give me a chance to talk, woman. Those are for you."

There was a huge bouquet of roses and a bowl of fresh strawberries sitting on the coffee table. She ignored the roses and his comment. She had been in the mood earlier but now she was angry because he was late.

"JP, where have you been?"

"Playing basketball with my boys."

"Basketball? You went to play basketball on my birthday? You should have been here when I got off work to help me celebrate my birthday."

"Day, we're celebrating your birthday tonight with the family and I'm here now."

She glared at him as she dropped the towel and walked into her closet. He followed her inside, cut off the light, and enveloped her in his arms enjoying the smell of her clean body.

"Go away, JP. You stink."

She pulled away from him and began putting on her underwear.

"What are you doing? Don't you want to have a quickie?"

"No." She wanted it more than he did but she was hurt because he had chosen to spend the time with his boys rather than her.

"No?" Now he was hurt.

"No."

She fastened silk stockings to her garter belt and pulled the chartreuse beaded party dress over her head.

"You're serious, huh?"

She picked up a new pair of gold sandals and walked past her husband out of the closet.

"What? I can't get no kiss either?"

He watched Vadé drop a strawberry into her glass of champagne before he walked into the bath and turned on the shower. She had never turned him down for a tête-à-tête between the sheets. She was sitting in front of her dressing table when he came out of the bathroom. He glanced at her as he went into the closet to dress in his favorite hip-hop attire, baggy jeans and an oversize shirt.

"Don't tell me you're wearing *that* to my party."

"Why? What's wrong with it?"

"You look stupid. That's why. Why don't you put on one of those suits we picked out for you in Paris?"

"Because those suits are too small for me now and I happen to like what I have on."

"If you want to look stupid that's fine with me. You Americans have no sense of fashion anyway."

She turned toward the mirror to make finishing touches on her makeup. Vadé thought JP looked cute in whatever he put on; she just wanted to fight.

"You're the one who looks stupid. You're twenty-one and you dress like you're thirty. Why don't you act like a young person sometime?"

"You mean be irresponsible like you? I'm the one with all the responsibilities around here. I'm working every day doing a job I hate while you're out playing basketball with your boys."

She sprayed perfume and left the room.

Left Bank had a considerably large crowd of young people, especially women, gathered around the huge wooden bar and dancing on the hardwood floor. Laurent and Little Claude were at the family table having drinks.

"Where did all these kids come from? The club never has such a young crowd and so many ladies."

"I think it's great."

Little Claude grinned at Laurent, who was beaming.

"What are you two up to?"

"Nothing, Day. Happy birthday."

"Yeah, happy birthday." Little Claude saluted her with his Long Island iced tea.

"Where's JP?" Laurent stood up as she sat down.

"I don't know. Where are you going?"

"We'll be back."

She watched Laurent and Little Claude disappear into the crowd as Vicenté and Martine walked up with a group of girls.

"Happy birthday, girlfriend. You're looking fabulous like the princess sister you are." Martine kissed her on the cheek and smiled.

"Happy birthday, Vadé. Where's Lar?"

She extended her cheek to her brother. "I don't know. He and Little Claude were just here. They're around here somewhere."

"That dress is gorgeous. I know, you got it in Paris."

Vadé laughed. "*Oui*, mademoiselle." She saw Tia take off a jacket to expose a sheer black lace bodysuit. Her black hair was braided into a long thick ponytail. She stuck a cigarette between her full red lips and lit it.

She has absolutely no class.

"Vadé, I want you to meet my little sister, Juliet."

Martine grabbed both girls by the hand. Vadé was surprised when she saw the tall, slender girl with a beautiful figure. She was the color of honey, and her hair had been lightened to match her skin with golden highlights. Her eyes were the same color as her hair. She was the most sophisticated American girl that Vadé had encountered during her years in New Orleans.

"Bonjour, Vadé." She extended a hand to Vadé.

"Bonsoir," Vadé corrected. For some reason she felt intimidated by Juliet and she needed to feel that she was the better. "Please have a seat at my table."

She looked around for her husband and wished she hadn't been so mean to him so they could escape to their bedroom and she could ditch the table of females. Little Claude walked onstage and stood in front of a microphone as JP and Jeffrey dressed in the latest hip-hop fashion slid into chairs on the other side of the table.

"Good evening and thank you for coming out to Left Bank for just one of our many Mardis Gras celebrations. We've got a special treat tonight."

Vadé wondered what Little Claude was talking about as the women in the club began screaming.

"I'm pleased to announce the debut performance of Lar Legrande at Hotel de Chevalier. Happy birthday, Mrs. Vadé Olivier. This is for you."

The club darkened and Vadé saw Laurent walk onstage as an up-tempo track filled the speakers of the club.

I knew they were up to something.

The women in the club began screaming when a single spotlight illuminated Laurent's gyrating body. As soon as he began singing everyone rushed the stage to get a better view of the smoothly executed routines he danced with hip-hop dancers.

"Isn't he fantastic?" Martine yelled over the music and screams. "Yes."

She was happy to see her brother doing what he loved most in the world, but had to wonder why he had gone to such lengths to keep everything a secret from her. She was saddened that he had not shared something so important.

"Chevalier, the boys have stolen our club," Big Claude teased. "This place is packed and Lar is bad. He's going to be a superstar."

Pierre was silent as he watched the young girls clamoring after his youngest son. This was not the kind of life he had planned for him. Laurent finished his three songs and left the stage. He could still hear the girls screaming back in the dressing room.

"You were the bomb, man. I knew it was going to be like this. Did you hear all those ladies screaming their heads off?"

Little Claude paced the black and white marble-tiled floor in the dressing room excitedly.

"I could barely hear the playback through my monitor."

There was a knock on the dressing room door and Little Claude snatched it open.

"There you are. Come on in, man."

Laurent looked up to see a young, attractive sandy blonde enter the room.

"This is Greg Giagrossi from Virgin Records in LA. He flew in to see your showcase."

"That was a fantastic show, Lar." Greg looked to be only a few years older than the two of them.

"Thank you. You flew out just for my show?"

"Claude sent me a track and some photos a few months ago. We've been on the phone ever since. I want to sign you to a deal with Virgin."

"Lar, how dare you do all this and not tell me?"

Vadé walked in and interrupted his conversation.

"Did you like it, Day?"

She wanted to be mad but she couldn't. She was happy to see her little brother performing. Little Claude ushered Greg Giagrossi out of the dressing room and into the club while she continued speaking to her brother.

"I loved it. You were great. Did you hear all those girls screaming?"

"I would have told you, but you're always so busy with JP. I miss you, Day."

"I know. I miss you too, little brother."

"So where is the budding attorney?"

"I don't know."

"What did you do?"

Vicenté and Martine burst into the dressing room with an explosion of color and energy.

"You turned it out, little brother." They laughed and screamed while Laurent beamed with happiness.

"Hello, family." Laurent hugged his brother and kissed Martine on the cheek. "You are looking beautiful as usual, Madame Chevalier."

"You were great."

"Martine and her crazy cousins were standing on chairs screaming for you."

"We sure were. So were a lot of other girls. I am so glad that you are my brother-in-law."

Laurent smiled as he focused on the eyes of a stranger. There was something about her eyes that made his soul tingle and his spirit dance.

"Lar, I want you to meet my sister. This is Juliet."

"Bonsoir, Laurent."

She was so beautiful she took his breath away, but it was more than her physical beauty. There was something else . . . in her eyes . . . something he had never seen. Juliet was dressed simply but elegantly in a black jumpsuit. Classic but still sexy, especially the way the Italian suit clothed her gorgeous figure. For the first time in his life, Laurent was at a loss for words.

"I knew it," Martine whispered just loudly enough for Vicenté to hear. "He's sprung. He can't even talk."

They walked over to the buffet table to speak with Vadé.

There were so many thoughts and feelings running through his mind that Laurent didn't know what to say. He didn't want to say the wrong thing either.

"I am in love. "

Juliet smiled and Laurent's heart melted.

"I am serious."

Her smile intensified and Laurent realized it was her eyes. . . . A passionate glow radiated from them, out the depth of her soul. Laurent was raptured, lost inside her . . . as time stood still.

They stood there smiling at each other as Pierre and Big Claude walked into the dressing room.

"Chevalier, he's got our dressing room, too. We're as good as gone."

"What did you think, Papá?" Laurent managed to find his voice and his mind with the appearance of his father.

"He knows you were the bomb, little brother."

"Wasn't he fabulous, Papá?"

Vicenté and Vadé had joined their brother and Pierre and formed a small circle. They were all anxious to hear his response.

"I don't want to see anything on your report card but A's and B's or you will move out of this hotel and I won't give you another red cent."

Pierre glared at Laurent as he stormed out of the dressing room.

"What was that all about?" Vicenté was hot.

Laurent said nothing. He looked like he wanted to cry.

Vadé shuddered at Pierre's words because she knew he meant everything he just said. She hadn't seen her father that angry since he had found her and JP in bed.

TWENTY-FOUR

It was an extremely warm day for February, but things always get out of sync during the Mardis Gras celebration season, especially for the family. It was a tradition. Something crazy was bound to happen and sometimes the craziness was wonderful.

"Are you really in love with me?"

Laurent watched the wheel of the paddle boat shovel water out of its way as it clipped along the Mississippi.

"Laurent, are you really in love with me?"

She was too beautiful to look at and he had already made a fool of himself too many times so he chose the water. It was hypnotic and soothing as it splashed through the paddle wheel.

"Yes."

"I'm scared, Laurent. Please don't break my heart. I've never felt like this about anyone and I don't want to get hurt."

He had to look at her now. He pulled Juliet into his arms and held her so they both faced the water.

"I'm scared, too. I won't break your heart. I promise."

He wanted to stand there holding her forever. With Juliet, all the bitter, painful experiences of his life suddenly became sweet. He didn't even know he had been in pain until that gnawing ache disappeared the first time he looked into her eyes.

"I haven't been on one of these boats since I was a little girl. My daddy took us out for lunch one Sunday after church."

"We've lived in New Orleans almost six years now and this is the first time I've ever been on one of these riverboat cruises."

"Nawlins is quaint. How do you like living here after growing up in France?"

"It's okay, but no comparison to Paris. I love it because the people I love are here."

"That is so sweet. I love working in Europe. I don't think I can ever live in Nawlins again. I'm spoiled."

"You deserve to be spoiled. What do you think about LA?"

"I haven't been there yet."

"I've been offered a record deal with Virgin. If I take it, I'll move to California."

"That's wonderful, Laurent. Are you going to do it?"

"I don't know. My father wants me to finish college first."

"How much longer do you have to go?"

"A semester. My cousin and I went to summer school so we could graduate early."

"You'll be finished in a few months."

"Virgin wants me in LA and in the studio next week. I'm only going to college to keep my father happy, but I don't think I'll ever be able to do that."

"So what do *you* want to do?"

"Go to LA. This is my dream."

"Well, it looks like you're going to LA."

"I haven't signed the contract yet."

"What's stopping you?"

"My father . . . the family. I don't know."

"Will you be by yourself in LA?"

"My cousin Claude is my manager. He's ready to leave on the next thing smoking. He plans on finishing his last semester in Los Angeles."

"Why don't you do that too?"

"Because once I hit that studio I won't want to look at a book. My sister didn't go to college, so my father wants me to be the graduate. Day was supposed to go back to Paris for college, but she hasn't made it there yet and she refuses to go here. My father lets her do whatever she likes. If I bring home anything besides an A or a B, he's going to throw me out of the house."

"No, he won't."

"He will. You don't know my father. Sometimes he acts like a madman. I wish my mother was here to chill him out."

"Where is your mother?"

"She disappeared during Mardis Gras three years ago. We haven't seen her since."

"Deep."

"I've got a crazy family."

"If your mother was here, what would she say about this record deal?"

"She'd be happy for me. My mother is a singer too. I walked onstage while she was performing when I was three. I've been singing ever since."

"That's so cute. I say take it. Do it for your mother. She might hear about you singing and come see you."

"That'll be the day. My mother's never coming back home. I think my father knows it, too, now. That's why he acts like an idiot."

"She could still come back. If your father was her true love she'll definitely be back."

"I thought he was her true love and I thought I was her true love but she's been gone forever. How could you stay away from people you love that long?"

"Maybe she was in pain and needed time to heal."

"For three years?"

"No one knows the pain of the heart except its owner."

"You are so easy to talk to. I've never talked about my parents to anyone but Little Claude. Not even my sister. And here I am telling you everything I've ever thought or felt."

"Your secrets are safe with me, Laurent Chevalier. I'll never tell anyone what we talk about."

"Good. And I'll never tell yours."

They smiled at each other as they became best friends. Laurent ran his hand across the golden hair that reminded him of his mother's.

"So did you always know you wanted to be a model?"

"Not always. I really want to be an actress. I did a little bit of everything trying to get noticed. My pictures were sent to a friend of the family and I've been modeling ever since."

"It's nice to have family support."

"It is."

Laurent closed his eyes and kissed her. From that moment he knew he'd never be the same. She was a dream come true. She was so beautiful and so sweet and she was shy. He had never met anyone like her and knew he never would. She was that one-in-a-million chance of a lifetime. She blushed as she looked into his eyes and silently stole another piece of the heart he thought was gone.

"You're coming to my show tonight?"

"Of course. There's no place else I want to be."

"Good."

They watched the boat dock and seconds later, heard the rumbling of footsteps on the wooden pier as passengers left the dinner boat. Laurent and Juliet held hands all the way to the car.

"I just love Martine and Vicenté's condo. It's perfect for them."

Laurent pulled his '65 Mustang to a stop in front of his brother's trilevel condo. Martine and Vicenté were peeking out the window while Laurent helped her out of the car.

"Look at them, V. They look so cute together. I knew they would hit it off."

"You're right, but who would have thought that skinny little kid would turn out like that?"

Laurent dashed up the back stairs in the hotel and ran smack into JP, who was going down the stairs.

"Hey, man. Where have you been?"

"Where have you been? That was some performance you put on the other night. Little Claude told me about Virgin. When are you leaving?"

"I don't know if I'm going."

"You have to take it. This is your dream. You know, like we used to talk about this back in Paris."

"I know, *mon ami*. I've got a decision to make. What's up with you and Day?"

"I don't know. She's been tripping ever since her birthday because I wasn't home when she got off work."

"Don't pay her any attention. You know Papá spoiled her. She'll be all right. It's just Mardis Gras."

"Yeah, you're probably right."

"I have to go prepare for the show. Are you coming?"

"You know it. I'm on my way downstairs now to get a drink so the queen can have the suite to herself."

"All right. Later, brother."

JP walked into Left Bank and was surprised to see Martine's cousin sitting alone at the bar. He slid onto the stool next to her.

"I'm JP and I know you're one of Martine's cousins from Puerto Rico, but I don't know your name."

"Tia." She smiled as she extended her hand to JP.

"Tia. That's a very pretty name. Would you like a drink?"

"A rum and Coke would be nice."

"Are your sisters still here?"

"No, they went back the day after Juliet's birthday. She's my favorite cousin so I wanted to stay a few days longer so we could spend some time together. I'll be returning home tomorrow, unfortunately. I've had such a wonderful time." She smiled warmly.

"I'm glad you've had a nice trip." He returned the smile and ordered the drink and a beer for himself.

Why is Day tripping so hard? We haven't made love for a couple of days now. He looked at Tia as he sipped his beer. *I know Little Claude tried to hit that. She looks like his type . . . beautiful and easy. Speaking of hitting it, I'm going upstairs and make love to my wife. That's all we need.*

He tapped Tia on the arm to tell her he was leaving.

"JP, what are you doing?"

Vadé was standing behind him looking at the both of them.

"Coming upstairs to see you. Why?"

"Your father's on the phone. He said it was important."

"Cool. Let the bartender know to put both of those drinks on the tab."

He dashed out of the bar as Tia gave Vadé a sly grin.

"Do not think you will ever get your hands on my husband, you little whore."

There she was, being a bitch again, but Tia deserved it.

"When your husband makes love to you, he's thinking about me."

Tia ran her tongue around the rim of her glass before she took it and sauntered across the club to a table. Every man in the room watched her as she walked.

It took every ounce of strength in Vadé's body to restrain her from leaping on Tia's back, snatching out every strand of her hair, and choking her with it. She wouldn't go back to her suite either because she knew she would pick a fight with JP. What she needed was to be alone. She ordered a double vodka and went upstairs to her office.

Laurent and Little Claude sat in the dressing room having dinner. Claude wasted no time putting away a bowl of gumbo while Laurent stared at his pasta and blackened rib eye.

"What's wrong, man?" Little Claude buttered a hard roll. There was nothing wrong with his appetite.

"I'm in love, Claude."

"Really? Who's the lucky lady?"

"Juliet."

"No stuff?"

"No stuff."

"She is too beautiful. I'd be her Romeo any day. Did you hit it yet?"

"It's not like that, man." He looked at his cousin and realized he wouldn't begin to understand his feelings for Juliet and it would be a complete waste of time to try and explain. "I'm just trying to decide what to do about Virgin."

"Lar, sign the papers. Dad and Uncle Rene got us a great deal."

"I know."

"So what's the problem?"

Pierre opened the dressing room door and came in.

"Your sister talked me into letting you sing tonight. There were a lot of phone calls about you. But I don't want to hear another word about you singing anywhere until you finish school."

He left the room as quickly as he had entered.

"He's the problem!" Laurent yelled, frustrated. "Sometimes I hate him."

"You know what you have to do."

There was a knock at the dressing room door. Little Claude got up and went to answer it.

"Your public awaits you."

He pulled open the door to find Juliet and Tia standing there.

"Ah . . . las mademoiselles. Come in."

"Laurent, you know my cousin Tia."

"Yes, hello. And you know my cousin Claude."

"We're just one big happy family here. May I offer you ladies something to drink or some dinner?" Tia was under Claude's spell.

There was a large vase of roses sitting on top of the grand piano in the suite. Laurent pulled out a single rose and handed it to Juliet.

"For the most beautiful mademoiselle," he whispered softly.

She smiled and stroked him on the cheek as Vadé threw open the dressing room door.

"Lar, the club is packed. Everyone in New Orleans must be here to see you."

She stood in the doorway in a dazzling white beaded gown with diamonds sparkling on her ears, wrist, and throat. When she spotted Tia and Juliet a crazed look came into her eyes.

How dare this whore who made a play for my husband come sit in my brother's dressing room! And does the other tramp kissing my brother actually think he is interested in her?

"Excuse me but didn't the maids take out the trash? I gave them explicit orders to clean this room thoroughly." She looked directly at Tia and then Juliet as she spoke.

"Vadé!" Laurent was unusually sharp with his sister as he gave her an imploring look.

"Tia and Juliet are our guests," Little Claude explained.

"Guests?" The word rolled off her lips like poison. She turned to her brother and spoke to him, her voice as sweet as sugar.

"Lar, you're going to blow them away."

"Thanks, Day. Do me a favor?"

"What, my sweet?"

"Take our guests to the family table and get them anything they like."

She saw him give Juliet a dove-eyed look and wanted to throw up.

He can't be serious, or maybe she is another one of the many secrets he keeps from me now?

"The family table?"

"The family table," Claude repeated. "We'll see you ladies after the show."

The girls followed Vadé out of the dressing room and into the club. She took a seat next to JP, who was sitting with Pierre, his parents, Big Claude, and Giselle, and ignored the girls.

"Bonsoir, *mí famile.* Hi, baby." She kissed JP and he smiled.

The Bárres girls stood there waiting for someone to offer them a chair. The rest of the family was busily ordering drinks and appetizers, so no one saw them. Finally Tia took the lead and pulled out an empty chair at the table. Pierre noticed the girls as they sat down.

"Is there something I can help you with?"

"They're guests of Laurent and Little Claude," Vadé offered nonchalantly.

"I see." Pierre eyed the ladies carefully.

"Pierre, this is Juliet Bárres, Martine's little sister, and Tia Bárres, her cousin from Puerto Rico," JP informed him.

"Please sit down. You're family. Vadé, why didn't you introduce me to these beautiful ladies?"

"I thought you knew who they were, Papá."

Vadé smiled sweetly at her father. Tia gave her a triumphant grin as a waiter handed her a fresh drink. Juliet sipped a glass of orange juice as she stroked her rose.

"Are you sure you wouldn't care for something stronger?" Vadé asked.

She took a sip of champagne and looked at Juliet. She felt JP give her a sharp nudge under the table, but she didn't care. She was tired of these women hanging around her family.

"If I wanted something stronger, I would have ordered it." Juliet gave Vadé a cool look. She was used to girls not liking her.

"Touchy, aren't we?" Vadé's smile did not melt her icy words.

"No, you are. And I've had enough of you and your rudeness. Come on, Tia. I'm sure there must be other seats available."

"Don't settle for another table. Why don't you just leave?"

"Why don't you make us?" Tia taunted.

"I will."

JP was unable to restrain her as she threw Juliet's purse and the rose on the floor. Tia took her rum and Coke and threw it in Vadé's face, who retaliated by slapping her as hard as she could. Tia didn't hesitate in returning the slap. JP held her as she screamed, "Get out! Get out! Get out!"

"What's going on?"

Pierre rose to his daughter's defense as conversation around them diminished. Tia stood waiting for Vadé's next move while Juliet gathered the rose and her beaded evening bag from the floor. Laurent walked onto the stage and greeted the audience, who applauded and cheered. The tracks kicked in and he began to dance. Juliet picked up the rose and looked directly into his eyes.

What's the matter? she read from them.

She broke into tears and rushed out of the club while Pierre and JP were in the dressing room trying to calm Vadé. She sat in front of the makeup mirror looking at her cheek.

"Papá, is there swelling?"

"No, Princess."

Pierre inspected her cheek while JP poured her a glass of ice water. They could hear muffled screams and Laurent singing. Juliet and Tia waited in the foyer for Juliet's taxi.

"You can't leave."

"I most certainly will. These are the rudest people I ever met. What kind of family did my sister marry into?"

"The same family you're going to marry into."

"Not in this lifetime. I'm going home." She hopped inside the yellow cab and waved good-bye to her cousin.

Tia walked back inside the club where Laurent was still performing. Young ladies were standing on chairs screaming. He danced across the stage in baggy jeans, rhinestone high-tops, and a baseball cap and jersey that said LAR. The family had returned to the table where Vadé was nursing a glass of champagne. Tia stood by the front door smoking a cigarette as the audience stood and gave him a standing ovation. A single spotlight followed Laurent as he jumped off the stage, ran through the audience and out of the club, pulling Tia along behind him.

"Where's Juliet?"

"She left."

"Why?"

"Your sister was rude to her."

"Come with me."

When he turned to go back into the club, he saw the rose lying on the floor where Juliet had dropped it. He picked it up and grabbed Tia by the hand. The audience saw him when he came back into the club and began yelling for an encore. Instead of going on-stage, he marched straight over to the family table to Vadé.

"What did you say to Juliet?"

She had never seen Laurent this angry. She was so shocked she couldn't find the words to speak.

"What did you say?" He grabbed her sharply by the wrist and held her tightly.

"Ouch, Lar. You're hurting me." She looked at her brother as if he were crazy. They had never fought before.

Little Claude did a rap with Laurent's hip-hop dancers to keep the crowd going. The audience cheered and continued demanding an encore. Someone turned a spotlight on Laurent and it illumined the entire family.

"Laurent, this has gone far enough. Leave your sister alone and get back on that stage and sing."

He dropped his sister's hand and turned around to glare at his father.

"You disobeyed me," his father said. "You're the one who wanted to sing, now get back on that stage and sing before I give you a whipping you'll never forget."

The audience was elated when Laurent finally ran back onstage. He danced and sang hard, releasing all of his pain and anger. When the song ended, he ran into the dressing room and paced back and forth.

The only thing I ever wanted in my life, to sing, and to be in love, and the two people I love most are ruining it for me.

He sat down at the grand piano and pounded the keys in a melancholic melody until he was too exhausted to move. He collapsed on the piano and cried from frustration, pain, and loneliness. When his tears were finally spent, he looked up and saw the vase of red roses sitting on top of the piano. He took his arm and swept the entire vase crashing onto the glossy checkerboard floor. The sound of glass breaking and marbles bouncing across the tile didn't shatter the words echoing in his head.

Mamá, why did you leave and why didn't you take me with you?

TWENTY-FIVE

Juliet Bárres sat in the bay window of her bedroom wearing green silk pajamas, clutching her teddy bear. Moonlight lit the dark, quiet street beneath her. An old automobile rumbled past the house, breaking the silence. She grabbed the bear tighter and tighter until she saw it. She was unable to contain the smile that spread itself across her pretty face as she ran down the carpeted stairs and threw open the front door.

Laurent slipped between her arms as if he belonged there, as if that spot had been made just for him. She was crying and she didn't know why. He tasted her tears as he tried to squeeze her inside his body, head, and heart.

"Marry me, Juliet," he whispered in her ear. "I want to be with you the rest of my life."

He bent down on his knee, took a tiny silver ring out of his pocket, and slipped it on her finger.

"It fits perfectly." She knelt beside him and smiled into his eyes.

"That's because it's yours. I bought it years ago in a little art store in Paris. I always saw myself giving it to the girl I would marry. There's another piece that fits on top and they form a heart. I'll keep this piece and give it to you when we get married. The piece you have on is your engagement ring."

He laughed as he twisted the tiny silver band around on her finger and slipped the other half on top of it. Together, they formed a complete heart.

"It's beautiful, Laurent."

"It's not much. I'll buy you a better one later." He slipped his portion of the ring back into his pocket.

"No. This ring is absolutely perfect. Just like the story that goes with it. We can tell our children someday."

"You still haven't answered my question. Will you marry me and go with me to LA tomorrow night?"

"You'd better not leave without me. Yes. Of course I will."

She kissed him and felt herself melting in his arms.

"When are we leaving?"

"After the carnival. At midnight. I already signed the contract."

"Can we skip the carnival? I don't want to go to the hotel."

"I know, baby, but despite everything my family has done, I can't leave them without a performer for the carnival. It would be bad business for the hotel."

"I understand, Laurent. I just don't want to go back there."

"I don't either. I don't even want to see my father or sister but I have to perform."

"I don't know, Laurent. Why don't I just meet you at the airport?"

"Please? I want you there with me. It's a masquerade party so no one has to know you're there but me."

"I can come in costume?"

"Of course, silly. What do you think a masquerade party is?"

"I haven't done very much thinking since I met you."

"Me neither." He kissed her and smiled. "This will be our secret. We won't tell anyone. We'll send them a telegram after we get to LA and get married."

"This is going to be so much fun."

"Do you know what you're going to wear to the ball?"

"Yes. I'll come as a bride in one of those old-fashioned wedding dresses. I'll wear a white mask under my veil."

"That's perfect. After the show, I'll be dressed as a chef. I'll get my brother to give me one of his old uniforms."

It was four o'clock in the morning when Laurent rang his brother's doorbell. The French Quarter was still lively with activity. Vicenté answered the door wearing red silk boxer shorts.

"Sorry to wake you up, man, but there was no place else I wanted to go."

"My house is your house. Are you all right?"

"I'm fine now."

"Did you talk to Juliet?"

"I just left her house."

"Good. You hungry?"

"Yeah, man. I could eat a little something, something." Laurent spoke with a perfect Haitian accent.

He followed his brother into a large kitchen with bright green walls and shiny silver commercial appliances. There were copper pots hanging from the ceiling. A grill and a small stone silk were on a separate island.

"What will it be, Lar? Chef's surprise?"

"Cool."

Laurent watched Vicenté tie on an apron, wash his hands, and pull numerous ingredients out of the subzero refrigerator. Minutes later, he spooned the contents out of various sauté pans onto three plates as Martine shuffled into the kitchen looking more asleep than awake.

"Something smells good in here."

"Good morning, beautiful. Have some breakfast."

Laurent smiled as he picked up his fork and dug into the scrambled eggs with scallops, onions, and cheese. There was also bacon and fried plantain on his plate. He loved his brother's cooking. The combination of tastes and textures was soothing to his soul and delightful on his palette.

"I cannot believe what went down last night. Everybody went crazy. Vadé slapped Tia and threw her and Juliet out of the club. See what happens when we stay home, baby?" Martine chomped on a slice of bacon.

"Vadé slapped Tia and threw Juliet out of the club?" Laurent dropped his fork into his plate.

"You didn't know, man?"

"No. Juliet didn't tell me any of that."

Martine set goblets of fresh-squeezed orange juice by their plates. "I can't believe all of this went down while you were performing."

"Your father and sister showed out." Vicenté laughed.

"They are your father and sister too."

"Don't remind me, little brother, but we do have to take the bitter with the sweet."

"That's cold." Martine laughed. "But I don't understand why Vadé would treat my sister and cousin like that. She was so sweet the day of the wedding. I thought she was my friend."

"I don't know what's wrong with Vadé. She and JP are having problems, but that doesn't mean she has to take it out on everyone else."

Laurent saddened as he talked about his family. Martine picked up and changed the subject.

"Did you speak to Juliet?"

"I went by your mother's house and saw her."

"Good." She smiled at Vicenté.

"I'm in love with your sister."

"I know."

"How? Did Juliet tell you?"

"No. I predicted the entire thing. Tell 'em, V."

"She did, Lar. I didn't think you'd be interested in Juliet but Martine said she'd get you hook, line, and sinker."

"Why did you say that?"

"The two of you look like you should be together. God planned it like that and when the time was right, He brought you together. A match made in heaven or some craziness like that. I don't know."

Vicenté was laughing. "You're right, Martine. Juliet fits the part. The Hollywood rock star with his supermodel girlfriend."

The three of them laughed as they adjourned into the family room. Martine stretched her legs across the sofa into Vicenté's lap. He took a bottle of red polish out of his pocket and began painting her toenails.

"That's pretty romantic of you, big brother." Laurent watched him as he carefully polished her big toenail.

"I'll teach you how to love a woman right."

Laurent smiled as he fell asleep beside his brother and Martine on their comfortable sofa. Families were great. He had made a reservation for Juliet on his flight. They would take a red-eye to LA and get married the following morning. He drifted off into peaceful sleep.

When he opened his eyes, it was dusk. He had slept the entire day. He could hear music and laughter through an open window as Mardis Gras revelers in the French Quarter celebrated the night. He sat up on the couch as Vicenté entered the room.

"It's time to go, man. I've got kitchen duty for the party tonight. Martine has the car. She and Juliet went shopping and to get their hair done. I'm riding with you."

The sisters went in and out of dress shops as Martine searched for the perfect outfit for the ball.

"So things are cool between you and Lar?"

"Yes." She smiled as she twisted the silver band on her ring finger with her thumb.

"I'm glad Vadé didn't mess that up with her crazy self. I'm going to have a talk with her about what went down. Why didn't you mention it to Lar?"

"Because that is his sister, whatever her problem is. Things are great with us so don't make a big issue out of this. I know how you can get."

"All right, princess sister. Chill."

"We'd better hurry up and get your costume. It's getting a little congested out here. Do you have any idea of what you want to go as?"

"Any suggestions?"

"Martine!"

They strolled past the Voodoo Museum on their way to Martine's favorite dress shop. The building was overflowing with patrons. There was a line out of the door and around the corner.

"Those people are wasting their money." Juliet made a face as she spoke.

"They're just doing it for fun. Come on. Let's have our fortune told for Mardis Gras, and then we'll go home and change."

Juliet consented for the sake of time. She wanted nothing to do with spells, potions, or magic. She just wanted to get to the hotel and see Laurent.

The line for the fortune-teller barely moved. She fought to maintain her cool as they stood at the end.

"We've got plenty of time, Juliet. It's just seven-thirty. We'll leave for the hotel by nine. Laurent doesn't perform until ten-thirty."

Hotel de Chevalier buzzed with activity. Left Bank swarmed with all sorts of characters. They flowed out of the hotel onto the grounds and formed a line by the grill, where one of Vicenté's assistants smoked seafood and blackened steak.

Vadé rubbed almond cream into her freshly bathed body and fastened a thin gold chain around her waist. She sat down in front of the vanity mirror and carefully outlined her eyes with dark blue eye pencil and applied a pair of false eyelashes. After she highlighted her Egyptian eyes with sparkling gold shadow, she placed a tiara on her head. She was Sabre, an African princess.

She pulled the sheer emerald green skirt over her bare hips and fastened a bra made out of gold coins on her bare body. She would put the rest of the outfit on later. This dance was for her husband. She picked up a pair of finger cymbals and a silk scarf and danced into the bedroom.

"I am Princess Sabre from Africa. Your every wish is my command."

She tapped her cymbals together as she shook her hips and twisted her waist to the smooth strings and soft percussion on the tape she had inserted into JP's boom box earlier.

"You know what I wish, beautiful girl. Come here."

Vadé laughed as JP pulled her onto the bed. She hadn't made love to her husband in over a week and it was time she put a stop to that nonsense.

Laurent looked around his room for the last time as he got out of the shower. This would be the last time he ever dressed in this room as a single man. He pulled on a pair of shorts and went through his desk and clothing drawers removing personal mementos and tucking them into his suitcase.

As the clock in the hotel foyer struck nine-thirty, the girls slid into the red Jeep, sped down the street, and screeched to a stop. There were cars everywhere. Martine pulled into a lane of traffic that was standing still. A half hour later, they had barely moved a car length.

"This is awful, Martine. Is there any other way we can go?"

"They've got most of the streets blocked for the parade."

Juliet wanted to scream.

"If I can turn around, I can go the other way."

Martine pulled up over the curb and tied up traffic in the other direction as she turned around.

JP helped Vadé back into her Mardis Gras costume. It was just about ten-thirty and time for Laurent's final performance.

Martine and Juliet sat in traffic going nowhere in the opposite direction.

"Where's your phone, Martine?"

"Look in my bag, Juliet. It's in there somewhere."

Juliet was trying very hard to remain calm. So far she had succeeded in spending the day with her sister and not telling her a thing. She dug inside her sister's oversize purse for her cellular phone.

Vicenté walked out of the kitchen into the club as Little Claude announced Laurent. The screaming was so loud you could barely hear him.

"Your phone's not in here, Martine." Juliet tossed the bag aside and removed the wedding veil. She was starting to perspire. She saw a telephone booth, grabbed her sister's bag, and jumped out of the Jeep.

"Juliet! Where are you going?"

"To use the pay phone!" she shouted over her shoulder as she ran, in her wedding dress, toward the phone. She dug in the bag until she found a change purse and dropped several coins into the phone.

"Hotel de Chevalier." Jewel was on the desk that night.

"I need to speak to Laurent Chevalier!" she yelled into the receiver.

"I'm sorry, but I can't hear you." Jewel had to shout to be heard over the screaming.

"Laurent Chevalier!" Juliet screamed as loudly as she could. The party in the street cranked up another level. Martine was almost in the same spot she was in when Juliet got out of the car.

"He's onstage now." Jewel hollered back.

"Take a message. *I'm running late. Please wait. Love, Juliet.* Can you read that back, please?" She was practically screaming.

"*Running late. Please wait. Love, Juliet!*" Jewel hollered back.

"That's it. Thank you." Juliet slammed the phone back on the hook and sighed with relief. She reread the slip of paper she had pulled out of a Faberge egg on the way out of Madame Bijou's dress shop.

Love endures all things.

"Why are you screaming into the phone, Jewel?" Vadé came down the stairs with JP and stopped to speak to her. "Go on, sweetheart, I'll be right there."

JP blew her a kiss as he ran down the stairs into the foyer.

"I was taking a message for Monsieur Laurent and I wasn't able to hear the caller. It was very noisy. She sounded like she was calling from a pay phone."

"I'll see that Lar gets it. You take care of the phones."

"Yes, mademoiselle."

She handed Vadé a slip of paper from the telephone log.

"*Running late. Please wait. Love, Juliet* . . . Give me a break. Does she think my brother is going to wait for her before he goes onstage?"

She ripped the message into tiny pieces and tossed them onto a tray of dirty dishes a waiter was carrying into the kitchen. *I'm sure she and her trampy cousin are already on the way.*

She removed the green silk scarf draped over her golden brassiere and gently pulled it around her husband's neck. They were finally back on track and she wasn't going to allow anyone ever to come between them again.

Laurent exited the stage as the revelers began to dance. He slipped inside the dressing room and changed before anyone had a chance to see him without a disguise.

While Martine and Juliet were inching along in traffic as the clock struck eleven-thirty, Laurent was seaching the club for his bride. There was no sign of anyone dressed in what Juliet had described. He saw Vadé and JP dancing as he walked outside. Flowers floated in the pool and masqueraders sat at individual tables eating by candlelight. He had reserved a table for them but no one was sitting there. He saw Little Claude loading their suitcases into the shuttle.

He dashed back into the club and almost ran into his father as the grandfather clock slowly began to strike twelve. Laughter filled the club as masqueraders made their identities known. Laurent's heart sank with grief. He didn't see Juliet anywhere.

He ran to the shuttle where Little Claude was waiting.

"Lar, come on before we miss the plane. You know traffic is going to be bad."

"Have you seen Juliet?"

"I haven't seen anyone tonight. Let's go."

"Wait a minute."

He ran back into the ballroom still wearing his mask. The masquerade was over and now the beheaded characters danced with human faces.

I can't believe she didn't come.

He ran upstairs where the receptionist sat. Jewel was off duty and a replacement informed him there had been no calls for him. He walked in slow motion outside to Little Claude, who practically shoved him into the shuttle.

"What's wrong with you, man? I thought you were excited about this."

Laurent peered into the darkness for a glimpse of Vicenté's red Jeep, but there was no sign of a car for miles. The narrow country road loomed ahead endlessly in the darkness.

She lied to me. She said she loved me and she said she would be here.

As soon as the cousins were seated on the plane, Laurent put on the headphones to his Discman and feigned sleep while he fingered his portion of the tiny silver ring in his pocket.

TWENTY-SIX

Juliet ran up the red carpet and into Hotel de Chevalier while Martine left the Jeep with the valet. She ran into the club as the clock in the foyer signaled the half hour. It was twelve-thirty.

I know he waited for me.

The masquerade ball was still in full swing. Juliet wove her way through the dancing creatures looking for Laurent. She went out the back door and ran down the hall to the dressing room.

He must be in here.

She turned the knob but the door was locked. She knocked on the door and just as she was about to walk away, JP pulled it open and looked at the pretty young girl in the antique lace wedding dress who looked like she was ready to cry.

"Juliet?"

Have you seen Laurent? I was supposed to meet him here."

Vadé was stretched out on the chaise in her African princess attire. She sat up as Juliet came into the room.

"Day, have you seen Lar? Juliet is looking for him."

Vadé looked the young woman up and down, who looked more like a child in the old-fashioned wedding dress and Shirley Temple curls.

She does look like someone Lar could be interested in. She's definitely not older than him for once and she is Martine's little sister. It's that trampy cousin that I cannot tolerate.

"No, baby, now that I think about it, I haven't seen Lar all day except when he was performing."

She sat up and slid her feet into a pair of gold sandals covered with the same gold coins as her top. "He's around here somewhere. We'll find him."

The Oliviers ushered Juliet back into the club as they began to inquire of Laurent's whereabouts. They found Martine on the dance floor with Vicenté.

"Have either of you seen Lar?" Vadé yelled over the music.

"No," Vicenté yelled back.

"They must be upstairs in Lar's room. Let's go up."

She and JP led Juliet, Vicenté, and Martine to the elevator in the foyer. It was concealed from view unless you knew it was there. They rode up to the family's floor. Juliet hardly noticed the beautiful corridor and rooms as they walked down the long corridor. Vadé left everyone in the living room while she went to get Laurent.

"Lar?"

She knocked on the door and went in. The suite was overly neat as usual. His favorite pop station was on his stereo. She closed the door and swished back down the hall to the family room.

Juliet's heart sank when she saw her come back without Laurent. He was gone. He had left without her.

"He's not in there. Where are they?"

"I thought I heard voices." Pierre came out of his sitting room wearing a gray smoking jacket, and carrying a book.

"Papá, have you seen Lar and Little Claude?"

"No. I haven't seen anyone. I've been in my room all day. Is something wrong?"

"No. Juliet is here to see Laurent and we can't find him. No one has seen him or Little Claude."

Vadé was starting to feel a little uneasy. She knew she had thrown away Juliet's message to Laurent. She had said to tell him she was going to be late and to wait.

Lar went somewhere and he was going to take Juliet.

"Did he do the set?" Pierre looked concerned.

"I saw him," Vicenté offered. "He turned it out once again."

"His car is here." JP closed the window and returned to his w side.

"They must be at Big Claude's."

Juliet watched Pierre dial a number.

They don't know. It really was our secret. But why did he leave without me? He should have waited. He said he wouldn't leave without me. He lied.

Big Claude and Giselle walked into the suite.

"Hello, family."

"Hi, babies." She blew kisses at the kids.

"Claude? I was just getting ready to call you, man. Are the boys at your house? There's a pretty lady here waiting to see Laurent and we don't know why he's not here."

"Pierre, the boys aren't there. We didn't think you'd realize they were gone for another few days."

"Gone? Gone where?"

No one dared to breathe as Pierre's face clouded like the sky before a thunderstorm.

"The boys are on their way to LA. Laurent signed a deal with Virgin and they want him in the studio."

"LA? A deal?"

Lar signed a deal with Virgin Records. He went to LA and didn't tell me and he was taking Juliet with him. Vadé felt as if someone had hit her in the stomach. She clutched JP's arm a little tighter.

"Claude, what are you talking about?"

Vicenté wanted to laugh. *Baby brother left them in a tailspin. Way to go, Lar. But why did you tell Juliet you were going to meet her and leave?*

He looked at his wife's little sister, who looked as though she had lost her best friend.

"Rene signed Laurent to a deal with Virgin Records."

"You mean you knew about this and didn't tell me?"

"Pierre, you know you have always been bullheaded when it comes to Laurent having a professional singing career."

"I don't care what you think, Claude, Laurent is my son. I have plans for him."

"*You* have plans. That's why your son is gone, Chevalier."

"Get out of my house, Claude. I never thought I would have to say something like this to you. Get out."

"Gladly. Come on, Giselle." He finished his drink and set the glass on the bar as she stood up and smiled at the kids.

"Good night, babies. Y'all know we love you."

"Papá! Stop them. Don't let Big Claude and T leave like this."

"Mind your business, Vadé."

Pierre threw ice cubes into a glass, picked up the decanter of Chevis Regal, and slammed the door as he went into his bedroom.

"Lar went to LA and signed with Virgin. He's blowin' up!"

Vicenté and JP slapped a high five in honor of Laurent's accomplishment. Vadé headed toward her room to find something to soothe the pain over her brother's secret departure, and now Big Claude and Giselle leaving.

"Juliet, didn't you call the hotel and leave Laurent a message telling him you were going to be late?"

Martine sat down next to her sister, as Vadé froze midway between the family room and her sitting room. After everything that just happened, she had completely forgotten about that message until Martine brought it up again.

"Yes, I did. The receptionist said she would give it to him. I forgot that I called."

Double damn. Would they forget the stupid message?

"Maybe he didn't get it." Martine looked at Vadé. She had been rude to Juliet. She knew Vadé could be underhanded, but not with her sister.

"The receptionist has a logbook. We can look in it and see who took the message." JP jumped up and headed for the door.

"Sweetheart, I'm sure Lar received all of his messages." She smiled sweetly at Juliet.

"It's no problem." JP ran down the hall and down the flight of stairs and was back in minutes. He sat down at the table and began to read the telephone messages that had been received that evening.

"You see anything, man?" Vicenté stood over him as he pored over the book. Vadé poured herself a double vodka. It did a good job of calming her during family crises.

"Here it is. The message came in at ten thirty-one. Laurent was onstage."

"Which means he didn't get it when it came in."

"Jewel took this message. It says, *Please wait. Running late. Love, Juliet.*" JP read the phone log and looked at Juliet. "He was going to take you to LA on the down-low. This is Lar's little honey. No wonder he was so excited when I saw him the other night. I'm sorry, baby girl."

Juliet smiled quickly and wiped a tear. She didn't want any of them to see how much pain she was in.

"Call Jewel and see if she gave that message to Lar," Vicenté demanded. "If she did and Lar stood Juliet up, then I'm going to kick his little ass the next time I see him. He can't trip like that because he got a record deal."

"That's really not necessary." Juliet stood up and tried to stop them. *If Laurent didn't get the message he still should have waited. I told him I would be there.*

"Yes, it is." Martine joined the group at the table.

"Jewel's probably at home in bed. I won't have you waking my employees. Ask her about that message when she comes to work tomorrow."

"In bed? Jewel's downstairs partying. I'll go down and get her."

Vicenté was on his way down the hall before anyone could say a word.

Now what am I going to do? Laurent's already gone so he can't get mad at me. He can call her tomorrow.

Vadé calmly sipped her drink as Vicenté and Jewel came into the room.

"Jewel said she gave that message to Vadé, and you said you would give it to Laurent."

Vicenté looked directly at her. He looked just like Pierre did right before he threw Big Claude out of the hotel.

"Mademoiselle, you remember the message I gave you?"

Every eye in the room was glued on Vadé. Their eyes bore holes through her soul, but no one was going to make her tell a lie. She hated to lie.

"Of course I do." She felt hot all over as she sipped the vodka.

"You little bitch. Why didn't you give it to him?" Vicenté was seething.

"Don't go there, V." JP stood to his wife's defense. "What happened to that message, baby?"

"I threw it out." She spoke coolly.

Whatever happens, I still have JP.

"You threw it out?" Martine was in her face. "Why?"

"Because he was onstage and he couldn't get it anyway. I thought she would be here by the time he completed the set. If I saw him I would have told him. I didn't know he was going to LA."

"Nobody did. But you should have given him that message." Martine was fuming.

"What's the big deal? He can call her later." She went to the bar and poured herself another drink.

"The big deal is you should have given him the message. But you didn't, you threw it out, probably because you think my little sister isn't good enough for your little brother, you stuck-up bitch."

There was that word again coming from someone she loved and someone who she thought loved her.

"That's not true."

"Oh, no? I never told Vicenté what you said."

"What did she say, baby?" Vicenté and JP both looked at Vadé.

"The day we bought the ring she congratulated me for getting my hands on a Chevalier, even if he was the poorer brother, and not to think that I would ever get a penny out of this hotel because it all belonged to her mother."

"That was before we were friends and I apologized."

"Friends? We're supposed to be family. I can't believe you'd treat my sister like this."

"Vadé, tell me you didn't say that." JP gave her a funny look.

"She said it. I know she said it." Vicenté still looked a lot like Pierre and he yelled a lot like him too.

"What's going on out here?"

Pierre snatched open the door of his private sitting room where he had been sitting by the fire reading. Tears were streaming out of Vadé's eyes.

"It's not like that now."

She looked at JP, who turned away.

"I've had enough of this. Let's go, Martine." He turned and looked at Vadé again.

"I asked what's going on out here. Why is my daughter crying?"

"Your son's wife called me a bitch, Papá!"

"She only said it because you act like one and you need to mind your own business."

"I said what's going on in here? I want to know something right now." Pierre glared at Vicenté and then JP.

"The both of you tripping . . . always thinking you're better than everyone else."

"Let's go, Vicenté." Martine got up to leave.

"I said what's going on? Vicenté!"

He turned around and faced Pierre.

"You want to know what's going on out here? I'm glad you asked that because you need to hear this. In fact, you're the one responsible for all of this anyway."

"All of what?"

"This . . . the family."

"Vicenté, I asked you a question."

"All right." He stood there a moment longer before he spoke.

"You know . . . when I was a little boy in Haiti all I ever dreamed about, all I ever thought about, was a family. Mamá slaved over that hot stove every day talking about how we were going to be a family when you came back. And it was going to be fine like wine in the summertime. But you never came, man. You never came. And finally Mamá just stopped talking and then she died. I came looking for you. I was going to make you pay for breaking my mamá's heart like that. Pierre Chevalier, the world-famous musician. So I get here and I find out Papá's got a pretty little wife, and a pretty little daughter, and a pretty little son . . . so there's no room for me or Mamá even if she was still alive. And I hated you. But I couldn't get rid of that nagging little desire to have a family. And I thought, maybe, just maybe, I can be a part of his family."

"Vicenté, what is this about? I welcomed you with open arms into my family."

"You sure did, Papá. You gave me a job, and a car, and told everybody I was your son. You played the part real well. Only every time I look into your eyes, I feel like you wish I would go away."

"That is not true, Vicenté."

"It's not? Then why haven't you ever been to my house, invited me to have dinner, or have a drink in your room, just you and me? Man, you don't care anything about me. You wish I would go away."

"Vicenté, son . . . that's not true."

"Save it, Papá. And you, my beautiful little sister, with skin like the beautiful women on the island, and eyes as green as the sea, you're no better. You walk around here with your head held so high you can't see anyone but yourself. Some princess you are."

"Papá! Tell him he's wrong about everything. I'm not like that."

"Yes, you are." JP got up and went into their bedroom.

"No wonder Lar ran off to Hollywood without telling any of you. You ran him away. You don't have to run me away because I'm leaving. I don't want or need any of you. My little brother's on his way to LA. There's nothing here for me now."

Vadé watched them walk out of the room and head toward the elevator.

"Papá! Aren't you going to make them stay?"

"I can't make anyone do anything they don't want to do." He got up and walked back into his sitting room and Vadé followed him.

"Yes, you can, Papá! You just won't."

"I can't, Princess. Please, not now."

"Why do you make me do everything I don't want to do? You made me leave Paris and move to America. You made me marry JP."

"I said, not now, Vadé."

She stormed out of his room and into her suite where JP had a suitcase open on the bed.

"JP, what are you doing?"

She watched him toss in all of his clean underwear.

"Packing."

"I can see that. Where are you going?"

"I don't know. Anywhere. Away from you."

"Away from me? Why?"

"Because you are exactly what V said you are. A stuck-up little bitch."

"I am not, JP. You know me better than anyone."

"I thought I did, but I don't know who you are anymore. I can't believe how you hurt people to get your way."

"I thought I would see him. Isn't anyone listening anymore?"

"Not to you." JP continued packing.

"You can't leave me here. I'll go with you. I have money saved from work. We can get a place in the French Quarter or by your school until we move to Paris."

"I'm not going to Paris with you or anywhere else."

"But you love me, JP. I need you, and you need me."

"I do, but I can learn to live without you."

"I can't believe you're leaving me because I didn't give Lar a message."

She put her hands on her hips and watched him as he locked the suitcase and picked up his book bag.

"You'll have to deal with Lar about that yourself. I can't believe you would interfere in his life like that. But you interfere in everyone's lives to make them do what you want them to do. Just like your daddy. But then maybe that's why T left him. We know that's why Lar left."

He picked up the suitcase and started walking toward the door.

"JP! You're wrong. I threw that message away because of Tia. She said she—"

"Save it, Day, because no matter what, it's always about you and what you want."

"Why is everyone so mad at me?"

She screamed as he walked out of the sitting room and down the hall. The pain in her stomach moved into her heart and finally exploded inside her head. She threw herself on her bed and cried until there were no more tears to cry.

Hours later she awoke to sunlight in her eyes. The family floor at Hotel de Chevalier was completely silent.

Her body and soul ached for her husband, but sometimes a girl has to do what a girl has to do to survive. She jumped in her steam shower, dressed, and packed.

Vadé marched down the hall beside the bellboy with her Louis Vuitton luggage. She would not leave as the others had, secretly, stealthily, at night. She left boldly, during the middle of the day, while the birds sang, and Right Bank buzzed with luncheon activity. As she strolled through the lobby and out of building, she noticed the remnants of last night's Mardis Gras celebration had been swept away.

It was a grand exit out to the limousine. Vadé was the epitome of Paris haute courtier fashion in a green wool suit trimmed with mink around the cuffs and collar. As the bellboy loaded her suitcases into the limo, she kept hoping someone would stop her, and beg her to stay. There was just one problem. Everyone she had ever cared about was already gone.

TWENTY-SEVEN

St. Tropez, the playground of the rich and famous, was always beautiful at this time of the year, when the super rich were on holiday. Hundreds of tanned, oiled bodies sun-worshiped on the powder-white beaches of the coast. Jet-skis bounced across the vivid green Mediterranean while boats with colorful sails dotted the horizon.

Pierre sat on a fishing boat with his pole in the water and his feet propped up on top of the railing around the deck. There was a cooler with fresh-squeezed lemonade, lobster and fruit salads, and croissants. A thick novel lay opened on the chair next to him. He had come there searching for peace and the memory of her. He had left New Orleans several days ago on an early flight, the morning after.

He had thrown his best friend out of the hotel, driven both of his sons away, and lost the respect of his daughter all in one night. When he made plans for his family, he hadn't planned on any of those things happening. He had only tried to love them all the best way he knew how. Protect them from the world, give them a roof over their heads, clothes, food to eat, and a few little trinkets on the side. Wasn't that what a father was supposed to do? Then how did he make such a mess of things?

Pierre looked like a man without a care in the world. The Grambling University T-shirt looked good on his well-toned chocolate body. He had hit the gym to help him unwind as soon as he checked into the hotel. He had retreated to the south of France for its solace and wonderful memories. He had thrown away the cigarettes and refused to take another drink of scotch. Pierre drank steadily through the years following Desiree's disappearance and it barely numbed the pain. Now it was time to face it like a man, and the placid aquamarine water was soothing to his restless soul.

Moonlight spilled into the harbor and the bay looked like a silver reflecting glass when Pierre docked the boat and carried the empty cooler and his fishing gear to the rented Range Rover. He was in St. Tropez for the night. Tomorrow he would drive out to Antibes, to the villa that had served as income property for the family since they left Paris. No one from the family had been there for years. He had been waiting for an available room. The family suite was booked too, but its occupants would be forced to find accommodations elsewhere now that Pierre was on his way.

The villa's pink-washed structure brought back memories of good times when things were simple and easy. He was amazed by how much Hotel de Chevalier reminded him of the villa. There was a cool elegance yet a definite sense of formality about the salmon and black marble floors, ceiling fans, and bamboo furnishings. He had let Vadé supervise the decorating of the hotel. He was too distressed over Desiree to pay anything much attention. He just knew it looked nice. The rest didn't matter.

He caught a glimpse of a petite woman in a large black straw hat and dark sunglasses stepping out of the elevator and watched her swish out the front door of the villa. He smiled when he caught himself staring. She reminded him a lot of . . . He ran out the front door after her but the lady in black had vanished.

Later, Pierre sat in the one-bedroom hotel room puffing on a *galouise*. A glass of zinfandel sat beside the ashtray. He had reneged on the cigarettes, but he refused to give in to the scotch.

Could Desiree have been living here in the villa all these years?

He had thought to come to Antibes himself to get away from all the craziness, but he couldn't stand the thought of being there without her so he never found the time to get away. He called the receptionist and spoke to her in French, asking for Desiree Chevalier, Desiree Legrande, but there was no one registered by that name. She refused to disclose the names of the occupants in the family's suite. He could take that up with Monsieur Gilbert when he returned from his holiday next week.

Pierre dressed and went downstairs to the restaurant. He hated his small room. It made him feel claustrophobic. He had to sit at the bar while he waited for a table because it was so crowded. It was nice to see that business was going well.

There was a sound of light conversation and tinkling glasses when she sat down at the piano and sang into the mike. Her accompaniment was an acoustic guitar, a cello, violins, and bongos. Her voice was as cool as the wind and easy, like flowing water. It commanded everyone's attention. It was the blues sprinkled with jazz, sung like he never heard them sung before.

"Dez!" he whispered to himself.

She was marvelous and ever so stunning in a fabulous emerald beaded gown. Her hair was different, chic, cut to the nape of her neck, but it was still Dez. He ordered another glass of wine as she continued singing.

What do I say to her?

It was obvious that she didn't want him in her life anymore, or why would she keep herself hidden from him all these years?

She has another man.

Although they were still legally married, it had been three years since they lived as husband and wife. He glanced around the bar and lounge looking for his wife's potential companion. There was a very distinguished American seated at a table in front, hanging on to her every word.

She's with him.

Desiree finished the set and joined the American at his table. Pierre had a coughing fit when she kissed him. A waiter arrived and finally ushered him through the restaurant to a booth. He ordered barbecued chicken and pasta without looking at the menu just to get rid of him. He covered his face with his hands and shook his head.

Dez has another man. I was a fool to think she was somewhere missing me just as much as I was missing her.

He chewed the chicken, pasta, and green salad. It tasted like straw. He just wanted to get out of the villa and away from the south of France as quickly as possible. There was no longer a reason to dream about her, no reason to hope. She was really gone.

He took one last glance in her direction as he signed the check, and rushed out of the restaurant toward the elevator. She and the American were gone. The elevator doors opened and he rushed in blindly, bumping into the guests coming off the elevator.

"Pierre!"

His eyes focused on Desiree.

"Pierre! It's really you!"

She jumped on him as he tried to figure out what was happening.

"Pierre, it's me, Dez."

"Hello, Desiree." He didn't know why he was being so cool with her.

"You finally came. Oh, baby. I didn't think you would ever come for me."

She forced her way between his arms into the spot that was reserved exclusively for her body. She cried as she kissed him.

Pierre was afraid to respond to the kisses he had dreamed of in his fantasies. He was afraid to embrace what could never be his again. He looked around for her handsome American as they stepped out of the elevator back into the small lobby.

"What's wrong, darling?"

He gazed into her green eyes and wanted to cry.

"Nothing."

"I knew better than to expect you to act like I never went away." She was almost pouting and she reminded him of Vadé.

"It's been a long time, Dez, and I realize things have changed. . . ."

"You have someone else." She pulled away from him and cried real tears. "I should have known better than to think you'd sit around waiting for me. Giselle always said you were quite the ladies' man."

"I have someone else? What about you and your handsome American?"

"Handsome American? Are you talking about Greg? He's from Virgin Records in LA. He arrived a few days ago. He wants me to record an album for them and they're thinking about releasing it in the States. My handsome American is here on business."

Pierre couldn't control the laughter that bubbled up from somewhere deep inside him.

"Virgin? Your son just made some deal with Virgin and ran off to LA."

"He did? Did Mother tell you I was here?"

"No. I came on my own. I really screwed things up. The kids are all pissed at me, and Laurent ran off to LA without telling one Chevalier."

"Oh, honey." She was back in that spot made just for her.

"I've missed you and my babies so much. I told Mother to tell you I was here from the very beginning. Well . . . after I was over being upset with you about Vicenté."

"How long ago was that?"

"About a week after I left."

"What?"

"I should have known Mother didn't tell you. I thought you hated me for all those horrible things I said to you."

"I thought you hated me because I wouldn't let you sing."

"I could never hate you for that or anything else. Father told you not to let me sing, didn't he?"

"He said I'd have problems with the hotel. He also told me not to tell you about our conversation. I didn't want to cause problems between you and your family. We had just come back to New Orleans."

"I know, baby. Father knew that, too, and took advantage of the situation. Why do parents try to control their children's lives?"

"And why do married people keep secrets from each other? I should have told you everything."

"You couldn't have told me about Vicenté."

"Vicenté surprised us all." He sighed and looked at Desiree. "I've blamed him for you leaving."

"Pierre, you didn't."

"Not with my words, but my actions. I really messed up."

"He'll forgive you."

"He was right. He said I played the part of being Papá well."

"That relationship is going to take time. You can't make up for twenty-eight years in three. And I know Lar left because you were making him go to college when you know he wants to sing. Pierre, you've got to stop interfering in their lives. They're grown. If they make mistakes, we'll be here to help them. Look what our parents interfering did to us."

Pierre glanced at Desiree like a child. "I just wanted Laurent to be able to make a way for himself in life. That boy can do anything he wants."

"And he's doing it, Pierre. He's wonderful. He's always had that special something that makes everyone fall in love with him. He's going to be a huge success. Virgin is a great label for him because they can make him an international superstar."

"I've been a bad boy. I don't do well when you're not around."

"It's okay, baby. He'll forgive you, too."

He laughed happily for the first time in years. Desiree always had a way of showing him things were not as bad as they seemed.

"You always did know how to make me feel better."

He took her into his arms and kissed her. She felt so good he wanted to shout.

"Where are you staying?"

"I thought you'd never ask." She pressed the button for the elevator. "I was starting to think I'd have to jump on you right here in the lobby."

The doors opened and they rode up to the family suite together.

"They told me there was no guest in the hotel registered under Desiree Chevalier."

"Of course not. I'm not a guest, nor does the staff know me as the owner. It's simpler that way. I have a private line. People who really need to get in touch always find me."

"We sure do."

Desiree had redecorated with furnishings from the house in Paris. Pierre immediately felt at home.

"You know we're never going back to New Orleans," he whispered in the darkness, enjoying the feeling of her nude body next to his.

"Yes, we will. Eventually." She turned over to face him. "You never did finish telling me what you did to screw things up with the children so badly. What else did you do?"

Pierre was laughing again. "I threw Big Claude out of the hotel."

"What?" Desiree was laughing too. "You and Big Claude got into a fight? Did he sit on you?"

"No. It didn't come to blows. I asked him to leave because he was in on Laurent's record deal."

"Well, thank goodness someone in the family helped him. What did Giselle say?"

"Nothing. Blew kisses at the kids on her way out with Claude."

"Sounds like G. Claude will forgive you, too. How's my daughter?"

Pierre was silent awhile before he spoke. "I may have screwed that up the most. I really disappointed her."

"I heard about that sudden marriage to JP. Did you have anything to do with that?"

"Yeah. I caught them in bed together so I made them get married."

"Pierre!"

"I warned her, but she's okay with me about it now. I always knew those two would be married eventually. No telling how long they'd been messing around."

"Pierre, things are different now. Kids do things that way now."

"Not my daughter. I told her if she wanted to have sex she was going to get married."

"Pierre, you and I would have done the same thing."

"That's not the point. And I never laid a hand on you until we were married. You were something special."

"Was Vicenté's mother special?"

"She was at the time, but we were just kids. We never shared anything together but the island. We have everything, baby, don't ruin this. I love you. You're the only woman I've ever loved, woman."

"I'm sorry, baby. I won't ever bring her up again."

She rubbed his head as they lay there in silence.

"Well, Vadé doesn't seem like she's mad at you about JP."

"She's not, baby. But I let her down. When Big Claude and Vicenté were leaving, she begged me to make them stay and fix things. But I wouldn't do it. I couldn't. I should have tried, but I didn't. Me and my pride. I never saw her look at me that way."

Desiree pulled her husband's arms around her. Things had been extremely painful for everyone and it was time to make them better.

"Your daughter will forgive you, too. You're her first love."

"What do you think the kids will say when they see you, Dez?"

"I don't want to think that far ahead. I know my son will forgive me."

"You know your daughter is going to demand some sort of explanation."

"I know. But she's a young woman in love with a husband now. I can only hope she'll understand."

TWENTY-EIGHT

The Santa Monica Promenade is always bustling with activity, especially on Saturday. People of all ages eat, shop, and see movies, browse bookstores, or sip flavored and iced coffees while magicians, musicians, and mimes provide sidewalk entertainment. At the nearby pier, lovers hold hands on the Ferris wheel as others stroll on the boardwalk, jog, ride bikes, and roller-blade along the coast of the Pacific Ocean.

Little Claude drove as quickly as traffic allowed down Wilshire Boulevard in the Land-Cruiser. He and Laurent had spent most of the afternoon in the Santa Monica City College Library. Final exams would be over in two weeks and they would be college graduates.

Laurent had refused to go at first but Little Claude persuaded him. He registered his cousin for school despite his protesting. They had done everything together since they were born, and they would also graduate together. Little Claude insisted that it would look good in Laurent's bio that he was a college graduate and a successful musician.

Little Claude rewound a studio tape of the single they were working on with Wyclef Jean. It was going to be the first single from the album. The record company was spending major dollars. They were already lining up his promotional tour, which included dates on MTV and BET.

"I am so glad that Dad hooked us up with the condo on the beach. I didn't think he would say yes, but he did. He said we could always rent it out and that we would enjoy working by the water, which we do."

"Big Claude really took care of us. All we have to think about is getting this album recorded and finishing school."

"Yeah. It's not like we're out here working in Burger King trying to pay our rent."

"Thank you, Lord. It's nice to have someone in the family support us."

Laurent stopped talking and looked out the window as Little Claude drove down a shady street and turned up into a small gated community. He watched the black gate roll open and pushed thoughts of Juliet out of his head. It was a constant battle, day and night.

"This record has got to be huge, not just for me, but for everybody who believes in me. I want them to be proud."

"You want to show Pierre, too."

"You know, man, I used to want to show him, but if I sold a zillion records he wouldn't be proud of me because I'm not doing what *he* wants me to do."

"I don't get it. I just don't get it. Especially since he's a musician, too."

"I don't even want to get into that, man. I've got better things to use my energy on."

"Yeah, like those fine honeys we had at the house last night."

"There you go." Laurent jumped out of the gold SUV and closed the door.

"Lar, you need to loosen up, get a little crazy. You need to be having the time of your life. You're a young, single, good-looking man who's about to blow up on the music scene. You can have any woman and as many as you want."

Laurent unlocked the door and quickly punched a code for the alarm system.

"I only need one woman, Claude."

And the one I want doesn't want me.

"You want something to eat, man?" Little Claude opened the refrigerator, and took out a carton of juice.

"Whatever you want to do, *mon ami*. Hook us up. Order something if you want. I'm going upstairs for a minute."

There were two master bedroom suites, one up and one down. Little Claude chose the one downstairs, he said, because it was close to the pool. Laurent knew he had girls making booty calls all night. He liked being upstairs alone. He went into his bedroom and turned on the television set. There was a king-size water bed, a CD player, and a red director's chair. He never had to do much decorating. If Vadé had been there she would have his room looking great.

He hadn't spoken to his sister or anyone else in his family since he arrived in LA. He sent a telegram to his father at the hotel, but there had been no response. Big Claude hadn't seen or heard from anyone. Giselle said neither he nor Vadé was at the hotel and they hadn't tried to contact him. JP was back at home with his parents. He hadn't heard from Vadé and had no idea of her whereabouts either. He was coming to visit them in LA as soon as he could. The Oliviers kept in touch. It was the Chevaliers who weren't speaking.

Laurent felt guiltier by the day for not contacting his brother. There was only one reason why he hadn't called Vicenté, and that was that he was married to Martine, and Martine was Juliet's sister. Somehow things always got back to her.

He opened the door and stepped out of the shower and rubbed his butterscotch skin, tanned copper by the sun, with a green velour towel.

She never tried to get in touch with me.

He sprayed his skin with a light body oil, pulled on a pair of Nike sweats, lay across the cool water bed, and placed a set of headphones on his ears. He was ready to do some intense soul searching. He had opened the Juliet door in his mind once again, and now he was ready to go through it.

He had picked up the phone so many times to call her, but he didn't know what to say. *Hello, beautiful. Would you like to tell me why you stood me up for our wedding?*

He was too embarrassed to talk about it with anyone. Little Claude confronted him once, shortly after their arrival in Los Angeles. He had spoken to JP, who said Juliet arrived at the hotel late . . . that Lar had planned on taking her to LA, but Vadé had thrown away some message and everyone got into a huge fight.

Laurent had denied everything emphatically.

She told everyone our secret. . . . If what JP said was true, why didn't Juliet call me and tell me that herself? She knows I signed with Virgin. She could call and leave a message for me there if she really loved me. She could have told Vicenté to call me. He hasn't called me either.

He sat up and snatched the headphones from his head. He had gone too far. Little Claude tapped on the door and opened it.

"I cooked, man."

Laurent sat up and found his sandals. "What did you cook, gumbo?"

"All right."

Both of the boys laughed as they went into the kitchen.

"I made Mexican."

He lifted the lid on a skillet of shrimp fajitas. There was a clay pot with warm tortillas. Tomatoes, lettuce, several types of cheese, and sour cream were neatly lined up on the tile countertop.

"Look at you, man. Are one of your girls coming over?"

"Maybe later. I did all of this for you."

"No stuff?"

"No stuff. You look like you could use a little cheering up. I made a big pitcher of strawberry daiquiris, too."

"You're the best, Claude. I don't know what I'd ever do without you. I love you, man."

They both laughed as they went outside on the deck with the food.

"Since you love me, can I ask you a question?"

"Sure, *mon ami.*"

"Did you ever call her?"

"Call who?"

"Juliet."

Laurent swallowed the food he was chewing.

"No."

"Why not?"

"It's not important."

"It's not important and you've been dragging around ever since we got here. Call the girl."

"Why are you making an issue out of this, Claude?"

"Because you are."

"I am not."

"You are, Lar. You're just trying to be real careful and cool. She's not like the others. This one got you and you don't want to give in."

"Give in? I asked the girl to marry me and she never showed up."

"You and Juliet were going to get married? Why?"

"I wasn't going to bring her out here just to sleep with her. I wanted to spend the rest of my life with her."

"Then why did you lie? Why didn't you say something when I told you what JP said?"

"When JP gets his own love life straight with Day, then I might let him give me suggestions on mine."

"I agree, but I'm sure he was just trying to help you out. Maybe he knows something."

"If JP knew something, he would have told you. So do me a favor and keep JP out of my business. And you stay out of it too."

"I was only trying to help, Lar. Don't get mad at me. Vadé was the one who threw your message away."

"I'm not mad at you, and Vadé probably did throw away the message."

"Probably? She did."

"We weren't there."

"She's your sister."

"Our sister."

"True dat."

"No one would ever think you were born in Paris."

"True dat."

They both laughed.

Laurent was in the process of escaping to his room. "Whatever happened, it can't be undone."

"You don't know that, just call her."

Little Claude's final suggestion fell on deaf ears as Laurent covered them with the headset and cranked the volume on the CD.

TWENTY-NINE

It was Christmas in Paris. At least it was inside the building where Juliet strutted down the Claude Montana runway in the finest of his Holiday collection. The backless metallic gold gown looked as though it had been designed just for her. The meshlike fabric felt wonderful to the touch. Her golden hair and bronze skin made her glow. She was fashion's new hot golden girl.

Juliet was booked solid with almost every major design house in Paris. She had been in the city since February. She modeled their spring collections and spent the rest of March and April shooting swimwear and the *Victoria's Secret* catalogue.

Juliet smoothed sunblock on her freshly washed skin, applied mascara, and picked up her makeup case. Another day, another dollar. She loved modeling and she loved making money. She pushed open the door of the warehouse where she had been working, carrying the golden dress in a plastic bag over her arm. It was too fabulous to pass up.

The July sun was sweltering. At the Metro station she dug in her backpack for a token and sunglasses. She spent so much time in Paris that she had rented an apartment not far from the design houses. She glanced at the Eiffel and wondered what sort of home Laurent's family owned when they lived in Paris. She thought about him often. It was hard not to, knowing that this had been his home.

Juliet rode through two stops and walked through the empty train station. Nearly everyone had left the city for the summer holiday. The classical music playing through the speakers faded as she walked toward her building. She felt sad. There was a sense of loneliness she couldn't shake. It was also the reason why she had had to leave New Orleans. She was relieved when her agent had called and given her the extensive assignment in Paris because she needed something to do, to be busy, and away from her sister.

Martine kept telling her she should call Laurent in California, but Juliet felt he should have called her. He was the one who left without her because she was running late, after he said he wouldn't leave without her. Martine felt she was being stubborn and not giving Laurent the benefit of the doubt since Vadé threw away the message.

We made a plan. Message or no message, he should have waited.

She stopped at the gymnasium for her daily workout. She found the grueling sit-ups and weight lifting boring but they were necessary if she wanted to keep working, and they made her focus on something else besides her nonexistent love life. She pulled on her sweats and grabbed her towel as she went out into the Parisian night that was just about to come alive and ran down the street to her building.

Many of the models working in the city for lengthy stints lived in the ultramodern glass and chrome complex. Others used it as a home base while they traveled to locations around the world. It was often referred to as the Model's Building. There were several restaurants and cafés in the neighborhood and many times locals would frequent the eateries just to get a glimpse of the beautiful young women.

Juliet rang for the lift, a motorized Plexiglas cube that moved occupants from floor to floor. She stood there thinking about what she would eat and how she would spend her time for the remainder of the evening. A buzzer sounded and the lift was there.

"Want to go dancing with us, Juliet?"

Juliet looked into the honey-colored eyes of Simone Mousseau, a very beautiful French girl. She was several years older than Juliet and much more sophisticated. She was a favorite with the Collections as well. Simone always had a stream of male callers. Some said she was equally popular with the women as well. Juliet never saw her much outside of work.

"Come on, Juliet. Go with us. A lot of the guys have been asking about you."

"Oh?" Juliet looked interested. "Who?"

"That hot American who has the big exclusive with Calvin Klein underwear. I heard he has a thing for you real bad. I know I would. Give him some of your brown sugar."

Juliet ignored Simone's pass at her and laughed. She had never given much thought to dating a white guy even though he was cute, and she had no interest whatsoever in women.

"And that gorgeous Mustafa from Africa. He has one beautiful chocolate body."

"You're sick, Simone."

"So will you come with us or what?" Simone really looked like she wanted her to come and a night of dancing in Paris sounded like fun.

"Okay."

"Good. Meet me upstairs in two hours. I'm on the fourth floor."

Juliet watched her run through the lobby and out of the building as the motorized cube carried her to the seventh and top floor. She walked through the narrow glass hallway to number 714.

The large studio apartment looked like home with her things from New Orleans. Teddy, her favorite stuffed animal, was propped on a pillow on her brass antique bed. There was a large antique dressing table with a round mirror covered with makeup and perfume. French art posters and prints of black American art were framed and on the walls. A large Japanese screen separated her sleeping space from the rest of the room.

Juliet hung up the gold dress in a huge walk-in closet overflowing with shoe boxes and clothing and went into the bathroom to run a bubble bath. She pulled her sweatshirt over her head and saw the tiny funny-shaped ring she wore on a silver chain around her neck. She took off the chain and closely examined the ring before dropping it into a ballerina jewelry box on her dressing table.

It's definitely time to move on.

She brushed her hair, turned on the CD player, and relaxed in the tub. The new CeCe Winans CD sounded good and the jets in the whirlpool tub felt good. Two hours later she sat in Simone Mousseau's apartment dressed and ready to go.

"You look really hot, Juliet."

Juliet wore a red dress from an Italian design house and stilettos that showed off her lean calves nicely. Simone flitted through the room in something short, black, and French that flattered her body perfectly.

"Thanks. So do you."

"That's what we get paid to do. Want a glass of champagne?"

"Do you have a Coke?"

"Did you say a Coke or some coke. I've got both."

"I'll have the one in the bottle, thank you."

Simone laughed as she handed Juliet the soda.

"Don't you want a little something to party with?"

Juliet watched her sprinkle some of the powder onto a mirror.

"No. Thank you. How did you get started modeling, Simone?"

Juliet stood up to admire the photographs in frames all around the room. They were shots of her with various celebrities and some with people she didn't know.

I've always wanted to model. I've been around fashion and the Collections all my life. I used to model once in a while for fun, but when I graduated from college, Daddy said I had to get a job. I moved to New York to work for MTV and ended up getting discovered and here I am. I don't like working nine to five, so I intend to make this work until I marry some good-looking rich rock star." She giggled as she spoke. "I added on the good-looking rock-star part. Daddy just wants me to marry someone with money."

"Oh." Juliet gasped as she picked up a photo of Simone and someone who looked a lot like Laurent in ski outfits. "Who's this? Your boyfriend?"

She held up the photograph for Simone to see.

"That's Lar Chevalier. We used to go out. That was the last time I saw him. He came on holiday with me and my family to Switzerland. That's one holiday I'll never forget."

Simone took the picture from Juliet and looked at it before returning it to the table.

"I haven't seen Lar for years. I met him through friends at L'Ecole. He was younger than me but he was so hot. His sister Vadé was gorgeous too, but not real friendly. I don't think she liked me."

Some things haven't changed.

"Why, because he was your boyfriend?"

"He wasn't really my boyfriend, but we had great sex. I spent a week with his family in the south of France. That was one hot summer. His sister was pretty cool then, probably because of that gorgeous man she was with. He had a cousin, too. Claude . . . they were all really hot guys. I tried to sleep with his cousin too, but he wouldn't do it because he thought Lar and I were serious."

Juliet held on to the table to steady herself. She knew this was Laurent's hometown but she never imagined she would run into one of his old girlfriends and it would be Simone, of all people.

No wonder he left me. I don't put out like Simone.

"Were you?"

"What?"

"Serious?"

"Not really. There are too many good-looking guys around for me to get serious about one that lives in the States. I haven't seen or heard from Lar for years. We sort of lost touch after he moved to America. We tried to keep in touch. That was the last time I saw him on that ski trip. We talked about sharing an apartment together in California. I wonder what he's up to. He had this dream of becoming a rock star."

Simone went into the kitchen for more champagne.

How many people has he thrown this move-with-me-to-LA line to? He and Claude must have had a good laugh on me.

The door buzzer sounded and Simone floated back through the room.

"That must be the girls. Let's go, darling."

She opened the door and kissed all her girlfriends on the lips.

"Enchante, darlings."

She held the door open for Juliet, who was greeted by the girls the same way they had greeted Simone. She was too stunned to protest. Five of them piled into the lift and Juliet thought she was going to be sick. There was a horse-drawn carriage waiting for them by the door. Juliet allowed herself to be assisted into the carriage by the coachman with the rest of the girls and the white horses trotted off into the brightly lit night. She should have felt like Cinderella on the way to the ball, but instead Juliet wished she had just stayed home.

THIRTY

Vadé walked into what used to be Laurent's bedroom in the family's old house in Paris. It was the baby's nursery decorated with the palest mint green paint and wallpaper. Drapes and a baby comforter were custom-made for the windows and antique crib that a rocker sat close by. Framed photographs of the family sat on the baby's dresser. They was a chest of toys, a small blackboard with magnetic plastic letters, and a CD player for the baby's music.

Vadé felt the baby kick hard and rubbed her enormous stomach as she placed a stack of newborn T-shirts in a drawer and closed it. She went into her bedroom, stretched out on a chaise covered in emerald and jacquard, and pointed a remote at the thirty-five-inch television occupying the spot once held by her Louis III desk.

"I have a television set in my bedroom, Mamá."

She thanked God every time she remembered she was back in her family's old home by the Louvre, remembering the circumstances that had brought her there. She knew God had been with her ever since she left New Orleans. How else would she have been able to make it? This was the first time in her life she had ever been completely on her own and away from the family.

Vadé had returned to Paris on the first available flight, the morning after JP left her. After she checked into the hotel, she took a taxi to the house. It looked exactly the same. She had stood there for hours crying, remembering happier times.

She returned the following day to see her interior decorating instructor. He set up an appointment for her to meet Madame Divivier, the famous Parisian decorator, who was looking for an assistant to take over the smaller jobs. Madame fell in love with her minutes into the interview and offered her the job on the spot. Vadé had put together an excellent portfolio that included photographs of Hotel de Chevalier and Grandmother Legrande's house.

All of her projects had to be approved by Madame and the two of them got along splendidly. They shared similar tastes, even though Vadé was the same age as her granddaughter. Madame paid her well, but Vadé would gladly have worked for free. She loved what she was doing.

Vadé was so busy with her appointments she didn't have time to look for an apartment. Then she discovered she was pregnant. She got sick during lunch while she was discussing the plans for a client's chateau. It happened every morning for a week before she saw a doctor. She blamed her upset stomach on spoiled fish. She was totally amazed when the doctor informed her she was pregnant.

It had to happen the night of the masquerade ball, before the fight. We made love all that evening.

She had been so excited about making up with him she had forgotten to use her diaphragm.

Days, weeks, and months went by without a word from JP. She had left her phone numbers at the hotel but no one ever called, not even the family, so she assumed they were was still upset. She missed her family, but she was really upset with JP. If he couldn't call to see how she was doing, then she wouldn't call him either. No matter how much she missed his smell, his touch, and his dimpled smile, she refused to be the first one to give in.

He never even heard my side of the story.

She pulled on a pair of stockings and broke into a sweat.

I wouldn't want him to see me like this anyway. I am so fat.

She managed to pull herself up from the bed and waddled over to the dressing table to comb her hair and put on makeup. She had learned of the family's old town house while looking for fabric swatches for the bedroom of a local diplomat. When she mentioned the samples were for a diplomat, the sales clerk wanted to know if she was decorating the wonderful town house by the Louvre. Its former owners had vacated it.

Vadé called her father's old banker, who offered to assist her with the purchase. She still had most of her savings from her job at the hotel and with a loan from Grandmother Legrande she was able to reclaim her dream house. She had all sorts of ideas for renovations. The baby's nursery and her design studio had been first on the list. She redid Laurent's room and turned one of the two guest rooms below into her studio. She worked mostly out of the house. Once the morning sickness passed, she never missed another day of work. The baby was due any day and it was the day before Christmas Eve.

She waddled past the spot where there should have been a Christmas tree. There had been no extra time to shop for presents or a tree. She had put herself on a tight budget. The fact that no one was around to buy presents for made it a little easier. She made it to the Metro in time for the train. When the baby arrived she would have to buy a car. She thought about her Porsche in New Orleans and laughed. She could just see herself with a baby seat in a sports car.

She got off the Metro and walked the few short blocks to the structure and went in. The room was bustling with Parisians excited about the holidays and the fabulous Collections. She had Madame's seats right down front. Even in her enlarged state, Vadé was still elegant and very Parisian. It was nice to hear the greetings in French instead of in English with a southern drawl. She was back where she belonged.

The music started and she carefully studied the models' clothing, making notes on the selections she intended to buy. There were some beautiful American black women in the show. The blond one was very pretty. Something about her reminded her of Desiree. Maybe it was the hair color. Her mother's was natural, but this woman's dyed hair color was gorgeous. Vadé's eyes followed the model as she admired the beautiful young woman with the body of life.

She makes me feel really fat.

She held her breath as the baby kicked up a storm and then she slowly exhaled, relieved to find the sharp pain that accompanied the kicking gone. She looked for a handkerchief in her purse as she began to perspire.

Vadé sighed with relief when the show was over and made it back to the cocktail reception. She sat down and nursed a glass of orange juice while she chatted with a stranger about the Collections. She loved to talk. Outside of business, she didn't have any personal friends. Her friends had always been the family.

There was no line for the buffet, so she went to get some fresh fruit. She wanted the duck and exotic green salad, but was afraid it wouldn't stay down. She really wanted to go home and take her shoes off. If she was going to be sick, she preferred to be there. She stepped away from the table and felt a pain so sharp she screamed and dropped her plate. She clutched the table and slowly lowered herself to the floor.

"Help, someone, please help."

Simone, who had just walked into the reception after posing for photographs, rushed to her side.

"Are you okay?" She bent down to look into her face. "Vadé Chevalier? Is that you?"

She nodded her head in response. "Can you help me to a taxi?"

"I'll call you an ambulance."

"No. A taxi. It will be much quicker."

Simone helped Vadé stand up and walk toward the door. Conversations resumed when everyone realized she was up and walking.

"Are you sure you're going to be okay?"

"Yes." Vadé finally recognized the model as Lar's friend Simone. "I didn't know you were modeling."

"I worked a month at MTV in New York City after graduation. I met a photographer at a party. I didn't know you were married or pregnant." She pointed at the diamond rock on Vadé's ring finger. "Are you here with your husband? Can I call him for you?"

"I'm fine. I just need to get to the hospital." She grabbed her stomach and screamed.

"You are not fine. I'm going to the hospital with you. Don't go anywhere."

Vadé made a face and hobbled out toward the street. A driver jumped out of the car to assist her as Simone caught up with her and helped her into the cab.

"She needs to go to the hospital," Simone informed the driver. "We're going with you."

She took Vadé's other hand and nodded in the direction of the other young lady getting in the other side of the cab.

"That's my girlfriend, Juliet."

Juliet got inside the cab and recognized Vadé immediately. Although she had only seen Laurent's sister twice, she would remember her anywhere.

"This really isn't necessary. I'll be fine by myself. I'm only having a baby."

Vadé doubled over with pain again and held on to Simone's arm so tightly she knew it would bruise.

"Call my husband, Jean Paul Olivier. Tell him I'm having a baby and to get here."

She screamed again and held on to Simone and Juliet.

"My phone's in my purse."

"Get her phone, Juliet."

Juliet looked inside Vadé's bag and found the tiny cell phone. She had been trying to figure out a way to get away from Simone and Vadé, but now it was too late. She dialed the numbers Vadé yelled out and left messages on an answering machine and a pager.

They finally arrived at the hospital. After Simone ran in and screamed and shouted, someone ran out with a wheelchair. Minutes later they sat with a sedated Vadé in an observation room. Her labor pains had stopped for the moment. She lay there looking at Simone and her pretty girlfriend who had come to her rescue. She had said she didn't need anyone, but now she was glad they were here. She finally had recognized Juliet as the model with the golden hair like her mother's. She looked a lot younger and not as worldly without all the makeup, and very familiar.

"You're Juliet."

The phone was ringing and Juliet answered it.

"Did someone page me?"

"Yes. I'm calling for your wife."

"My wife? Who is this?"

"That's not important. Your wife's having a baby."

"A baby? Vadé? Where is she?"

"He wants to speak to you."

"Hi, JP." Her voice was groggy but calm.

"Vadé? Somebody just said you're having a baby?"

"I am."

"Whose?"

She could hear the jealousy in his voice and she covered her smile with her hand. *He still cares.*

"Ours, silly."

"We're having a baby?"

"Yes."

"When? How?"

"Just get on a plane as soon as you can."

He was so shocked he could barely speak.

"Hurry up and get here, JP, please. I really need you and I'm scared."

She yelled as fresh pain gripped her body. Simone took the phone as Juliet went for the nurse.

"Are you okay, Day?"

"You'd better get here as soon as you can. I don't know how much longer it's going to be."

"All right. Tell Day I love her and I'm on my way."

THIRTY-ONE

J ean Paul Olivier handed the flight attendant at New Orleans International his ticket to JFK. How he ever got on a flight on Christmas Eve no one will ever know, except God and the angels.

He slid into the first-class seat and clicked his seat belt together. He had just gotten off a flight from LA hours before he spoke to Vadé.

She actually called and said she needed me and we're going to have a baby. Hang on, Day. I'm coming.

It had been nine months since he had left her in her father's suite. Vadé had seemed a little weird ever since her birthday and they didn't have sex for an entire week.

I should have known she was just tripping because she didn't get none. Then, she put on that beautiful green outfit for the carnival and we tried to make up for a week in an afternoon. I don't even know why I left that night. If she hadn't left New Orleans, I would have been back at the hotel the next day. I did go back but she was gone.

JP glanced at his watch as the aircraft left the ground. It was a little after seven. He was flying out of Kennedy for Paris at midnight. If he made his connection he would be at the hospital by six in the morning.

He had just spent a week with his cousin and his brother-in-law in LA. Things were a little strained between him and Laurent initially.

Little Claude told him to overlook it because Lar hadn't really been himself since they had left New Orleans.

They spent most of the time with Lar in the studio while he was recording, but he was too busy to do much talking. The CD was almost finished. It was going to be a huge success. He had great material and the hottest producers. They had taken their time so Lar could get on some of their schedules. Greg really pulled in the favors. The first single would be released in January, although some stations were already playing it.

Little Claude had an endless string of beautiful women. He was managing Laurent's career, so he spent most of his time on the phone. The cousins tossed around the idea of starting a management company after Laurent's project took off.

JP enjoyed his time in LA with the fellas, but he didn't mind when it was time to return to New Orleans. They went to numerous parties, dinners, and clubs that were "about business" and had an exciting time, but it wasn't the same. Although they were together, no one was really there. Everyone was in his own world.

The night before he left, Laurent told him to take care of his sister. No one really talked much about the family. No one had heard from anyone. JP secretly hoped Laurent would have talked to his sister so he could find out if she had mentioned him. They didn't have a number for her either but Little Claude was pretty sure his mother knew something.

During the plane ride home, JP had finally made up his mind to call her for Christmas even though she hadn't tried to contact him once. He was overwhelmed when he saw the international code for Paris in his pager. Now he was in Paris and they were having a baby. What a difference a phone call can make.

JP found Vadé awake and the girls sleeping soundly in chairs when he arrived at the hospital.

"Good morning, beautiful."

"JP, you actually made it."

She broke into tears as he pulled her into his arms.

"Baby, I'm so sorry for everything. You were right and I am going to change. I do talk too much and—"

"That's all behind us now."

"Okay . . . I've missed you so much."

"You did?"

"Every minute of every day. I kept myself busy so I wouldn't think about you."

"Then why didn't you call me and tell me?"

"I don't know. I thought you were mad at me so I was waiting for you to call me."

"I came back the next day to make up with you and you were gone. No one knew where you were."

"You came back to make up? Baby, you did that for me? We would have had so much fun making up."

"I can't stay away from you, Day. I had made up my mind to call T to see if she had your number, but I got your page first."

"Aw, baby. That is so sweet. I love you."

"I love you, too, baby."

JP lay beside her on the bed and held her in his arms.

"You know your father left, too."

"Papá's not at the hotel? Where is he?"

"Nobody knows. Mrs. Lipscomb said she talks to him at least once a week. They hired two people to take over your job. Vicenté's still in the kitchen."

"I can't believe Papá left the hotel. Have you talked to anyone else?"

"Your brother is finishing up his CD. He's about to blow up."

"Really?"

She pulled him closer so she could whisper into his ear. "Is he seeing anyone?"

"I don't know. I didn't meet anyone. He's very busy."

"Guess who that is." She pointed to a girl still asleep in the chair.

"I don't know. Who is it?"

"Juliet."

"Get outta here." He wasn't whispering now.

"Shh. You'll wake them up. Remember Lar's friend Simone? That's her in the other chair."

"You're kidding? Where did you run into Juliet?"

"I ran into both of them at the Collections, yesterday. I started having the most awful contractions. They were both in the show. Juliet is so beautiful. No wonder Lar liked her and she's so sweet. They came with me to the hospital."

"Leave it to Miss Thing to be on the verge of giving birth and out looking for new clothes. Girl, are you crazy?"

She couldn't help laughing as he rubbed her stomach.

"Look at you."

"Don't. I'm fat."

"You're beautiful."

"I am?"

"Yes!"

"You look good, too."

"You like my suit? I only wore it for you."

"Baby, you look good in everything you wear."

"But you said I couldn't dress."

"You shouldn't have paid me any attention, I was only being a bitch. And don't say Vicenté was right."

"I wasn't going to say anything."

Vadé took a sip of water and yelled. Both girls sat up at attention as Juliet stumbled over to the bed and rang for the nurse.

"My husband's here now. This child must know its father is here." Vadé was panting. "Sweetheart . . ."

She couldn't finish her sentence for the pain. When she came to several hours later she was in a sunny hospital room and Simone was sitting in her room reading a magazine.

"It was a dream." She moaned and fell back into the pillows. "I thought my husband was here. Where's my baby?"

"JP is here. He is so excited. He took Juliet over to the maternity ward to see the baby. I didn't know Lar married her sister."

"Lar's not married. I have another brother, Vicenté. Could you find my husband for me, please?"

"Sure."

JP and Juliet walked into the room before she could leave. When JP saw she was awake, he rushed over to her bed.

"Day, she's beautiful."

"She?" She had been secretly hoping for a little boy who looked like JP.

"She."

"I should have known it was a girl, waiting for her daddy to show up."

JP beamed with pride. "I already named her."

"You already named her what?"

"Perri."

"Paris? What kind of a name is that for a girl?"

"It's French and American like her."

"How is Paris French and American?"

"You don't spell it like the city, Paris, but you pronounce it the way the French do. When she's in America everyone will pronounce it Perry."

"Oh, I see. That is cute." She sank back into the pillows as she thought about the name. "I like it."

"Good. I couldn't think of a middle name."

"Perri Michel. I wouldn't give Vadé to anyone. Those horrible kids in New Orleans used to call me shady Vadie."

JP let out a belly whopper while the girls laughed softly.

"I never knew that, shady Vadie."

He covered his mouth to keep from laughing again as she punched him in the arm.

"One of the many trials and tribulations I had to endure living in America." Vadé yawned as if they were meager paupers boring her.

"Day, you're not a bitch. You're just you."

"I know. Now where's Perri? I'd like to meet her."

JP buzzed and asked the nurse to bring his daughter in to see her mother. Vadé could hardly keep still when the nurse walked in with the tiny baby in a pink blanket.

"You can feed her now." The nurse carefully placed the infant in Vadé's arms and pulled the curtain around the bed.

"Bonjour, *mon ami*. Happy *reveilion*. Merry Christmas. Look, JP, she is so sweet."

JP, who had been standing on the other side of the curtain listening, stepped inside.

"Hello, Princess." He cooed at the baby.

"Look at your itty-bitty hands and feet."

JP sat on the bed next to her while Vadé kissed her hands and feet.

"She's so light. Are you sure this is my baby?"

"JP!"

"I'm just playing."

"She'll get darker. She'll probably be the same color as you."

"With black hair and green eyes. Oh my God. She's going to be beautiful."

"We can't tell what color Mamá's baby's eyes are going to be."

The nurse helped Vadé out of her gown so she could breast-feed the baby.

"What do l do?"

"Just hold her up there and let her do what I like to do." JP laughed.

"JP." Vadé was blushing.

"Thank you for such a beautiful Christmas present, Day."

"You're the gift." Vadé looked into his eyes and smiled. "For both us girls."

They took the baby home in a taxi the day after Christmas.

"You don't have a car, Day?"

"No, I have a house."

The taxi drove through the light traffic by the Louvre. The Arc de Triomphe welcomed them as the taxi turned up a familiar street and stopped in front of the town house.

"We, I mean you live here?"

"Yes. What do you mean do I live here? Are you going back to New Orleans?"

Panic swept her and she broke into a sweat.

"I am home, baby. Wherever you and my daughter are, that's the only place I want to be."

"You are so sweet. I love you."

JP carried the baby as they walked to the back, to the servant's entrance, and down the back stairs to the nursery.

"I can't believe you bought this house. I always loved this house. I remember the first time I came over with Uncle Claude, I couldn't believe black people lived here."

"Really?"

"I had never met rich people like your father and Uncle Claude. I remember the first time I saw you. You were so beautiful, like a fairy-tale princess, and this was your castle. I was scared of you for the longest time. I never thought I'd be married to you and living in this house."

"You never told me this before."

He looked around the nursery as Vadé took Perri and carefully placed her in the crib.

"This used to be Lar's room, didn't it?"

"Yes. It's right next to our room." They walked through the nursery into Vadé's bedroom.

"Hey, I never saw this room." He stretched out on her bed. "I like this room."

"I'm sure you do." She tossed her coat over the chaise.

"Look at you, baby. You are fine. Got some of those Desiree hips now."

"No way."

She tried to see her behind in the mirror.

"Don't worry, baby. They're back there, but that's okay. Give a brother something to hold on to."

She laughed as she sat down beside him. JP made her feel beautiful, hips and all.

"I'm so glad you're here. Thank you for coming."

"You don't have to thank me."

"I know, but I want to."

"How long before you get your stitches out?"

"You are so nasty."

"Don't tell me you weren't thinking the same thing. I haven't had no lovin' since you had on that green thing for the carnival."

"That green thing? I was an African princess."

"You sure are."

"That's when we made Perri."

"I'm not surprised. I know we made something that day."

"You are so sick. You haven't done anything since then?"

"Nope."

She sighed happily. "Good."

"I'm a faithful man. It wasn't like I didn't have the opportunity either. Little Claude has a bunch of fine women."

"I can't believe he is such a dog. Was Lar with anyone?"

"He didn't introduce me to anyone and I was with him the entire time."

"Good."

"What are you thinking?" He sat up and looked at her. "There is something going on in that mind of yours."

"There is."

"Oh, no. What?"

"I want to get him and Juliet together. I don't know what will become of it. But I'd like to try. She's so sweet and not a tramp like that Simone."

"He was going to take her to LA with him."

"Who? Simone?"

"No. Juliet."

"How do you know? Did he tell you that?"

"No. But I know something was going on."

"Did Little Claude say something?"

"Little Claude mentioned something way back when they first went to LA, but neither one of them said anything while I was there."

"Juliet made me promise not to tell Lar I had seen her."

"She did? I wonder why."

"I don't know. But I feel like I at least need to get them in the same room. I owe them that much."

"But you told her you wouldn't tell Lar."

"I won't tell, but I've got to think of something. Will you help me?"

"Now you're including me in your meddling, but I like Juliet and I think Lar likes her, too. He's just being stubborn. Men act that way sometimes."

He looked at his wife and tried not to laugh.

"Yes, they do . . . but that's why God created women to help"

THIRTY-TWO

Vicenté stared at the Chevalier crest on top of the hotel's letter-head. Vadé had the crest designed by a Parisian and chose the palest mint linen parchment with gold embossing to display it. One sheet of paper was so expensive that she had a local printer attempt to duplicate it, reserving the French version for the exclusive use of her father. Vicenté carefully folded the fine sheet of paper and placed it back in the envelope. He couldn't believe what he just read.

He stepped out of his office into the hotel's busy kitchen where several chefs were preparing lunch for hotel guests, and locals who frequented the restaurant because the food was so delicious. Vicenté rarely cooked unless he was creating a new recipe, which he usually did at home. He spent three days out of every week teaching cooking classes featuring Creole, Caribbean, and southern cuisine. Most of his students were chefs and housewives. He taped *Cooking with Amour* the other two days and responded to mail on his Web site. A cookbook and a line of chef's aprons would be available by Christmas. Who would ever have thought cooking would turn into a million-dollar enterprise? He was definitely in the money . . . and now this.

Vicenté had almost quit his job at the hotel after he had it out with Pierre. He didn't *have* to work there. The cooking classes could support them until he was able to find another job. Someone was always trying to hire him away from Right Bank.

But he only stayed home one day, long enough for Martine to talk some sense into him and send him back. She told him he had no reason to be angry with his father. Vicenté had never invited Pierre to their home. What effort had he made to get to know his father personally? Pierre had welcomed Vicenté into the family with open arms. At least Pierre was trying. It was going to take time. She told him to "grow up, get over it, and stop feeling sorry for yourself." He had done that long enough.

Vicenté got mad and went out and got sloppy drunk, but he showed up for work on time the next day. But he decided to stay because no matter how much he tried to deny it, he really did like working for his father and being part of the *family* business. It was more than just a job.

He checked his schedule and dashed out to the topless Jeep. He wanted to talk to Martine before she left for class. He could hardly wait to share the contents of the envelope with her.

It was a beautiful summer day in the Crescent City. It was sunny and the humidity was unusually low. He cranked the volume on the radio. It was a great song with an infectious beat that had him hooked the moment he heard it. Vicenté almost ran into a parked car when he realized it was Laurent singing.

"Go head, little brother."

He threw his hands up in the air and danced along with the music at a traffic light.

"That's my brother!" he shouted to the driver in the car stopped next to him. The song ended and his head filled with thoughts of his brother.

Why haven't you called me, Lar? You goin' out like that just because you got a record deal? I didn't think you were like that.

He parked the Jeep in front of the town house behind Martine's Mercedes. He could hear Laurent's song blasting outside.

"Hi, baby, Laurent's CD is out. It's the bomb. I just picked up some copies from Blockbuster. Look. He thanked us in the credits."

He read *my big brother, Vicenté, and his beautiful wife, Martine. Thank you always for your love and support. I love you. Lar.* Martine watched his face for a response.

"That was nice, huh, baby?"

She took the CD cover from him and continued reading the liner notes.

"Yes, it was nice but why hasn't he called if he loves us so much?"

"I don't know, baby. He's probably busy."

"Too busy for your family?"

"Look, V. I wonder if he's talking about Juliet here. *I thank God for my beautiful Juliet. Love, Romeo.*"

"He's thanking God, Martine."

"But he's talking about Juliet, too. It's a message for her. You know, *Romeo and Juliet?*"

"Girl, you're crazy. Stop trying to see what's not there. Little brother kicked all of us to the curb."

"I know he's talking to Juliet. You just need to stop being mad because he hasn't called. I'm sure he has a good excuse."

"Yeah, like the bighead, bighead."

She laughed as the sound of a baby crying grew louder.

"Honey, could you go get Francois?"

"Sure. I have something to show you. Read this." He pulled the Hotel de Chevalier envelope out of his briefcase and handed it to her.

"I'm coming, Francois."

He dashed up the stairs and picked up the pretty chocolate baby with black hair like his daddy and kissed him. He laid the child on the changing table and talked as he changed his son's diaper.

"Come on, shorty. Let's go see that beautiful mother of yours." Francois smiled and Vicenté kissed him as he carried him downstairs.

"Pierre gave you fifty percent of the restaurant and ten percent of Chevalier-Olivier Enterprises stock? Dang."

"I know." He refolded the letter and placed it back in his briefcase.

"Pierre showed you much love. Is that his signature on the letter?"

"Yes."

"He must have had Mrs. Lipscomb send him that letter just so he could sign it himself."

"That's true, huh? I wonder if someone told him about Francois."

"Wherever Pierre is, he knows everything going on with his business and every detail of his children's lives."

"You think so?"

"He has to. He's been away a year and a half. Rich, powerful men like that can run their businesses from any part of the world. All you need is a computer and Federal Express."

"True."

"That's how I'm going to operate someday. That way I can take my boys to the beach."

"Do you have to go to class now? We could go to the beach."

"I can't. Finals. I have to leave as soon as I finish feeding him." She cooed at the baby while she spooned the contents from a jar of baby food that Vicenté created for their son. "You're going to be a big boy when your mommy goes back to school this fall."

"I don't know how you had him last September and still managed to complete all of your classes with A's, and look good at the same time."

"A girl's gotta do what a girl's gotta do. I don't know how I did it either. It must be those genius genes of mine, huh, Francois?"

She kissed him and handed him back to Vicenté and dashed out the door.

"Hey! Where's mine?"

"I don't want to be late. I'll take care of you later."

She blew him a kiss and he walked into the family room and sat down with his son.

"Hey, shorty. Hear that music? That's your uncle Lar. He's a big-time singer."

He picked up a framed photo of the family from the first Christmas he spent with them.

"I'm going to introduce you to the rest of your old man's family. They're real special people. I'm sure you're gonna like them. That's your grandfather, Pierre. He's a very powerful and wealthy man. He's a musician. He taught himself to play the piano. And that pretty lady is my sister, your auntie. Her name is Vadé. She's smart, too. She used to run the family's hotel. That's her husband, Jean Paul Olivier. You can call him JP. He's an attorney just like his daddy. That's Little Claude Olivier, my little brother's best friend, and his father, Big Claude Olivier, your grandfather's best friend. That's Big Claude's wife, Giselle. We call her T, that's short for auntie."

He placed the photo back on the end table.

"Well, that's your family on your dad's side, the Chevaliers. I'm sorry, but you only have one grandmother, that's Big Mamá, your mother's mother. My mother, your Grandmother Felicite, is in heaven. She would have loved you."

Francois was very quiet. He was listening and seemed to understand.

"The best thing you can ever have in this world is a family who loves you. And if you have a little money that's nice too. But family . . . that's what's important. I wish they were all here so you could get to know them. You're my father's first grandchild. . . . So what do you want to be when you grow up, Francois? You know you'll be able to be anything you want. With your mama's brains and my good looks you could be president of the United States."

Vicenté laughed as he picked up the remote for the CD.

"Wouldn't that be something? A black Frenchman as president of the United States."

He played the song he first heard in the car and picked up the liner notes from Laurent's CD from the table.

My big brother, Vicenté, and his beautiful wife, Martine. Thank you for all your love and support. I love you, Lar.

He stared at the photo of Laurent on the cover.

"I love you too, Lar," he whispered as he picked up the family photo. "All of you."

THIRTY-THREE

Martine pulled a baking sheet of Christmas tree sugar cookies out of the oven and slid them onto a cooling rack. They smelled delicious, and they were so rich and full of butter. Vicenté made the dough the night before. Now she was the baker. He came inside the kitchen with Francois right behind him.

"Look, Francois, I'm the Cookie Monster." He picked up a cookie and pretended to eat it with a series of grunts and growls as the child screamed with laughter.

"Y'all are crazy." Martine laughed as she placed another sheet of cookies in the oven and stood there watching Vicenté play with the baby until the phone rang.

"Ooh, I wonder who that is. Maybe it's Santa Claus." She made a silly face as she picked up the receiver.

"Merry Christmas!"

"Merry Christmas."

Martine recognized her caller the second she spoke, but it couldn't be, not after almost two years.

"Vadé!"

"Bonsoir, girlfriend!"

"It's so good to hear your voice."

"Yours too."

"It's your sister, V."

"Really?" He grinned as he came to the phone.

"What's happening, baby girl?"

"Merry Christmas, Vicenté. How are you?"

"Great. I'm celebrating my son's second Christmas."

"You guys have a little boy?"

"Yes. Francois Pierre Chevalier."

"You're kidding. I have a little girl now. Perri Michel."

"Martine! Vadé had a little girl!"

She snatched the phone from Vicenté.

"Girl! You had a baby, too? That's amazing. How old is she?"

"One year old, today. She's our *revelion* baby."

"One year old? Francois was one in September. What have you been doing?"

Vicenté snatched the phone from Martine.

"You have a daughter? How'd you manage that when JP was here until a year ago?"

"I was pregnant and didn't know it."

"You are too fresh. I'm glad you and JP got married or else I'd have to hurt that brother."

"Don't start. You know we just celebrated our fourth wedding anniversary."

Vadé laughed as she told her husband what Vicenté said. JP laughed and took the phone from her.

"I'm glad we're married, too. I don't need three of you Chevalier men breathing down my back."

"Just remember that, Olivier."

JP laughed and handed Vadé the phone.

"We just got in from Mass. What are you guys doing?"

"Baking cookies. I wish you were here. It would be so much fun."

"I know. You'll have to come to Paris next summer so we can go on holiday at the villa."

"You have a villa?"

"I don't, but the family does. The villa's in southern France, on the Riviera, but I did purchase my childhood home in Paris."

"The house you showed me in the pictures?"

"Yes."

"That all sounds wonderful, Vadé. I can't wait to come to Paris to see you and your little girl. And we can go to the villa."

"The children will love it. I know we did. But I was hoping we could

get together before then. And I also need your help." Vadé finished
the sentence in a whisper.

"What? What are you up to now?" She smiled as she waited for Vadé
to answer.

"Guess who is here."

"Where?"

"Here, at my house."

"Who?"

"Your sister."

"Juliet?"

"Do you have any other sisters?"

"None that I know about. What is she doing there? I want to speak
to her."

"You can't."

"Why?"

"Because she doesn't want Vicenté to know."

"Why?"

"Because he might tell Lar."

"Vicenté hasn't spoken to Lar."

"He hasn't?" Vadé was surprised.

"No."

"I haven't spoken to my brother either."

"What?"

"Not since the night . . ."

"Whatever happened that night?"

"That night is forgotten, forever. . . . I have so much to tell you.
Starting with how I ran into your sister."

"So you guys hang out?" There was a twinge of jealousy in Martine's
voice.

"Yes, whenever she's in town. We go shopping and out to dinner,
movies, and museums . . . everywhere. We take Perri and she loves it."

"I am so jealous. You always get everything. Now you're best friends
with my sister and you guys are running around Paris with your baby.
Francois and I will be on a plane tomorrow."

"Tomorrow's Christmas Day, silly, and you're not supposed to know
we're friends."

"Oh, yeah."

"Juliet is so sweet. I want to get her and Lar together."

"What?"

"Yes. JP thinks they had something hot and heavy going on but for some reason they won't talk to each other and that's where we come in."

"What do you want me to do?"

"I thought you'd never ask. JP found out Lar's schedule from Little Claude."

"JP is in on this too?"

"Yes, we're going to need all the help we can get. We need Vicenté, too."

"Cool. I love it. Dish, girlfriend."

"Lar's going to perform at Disney World."

"Really? We should go."

"That's the plan."

"But how are we going to get Juliet to Florida without her suspecting anything?"

"I'm going to invite her to come to Disney World with the family for a little vacation. I'll tell her I spoke to you and we decided to get together in Disney World with the kids."

"That's a great idea."

"I know. Now here's the good part. Little Claude knows we're coming."

"He's in on this too?"

"Yes. He's going to arrange a small party for the family afterward at a restaurant so we can get those two together in the same room."

"But she'll suspect something when we go see Lar perform."

"I know. There's nothing we can do once she sees him onstage except threaten her if she won't go to the party with us."

"I hear you. I don't know why she's being so stubborn about this."

"I told her I threw away the message but she still doesn't want to talk to him."

"I tried to get her to call him too before she went to Paris, but she refused to talk about it."

"We'll get her good and Lar won't suspect a thing until Little Claude brings him into the party and he sees her. I don't think he's been seeing anyone else. If he is, we'll just have to get rid of the bitch."

"Girl, you are so crazy. I've missed you so much. I'm sorry about . . ."

"I know, I'm sorry, too. I've missed you also and that night is behind us. Juliet is sweet, she's not wild and crazy like you." Vadé laughed.

"Not yet, but there's hope for her since she's a Bárres. So what do you want V to do?"

"Has he seen Papá?"

"No."

"You're kidding? No one has been in touch. That's awful."

"I know. V said he's coming back to New Orleans right after the first of the year."

"Good. We need him to get Papá to Orlando, too. Tell him to invite him on the trip so he can spend some time with his new grandson. I can't believe Papá is a grandfather twice."

"Your daddy is too fine to be anybody's grandfather."

"He is handsome and Vicenté looks just like him."

"Doesn't he?"

"It's scary. But don't tell Papá we're going to be there, and don't tell him about Lar either. I want it to be a surprise."

"Okay. Did you see what Lar said to Juliet on the back of the CD?"

"You thought he was talking about her, too?"

"Yes . . . this is great. I've been trying to think of a way for V and his father to get closer and this is perfect. And you don't know how many times I've been tempted to call the record company and leave a message for Lar with Juliet's phone number in Paris."

"She would have killed you."

"And I would have killed Lar if he didn't call her. Your way is much better. You are so good at this stuff."

"Hey, I didn't just get like this. It comes from years of practice, *mon ami.*"

THIRTY-FOUR

Vicenté held Francois up so he could press the button for the elevator. He pushed it and smiled at his father.

"Grandpère lives on three?"

"That's right, Francois. How many fingers is that?"

The toddler carefully held up three fingers.

"You are so smart. Come give your daddy a kiss."

Vicenté bent down to pick him up as the elevator doors opened. Upstairs, Francois laughed as he ran down the quiet hall. Desiree heard him and came out into the hallway to see whose child was laughing so happily. He ran straight to Desiree, who scooped him up into her arms.

"And who might you be, you fine little man?"

She smiled and he smiled back. It was love at first sight.

"Francois Pierre Chevalier."

When Vicenté reached the beautiful woman he gasped.

That must be Desiree. He's been with her all this time.

"Who's that out there with my name?"

Pierre walked to the door and stood next to Desiree.

"It's me, Grandpère."

He spoke with Pierre as if they were old friends while Desiree and Vicenté watched eagerly.

"Who's me?"

"Francois, Grandpère. Gosh."

He looked at Pierre as if he were crazy for asking such a stupid question as the adults screamed with laughter.

"Where did this child come from? Hello, son." He gave Vicenté a warm hug.

"Hello, Pierre." He was already feeling awkward.

"Vicenté, this is Dez."

"Hi, Dez." Vicenté gave her a kiss on the cheek. "Welcome home."

"Thank you, Vicenté. It's a pleasure to meet you. I'm in love with him." She swooped up the baby and gave him a kiss.

"Oh no, don't you get any ideas."

"Honey, remember when Laurent was this small? It wasn't that long ago."

"I know. Nobody asked me if I wanted to be a grandfather. I'm too young. Come here, boy." He grabbed Francois from Desiree. "Come give your Grandpère a big hug. Vicenté, fix yourself a drink."

"I'll fix it." Desiree sprang over to the bar. "What would you men like to drink?"

"I'll have a Coke, baby."

"I'll have one, too."

"And Francois, would he like some juice?"

"I brought some juice for him."

He opened Francois's bag and pulled out a bottle of apple grape juice.

"Oh, please, let me." Desiree handed Vicenté a glass of Coke and took the baby bottle.

"Come to Grandmère. Let's go out in the kitchen and see if we can find you a cookie to go with that juice."

"Oh no." Pierre smiled as they watched her leave with the baby.

"What a wonderful little boy. I'm so glad he's my grandson."

"Thank you. I'm glad he's your grandson, too."

Vicenté took a deep breath and continued speaking.

"It's good to have you back, Pierre."

"I'm glad to be back, too, especially with Dez."

"You look wonderful, man. I don' know when I've ever seen you look so well."

"Let Martine disappear on you for just a week. I'd hate to see how you would look."

"All right, man, I'm feeling you."

"You've done an excellent job with the kitchen. I don't know if I would have been able to stay on such an extended vacation if you were not here."

"Just doing my job. I'm glad you enjoyed yourself."

"Mrs. Lipscomb gave you my letter?"

"Yes. Thank you, Pierre. Thanks a lot."

"You're welcome, Vicenté. The restaurant accounts for a large percentage of the hotel's income and I know it's because of you. I was reading about the restaurant and your cooking show in one of those magazines on the plane. Both of my sons are celebrities."

"Me, a celebrity? Ha! Where were you coming from?"

"The south of France. The family owns a villa over there. That's where I ran into Dez."

"The French Riviera? Really?"

"I took off the day after you chewed me out. I ran into her when I checked in."

"I'm sorry about all that. . . . You own a hotel in the south of France?"

"It's not really a hotel. It's a little smaller than this place. There's a restaurant and a lounge. Dez was over there singing."

"You're kidding."

"I thought she had another man at first. It turned out to be someone from a record label. They just signed her to the same company as your brother."

"Did you hear the CD?"

"Yes. Greg sent us copies before it was released. I like it. Dez plays it so much, we know all the songs."

"So do we. Francois even has a cassette in his room."

"My grandson is a mess. How's Lar?"

"I haven't spoken to him since he went to LA."

"That's strange. I just knew he was in touch with you."

"No. We haven't heard from him."

"I know Laurent was upset but I can't see him being out of touch with the family for this long. I'm going to call him."

"I'm sure he's just very busy, Pierre. I heard he was on tour."

They were too close to D-day for people to start talking now.

"Tour or no tour, he needs to keep in touch with his family. Have you talked to your sister?"

"We spoke during the holidays. She and JP are fine."

"JP's in Paris with her?"

Vicenté nodded yes.

"Good. I'm glad she's not over there by herself, not that she couldn't make it on her own, but women need the company of a good man."

"That's true. I'm glad he's with her too. She loves him."

"She can be so stubborn but I knew JP was the right man for her. That's why I made them get married."

"She's just spoiled. Daddy's little princess."

Pierre was laughing. "You're right. From the moment I laid eyes on her. Dez always had to keep her in check because I was too much of a softy."

"So you and Dez were at this villa in the south of France. Is it on the beach?"

Vicenté wanted to get the conversation off Vadé before he told his father that he had a granddaughter, too.

"Yes. We used to take the children on holiday every summer. We'll have to go soon and take the newest generation of Chevaliers. We'll have a lot of fun."

"That sounds really great, Pierre. Maybe we can go this summer when Martine gets out of school. This is her last semester."

"What is she majoring in?"

"Finance."

"Good, very good. She'll have to work for the family. We don't have any accountants."

"I'll mention that to her. Companies are already contacting her."

"Great. Tell her to call me."

The men smiled as Dez and Francois came back into the room.

"Daddy, Grandmère has a picture of you in her bedroom."

"That's not me. That's Grandpère."

"Oh."

"Grandpère's my daddy like I'm your daddy. Remember when I explained that to you?"

"Yes, Daddy."

"He speaks and understands so well to be so young."

"That's because Martine and I talk to him all the time."

"Where is your wife? I want to meet her."

"She's at home studying. She sent me and Francois off to do a little male bonding."

"She sounds like a smart lady. I like her already. Have her call me soon and we'll have tea."

"Okay. Pierre and Dez, we were wondering if you could join us for a weekend in Disney World when we take Francois."

"Of course we will." Desiree answered for them. "When do you want to go?"

"The weekend of the carnival. We thought we'd take Francois to celebrate Mardis Gras."

"Oh, what a wonderful idea. We wouldn't miss it for the world." Desiree picked up Francois and kissed him. "Grandmère can't wait to spend the weekend with her grandson."

Vicenté smiled at his family. Things went better than he had even imagined. Dez was coming, too. No one ever factored her into the plan. He ran his hand over Francois's black silky hair, which was combed into one long braid, as he placed him into the car seat in the Jeep.

"Good job, little man, using that Chevalier charm on Dez. Your grandpère and grandmère are going to be so surprised and so will everyone else. But we'll keep Grandmère our little Mardis Gras secret."

THIRTY-FIVE

L aurent and Little Claude were oblivious of the activity around them as they stood in the airport gift shop at Los Angeles International reading magazines. The flight to Orlando would not board for another ten minutes. Laurent's bodyguard, Goldie, watched them as they conversed about various items. The fanfare had escalated to the point where the guys had to have someone with them all the time.

"This is one gorgeous honey."

Little Claude licked his chops as he smiled at the photo of the beautiful girl gracing the cover of the *Sports Illustrated* swimsuit issue.

"She is beautiful. A sister, too."

Goldie picked up another copy of the magazine and opened it to the centerfold. The model's beautiful copper skin was the same color as her eyes and her hair that was wet and glistening. Her generous hips and breasts were somewhat covered in a gold bikini.

"Let me see who you dogs are drooling over now."

Laurent tucked a copy of *Bon Appetit* under his arm and picked up a magazine.

"It's Juliet."

"That's Juliet on the cover of *Sports Illustrated?* Man, I told you to call the girl. Now you're hallucinating."

Little Claude flipped through *Billboard* as Goldie laughed.

"I'm not tripping, *mon ami,* that's really her." He took his magazines to the counter and pulled out his wallet.

"Here, get these, too." Little Claude handed him the *Billboard* and a *Hollywood Reporter.*

"Let me see that *Sports Illustrated.*" Little Claude held out his hand for the magazine as soon as they were seated together in the first-class section of the plane. Goldie was sitting behind Little Claude on the aisle. Laurent handed it to him as he flipped through *Bon Appetit.*

"Look, man. There's an article on V and the hotel in *Bon Appetit.*"

Their heads drew together as they looked at the photo of Vicenté in front of Hotel de Chevalier.

"He looks great. Look, it says he has a son, fifteen months old."

"Get outta here. I'm an uncle and he didn't even tell me."

"It's not like you've been running to the phone to call him either."

"I haven't called anyone."

"I know. They're all calling me."

"That's your job, man." Laurent was laughing. "But I really do need to call my brother."

"And your sister and your dad."

"I think about them all the time."

"I sure wish she would call me looking for you."

Little Claude grinned at Laurent as he opened the magazine back to the centerfold.

"I wish she would, too. Man, she is so gorgeous, she can have any guy she wants."

"And you can have any girl you want. That's why it's a match made in heaven. I told you to call the girl. It's not like you couldn't find her if you wanted. Your brother is married to her sister."

Little Claude couldn't resist the opportunity to pump Laurent up about Juliet. He knew his cousin would see her at the surprise party later tonight along with the rest of the family. He had been planning the weekend with Vadé, JP, Martine, and Vicenté for the last month.

This is going to be so great and Lar has no idea.

He coughed and covered his mouth to keep from smiling.

"I'll call V and Martine after we finish the show in Orlando. Hey, they could meet us in Orlando and bring my nephew. I'm going to call them now."

He pulled the air phone off the seat and quickly dialed his brother's number. Little Claude held his breath and prayed no one was home. They should already be in Orlando, at the hotel.

Little Claude had made reservations for him and Laurent to get into Orlando by five. Laurent would go on at ten before Destiny's Child. The girls would make sure the family would leave for dinner by five-thirty and be on their way to the show by eight. Laurent and Little Claude would arrive at the hotel by six. They wouldn't leave for the Magic Kingdom until nine-thirty.

"No one was home."

Little Claude sighed with relief.

"I left a message at the house with the number to my cell phone and pager."

"Cool, man. Are you ready for the show?"

"Yes, but I'm looking forward to the big tour with Janet Jackson. I can't believe she wanted me to open for her."

"You're the man, Lar. I was just reading a write-up in here about you and the new single. It's moving right up the chart."

"MTV, dude."

They laughed as they thought about Beavis and Butthead. At one time the boys had been fascinated with the cartoon.

"Oh, snap." Little Claude was too funny when he spoke American slang with a French accent. "I totally forgot."

"What, man? We didn't leave anything, did we?"

"No, we're straight. I just forgot that it's Mardis Gras."

"Oh, no."

"What?"

"Strange stuff always happens to the family during Mardis Gras."

"What are you talking about?"

"Every year something strange happens to the family around Mardis Gras."

"Like what?"

"Mamá disappeared the same night Vicenté arrived. That was during Mardis Gras."

"That was a coincidence. What else?"

"Well, it was carnival night when we left."

"That's when Day threw out Juliet's message and you've been crazy ever since."

"Stop clowning."

"My bad, but you're right. Stuff does happen. You don't think it's voodoo or something like that?"

"No way. I don't believe in that junk. I believe in Jesus. I think it's the angels mixing things up."

Laurent closed his eyes and dreamed of Juliet.

Little Claude stared out of the window at white cotton candy clouds and thought about the celebration he and his cousins had planned unknowingly during Mardis Gras. Maybe there was a grain of truth to what Laurent said about all the weird things that happened to the family during Mardis Gras.

Was it also a coincidence that Vadé had made reservations for the family at the Disney Port Orleans Resort? There would be some sort of Mardis Gras celebration going on in the club where they had planned the party. Little Claude closed his eyes and slept. It was all too mind-boggling. Time answers all questions and now it was only a matter of hours.

THIRTY-SIX

Vadé and JP walked Perri up another cobblestoned street in Disney World's replica of the French Quarter. The park had actually duplicated the ornate architectural details of the historic Vieux Carre. The intricate railings and stone fountains did indeed capture the romance and charm of the city.

"Look, sweetie. Remember when we first moved to New Orleans and you took me to that jazz brunch and told me all about the railings?"

"I'll never forget that day. That was our first official date. When you came to the door with that green suit on, I knew I was going to marry you."

Vadé smiled into his eyes. "Look, Perri. See those railings? African slaves brought that artwork to America. Isn't it pretty?"

She lifted the little girl up in front of the railing and JP took a picture. Perri was adorable in a green sundress. Vadé had brushed her jet-black hair up into a ponytail and tied it with a green ribbon. She did possess the same café au lait skin as JP, her eyes were green, and like her father predicted, she was beautiful.

"Carry me, Daddy." She spoke English well with a slight accent.

"Okay, Princess."

Vadé smiled knowingly every time he called her Princess. Perri adored her father and she was definitely a daddy's girl. He took care of her while Vadé continued working. JP would never admit it, but it was killing him to let Perri attend nursery school at L'Ecole in the mornings. They reminded Vadé of her and Pierre and she loved it. She got to work knowing her baby was well taken care of, and Perri loved her daddy. Vadé would see her own father soon. She hadn't seen him for two years, but she would see him tonight.

Martine had left a message that said Pierre and Vicenté were out playing golf. They had taken Francois, so she was treating herself to a massage at the day spa. They would meet them in the lobby at five for dinner.

Things were running smoothly so far. There was just one tiny glitch in her plan. Juliet had an important shoot come up at the last minute and had to take a later flight. She was scheduled to arrive at the hotel by four and it was three-thirty.

"Come on, you two. Let's get dressed for dinner and see if Auntie Juliet is here yet."

Martine and Desiree sat waiting for their nails and toes to dry. They had spent the entire day pampering themselves while their husbands played nine holes of golf. They had arrived at the hotel around eleven.

"Are you sure my daughter has no idea I'm back?" Desiree blew on a freshly painted nail. Diamond rocks sparkled on both of the ladies' hands.

"I didn't even know you were back until I saw you at the airport this morning. I can't believe V kept it a secret from me. He told me this morning that he and Francois had a secret, but that was all."

"Your son is too adorable. We fell in love at first sight."

"He came home talking about Grandmère one night and V told me he was talking about my mother. I should have known then because he calls her Big Mama."

"That's grandmother in French. You don't mind, do you?"

"Oh, no. I'm glad and Vicenté is too. His relationship with his father's family is very important to him . . . and me."

"I understand they were having problems, so when he suggested this trip, I said yes right away. I knew it would give them a chance to get together, away from the hotel. And we adore our grandson."

* * *

Vadé rang Juliet's room but she still hadn't checked in yet. It was four-thirty and she was beginning to worry. She jumped in the shower with her husband while Perri took a nap.

"I'm worried, JP. Juliet's not here yet."

"She'll get here." He kissed her on the neck.

"Don't start that now, JP, or we'll never make it to dinner."

"Then why did you get in here with me?"

"To take a shower. I don't want us to be late for dinner with Papá. We don't want to be in the lobby when Lar and Little Claude arrive either."

She jumped out of the shower and began drying off while JP turned off the water.

"How do I look, darling?" Desiree twirled around in a lime-green dress and matching sandals.

"Fabulous as always. You would still look like that twenty-year-old girl I fell in love with if you hadn't cut your hair."

"Well, I don't want to look like that twenty-year-old girl. But I do want to look nice for my first carnival night with you in years. Oh my God. Pierre, do you realize it was five years ago, exactly today?"

"I don't want to remember the day you left me. I just want to remember the day you came back."

"That was the stupidest thing I ever did." Her face clouded over as she sat on the bed.

"If the children hadn't upset you, you probably never would have come to the villa."

"I started to go down to the Caribbean, but I wanted to be someplace that reminded me of you. Remember that summer we went fishing?"

"We had the best time. I saw something about chartering boats here. Maybe I'll take my son and Francois."

"You'll have to take your daughter when we go to the villa this summer."

"Princess, on a fishing boat? She is too Parisian. If she allows it, I'll take JP."

"That's a good idea and then we can have some time together. Martine told me all about how she and Vadé became friends. It seems like they disposed of one of your female callers."

"Female caller? I haven't had any female callers."

"Martine said her name was Fleur."

"Fleur?" Pierre looked puzzled. "Fleur La Tiff? Fleur thought she was Josephine Baker. I was never interested in Fleur. I was never interested in any other woman. Is that why she left the hotel so suddenly?"

"They got some stationery from one of Martine's friends who works at a radio station and had JP write her about some fantastic singing engagement that she had to take."

Pierre fell out laughing. "That sounds like something my daughter would do."

"Our daughter. She was looking out for her mamá's man."

They laughed as they walked down the corridor. Vicenté, Martine, and Francois were already downstairs.

"Come here, Francois."

Martine took a baby brush out of her purse and brushed her son's black silky hair that had never been cut. His father kept it braided in a ponytail and it was almost to his waist. He pulled away from her and danced in the mirror by the elevator.

"V, when are you going to cut your son's hair?"

The elevator opened and Vadé and JP stepped off with Perri. The girls ran toward each other screaming.

"Look at you, you look gorgeous, and I can't believe you cut your hair."

"Thank you. You are also looking quite gorgeous, too. Madame in red."

"But of course, darling." She twirled around and touched Vadé's hair. "I still can't believe you cut all that hair."

"I got tired of it. I would have done it sooner but there was no one I trusted in New Orleans."

"But of course not, darling. Look at Perri. She's beautiful. She could be Francois's little sister."

"She is his little sister. She reminds me so much of your cousins from Puerto Rico."

"I know. They're so beautiful and exotic looking with that skin and black hair. You know Miss Tia keeps in touch with Claude. They went out while the guys were in Puerto Rico. Oh, girl, I have so much to tell you."

"Me too. But I want to go speak to my brother before he disowns me."

She walked over to the elevators where the men were standing with the children.

"Hello, big brother." She gave Vicenté a warm hug and kissed him on the cheek.

"Hello, Princess Sister. It's good to see you."

"You too. So you were the first to give Papá a grandchild."

"Yes, I was the first." He grinned.

"I'm glad. Now Perri has a big brother like I do. Little brothers are great, but a girl needs an older, wiser man to look out for her who's not her father."

"That is so true. I just wish I had been around sooner."

"Me too. But, then, I don't think JP would have had a chance with you, Lar, and Papá."

"Francois, come meet your auntie, my sister Vadé."

"Bonjour, Auntie Vadé. Daddy, what kind of name is Vadé?"

The adults screamed with laughter while Vadé tried to keep a straight face.

"I've always wondered the same thing, so you just call me T." She took the child in her arms and kissed him. "Martine, look at this hair as long as my daughter's, and he looks so much like Papá."

The elevator doors opened and Pierre and Desiree walked out.

"Mamá?"

Vadé took a few more steps to make sure she was seeing clearly.

"Oh my God, it's really you."

She flew into her mother's arms while the others smiled as they looked on.

"Hello, *mon ami*."

They were both crying.

"Mamá, where did you come from? Where have you been? Oh, I missed you so much. I don't care why you left, I'm just glad you're back."

They were hugging again and Pierre cleared his throat.

"Excuse me, but can your old papá get a little love?"

"I'm sorry, Papá." He kissed her and rubbed her cheek with his silky beard.

"Oh, Papá, I've missed you so much." Her eyes watered up again. "You haven't done that since I was a little girl. . . . Oh, my goodness. Perri, come here, baby."

Pierre's and Desiree's mouths dropped open when they saw the beautiful little girl with green eyes.

"This is Grandmère and Grandpère Chevalier."

"Bonjour." She spoke French as well as she spoke English.

Pierre picked her up while the entire family made a fuss over its newest member.

"God gave me une petite princess. Hello, Perri." He kissed her and handed her to Desiree.

"Oh my God, she has my eyes. You're gonna be nothing but trouble, just like your mamá. I just know JP is spoiling you, just like your mother's father spoiled her, because you are too precious."

She kissed her on the cheek and handed her to JP, who was waiting with open arms.

"He's worse than Papá. I had to send her to school so he could get back to work."

"Excuse me, family, but we'd better get going, we have dinner reservations. It's five-fifteen." Vicenté led them out of the hotel toward the restaurant.

"I'm glad you were watching the time, Vicenté."

"We don't want Lar to walk in the hotel and see us. So far, everything has gone perfectly."

"Things are better than perfect with Mamá here, but we have one small problem. Our guest of honor hasn't arrived yet."

Sister and brother were whispering as they strolled through the replica of the French Quarter.

"Are you talking about Lar? He's not supposed to be at the hotel until right about now. That's why we had to get out of that lobby."

"I'm talking about Juliet."

"Oh my God, Juliet, where is she?"

"Good question, her plane arrived at four."

"She should have been at the hotel by now. Martine?"

Martine was walking up ahead with JP and Francois. She fell back a few steps to walk with Vicenté and Vadé.

"Juliet's not here yet," Vicenté whispered loudly.

"Oh, no. I got so caught up into Vadé's reunion with her mother, I completely forgot about her. She was supposed to come with you."

"She was coming with us until she got a last-minute photo shoot. She had to take it. It was for one of the really big houses. One of her best clients."

"She's not coming. . . ."

"She is coming. She was supposed to take a later flight. I already tried her in Paris and she wasn't home so we can only hope she makes it here in time. But she should have been here by now."

"What do we do?"

"The only thing we can."

"What's that?" Vicenté and Martine spoke in unison.

"Pray."

THIRTY-SEVEN

Laurent and Little Claude climbed into a limousine at Orlando International. Goldie climbed in behind them and the driver closed the door and sped off into the dark balmy night. Laurent tingled with excitement. He felt like something wonderful was about to happen but he didn't know what. He loved performing and he had always wanted to go to Disney World.

They went into the Port Orleans where Goldie checked them in and got the room keys. The cousins shared a suite with a sitting room and bar. There was always someone to entertain after the concert.

"So what's up for tonight?"

"You sing at ten."

"And after that?"

"Nothing much, why?"

"Because I want to go to Disney World."

"So do I. We'll do that tomorrow."

"Cool. But I still want to go tonight."

"You are such a kid."

"So are you."

As they walked into their rooms, Laurent made a face and Little Claude cracked up.

"Rotten egg."

"Cool."

The guys raced down the hall toward the room like children.

Laurent tossed his jacket on the bed. He would definitely be the first one dressed. It was six o'clock . . . four hours until show time. He was a time bomb ready to explode. He had too much energy to sit around in a hotel room in Disney World. He dialed Little Claude's room and the line was busy, so he picked up his jacket and strolled down the hall toward the elevator.

Juliet dug in her wallet for American dollars to pay for the taxi. A bellboy was already taking her Louis Vuitton luggage out of the car. She paid the driver and placed the matching train case with her makeup on the luggage cart as she stuffed her wallet back into a black oversize bag. She strolled behind her luggage thinking about what she was going to wear for dinner when she saw him strolling in the opposite direction out of the hotel.

"Laurent?"

He turned around and time stood still. Juliet was actually standing in front of him calling his name. He pulled her into his arms and hugged her.

"I can't believe it's really you. What are you doing here?"

"What are *you* doing here?" She gave him a smile that melted his heart.

"Forget that. The important thing is that you're here. And I am not letting you out of my sight." He looked at his watch. I have a show to do at ten, which means we have to be back by eight-thirty. It's six-thirty now, which means we have two hours to go to Disney World, come back, and get changed."

He pulled out a wad of cash and gave a twenty it to the bellboy with her luggage.

"Take these things up to my room. The penthouse."

"No problem, Mr. Chevalier."

He took Juliet by the hand and led her toward the limo.

"Laurent, what are you doing? I didn't even check in."

"You can check in when we get back."

"Okay. She knew he was taking her wherever Vadé and JP were, so she played along. Vadé had told her they were going to have a lot of fun in Disney World, but she didn't mention anything about Laurent being there. She took his hand once they were inside the car.

"It's so good to see you, Laurent."

"It's nice to see you too, Juliet."

He smiled and she was lost inside his eyes.

"Why didn't you wait for me?"

"I thought you didn't want to come."

"I told you not to leave without me."

"I wanted to wait all night, but I was afraid."

"Afraid of what?"

"That you didn't love me as much as I loved you."

"Oh, Laurent. I thought you didn't love me."

"It was scary . . . everything happened so fast."

"I know, baby. But that's behind us. What's important is that you're here now."

He pulled her into his arms and kissed her.

"And I'm serious. I'm not letting you out of my sight. I don't ever want to lose you again."

"And I'm not letting you out of mine."

They smiled at each other as the limo pulled up to the front gate of Disney World.

"Is this okay, sir?"

"Yes, thank you. We'll be back in a few."

Laurent paid their admissions and they walked through the gate holding hands.

"Laurent, what are we going to do in Disney World for one hour? We don't have enough time to go on any rides."

"I know. I'm too wired to sit in a hotel room. I was on my way over here when I ran into you. You still didn't tell me why you're here, but don't tell me the real reason. I want to keep thinking you're here to see me."

"Then, that's exactly why I'm here. *Just wait until I see Vadé and JP.*

Little Claude walked through the adjoining sitting room into Laurent's bedroom. He didn't notice the Louis Vuitton luggage by the door.

"Where are you, Laurent Felipe Chevalier?"

He walked back into his room and dialed Goldie's room.

"Have you seen Lar?"

"No, but he took the car."

"He did what?"

"The limo's not here. The bellman said he left in it with some young lady over an hour ago."

"That boy went to Disney World and he took Vadé. I'm going to kill him. I've got to get the airport to get my parents. They're expecting a limo. Leave it to Lar to change everything around."

As soon as he hung up the phone, it rang.

"Little Claude, it's Vadé."

"Hey, Day, what's up? Did you guys have fun in Disney World?"

"Disney World? We're not going there until tomorrow."

"Lar's not with you?"

"No, he's supposed to be with you. Where is he?"

"He's here." *Somewhere.* "What's up?"

"Everything. We've got a problem."

"What's wrong?"

"Juliet's not here yet."

"She's not?"

"No. And I'm afraid she's not coming. She had a last-minute shoot."

"Oh, no. We were just talking about her on the plane. She's on the cover of the *Sports Illustrated* swimsuit issue. I almost told him she was going to be here when he saw the magazine at the airport. Now I'm glad I didn't mention anything. Is everyone else here?"

"Yes, and you're going to be surprised." She couldn't wait for him to see her mother and daughter.

"Why?"

"I'm not telling you. I'll see you at the party. Au revoir."

He hung up the phone and smiled as he dialed Goldie's room.

"I've got to go to the airport and meet my parents. They were expecting a driver and I have no other way to get in touch with them. I keep telling my father to get a cell phone. You stay here and wait for Laurent and make sure he's backstage in that dressing room by nine-thirty. If for some strange reason we don't hook up at the concert, be sure he's at the Mardis Gras, the club downstairs, by eleven-thirty for the surprise party."

"Okay, man. I'll make sure he's there."

"And don't tell him I went to the airport to get my parents, that's a surprise too."

If Lar wasn't with Vadé, then who was he with? He may have made arrangements to have some other girl meet him in Orlando . . . and the family is here. I should have told him. These kind of surprises never work, but Vadé made me promise to keep everything a secret.

He ran past the Mardis Gras on his way out of the hotel where carnival revelers had already begun the celebration.

THIRTY-EIGHT

Vadé dialed Juliet's room one last time and hung up the phone when there was no answer. She looked at Martine, who stood across from her in the lobby of Port Orleans.

"The front desk said she still hasn't checked in."

"She didn't come."

The girls looked at each other with unhappy faces.

"Well, we still have a surprise for Lar. Your mother's here."

"Lar is going to go crazy when he sees Mamá." Vadé brightened at the thought.

"And your mother and father are going to be surprised when they see him. I heard Pierre say he was going to take your mother to LA to see him real soon."

"They'll see him sooner than they think." Vadé gave Martine a sly grin.

"Yes. And Lar is going to be so surprised when he sees all of us. So we still have a good surprise."

"Yes, we do. I just wanted Juliet to be here, too."

"I know, me too. Thank you for everything you've done for my sister."

"You don't have to thank me. She's my sister, too, sister."

The girls smiled and hugged.

"I'm so glad my family is your family, too." Martine took Vadé by her arm and the girls walked together to join the rest of the family, who were waiting to go to the Magic Kingdom to see the parade.

Little Claude met Big Claude and Giselle at Orlando International. He was surprised to see his Uncle Rene and Aunt Aubrey waiting with them.

"Everyone's just full of surprises tonight."

He grinned as he gave JP's parents a hug. This would be the first time they would meet their granddaughter, Perri, too.

"The star, my cousin, swiped the limo so we'll have to take a cab."

Little Claude looked at his watch as he got into the taxi. It was nine. He instructed the cabby to drop off their luggage at the hotel before they went to the Magic Kingdom.

Laurent and Juliet jumped out of the limo and ran inside the hotel where Goldie was waiting for Laurent in the lobby.

"What's up, Goldie? This is Juliet."

"Claude will meet you at the show. I'll see that you get there."

"Cool." He turned to Juliet. "Can you get beautiful in thirty minutes?"

"Excuse me, I don't mean to interrupt, Ms. Bárres, but it is a pleasure to meet you and you're already very beautiful."

Goldie was big and buff with skin the color of butter. He was Giselle's nephew and the guys' cousin. He kissed her hand and Juliet blushed. Laurent smiled and pulled Juliet into his arms.

"*Mon ami*, that's a given, but you don't allow a lady like this only thirty minutes to shower and dress. I wouldn't ask, but these are extenuating circumstances."

"That's okay, Laurent. I can do it."

"Cool. You can use my room. I'll use Little Claude's."

The three of them took the elevator upstairs where Laurent led her into his bath where he removed a few of his toiletries.

"If you need me, I'll be on the other side of the sitting area using Little Claude's shower."

Juliet blew him a kiss as he closed the door. She stripped and jumped in the shower. She could be ready on time if she hurried. Minutes later she stood wrapped in a towel, deliberating over her gold-mesh dress from the Collections.

Vadé and the rest of the family found the stage in the Magic Kingdom where a young rapper was already performing. The area was overflowing with families with kids and teenagers.

"This is wonderful," Dez whispered to her husband. "I love it."

"Me too." But Pierre was referring to Francois and Perri dancing in front of him.

Laurent slipped into the pants of his stage gear. He felt as if he were dreaming and didn't want to wake up. He couldn't believe Juliet was next door and using his shower.

Martine clicked off her cell phone for the last time.

"She's still not there. She never checked into her room."

"I wanted her to come so badly. Things would be perfect if she were here."

Juliet carefully pulled the gold full-length dress over her head, quickly applied her makeup, and brushed her hair. She put the finishing touches on her gold lip gloss as Laurent knocked on the door.

"I'm ready." She pulled open the door and he was standing there dressed to go onstage.

"You are absolutely gorgeous."

"It's not too much, is it?"

"No. It's perfect, just like you."

She had rendered him speechless as he stood there staring. Goldie opened the sitting room door with a key, and came in.

"It's nine-forty, Lar."

"We're ready."

Goldie walked them downstairs through the lobby. As they walked out of Port Orleans, the taxi with Little Claude and the Oliviers pulled out of the hotel drive, heading for Disney World. The bellboy glanced at Laurent and his entourage as he wheeled the luggage cart past them inside.

In the Mardis Gras, the celebration had just kicked into a new level as more people joined the party, but Laurent and Juliet were too engrossed in conversation to notice anything else going on around them.

Little Claude spotted the family as he led his parents into the Magic Kingdom. It was just about ten. He pointed Vadé out to his father and dashed off toward the stage. He had gotten all of the Oliviers to the park. She could handle things from there.

Laurent led Juliet to a special spot on the stage.

"This is where I used to sit when I was a little boy watching my mother sing with my father's group. Goldie will come get you when it's time to leave."

She blew Laurent a kiss as he walked away.

Big Claude tapped Vadé on the shoulder. She screamed when she saw all the Oliviers. Little Claude had definitely lived up to his part of the bargain.

"Big Claude. I'm so glad to see you." She grabbed Giselle and hugged her. "Your best friend is here."

"Dez?"

Vadé nodded yes as she smiled.

"Dez is here? You're lying. Where?"

"She's over there hugged up with her man."

Vadé pointed her mother out to Giselle, who screamed. Desiree turned around, saw Giselle, and screamed with her as the two jumped around in a circle. Big Claude and Pierre hugged as Rene and Aubrey fussed over their granddaughter.

Little Claude pushed his way through the mob and backstage where he found Laurent in the wings drinking a cup of tea.

"It's about time you got here, man."

"Lar, where have you been?"

Laurent laughed and pushed him toward the stage. "We'll talk later. It's time for you to do your stuff, man."

Little Claude walked onto the darkened stage with a mic and the girls began screaming. He always introduced Laurent with a rap before each performance. The record company got so many requests for C-Note that there was a lot of discussion about him recording an album.

"Are you ready to party?" he yelled into the microphone as the audience yelled back. The drumbeats started, the lights came up, and Little Claude ran onto the stage. The family screamed right along with the rest of the crowd as Little Claude worked the audience to a deafening level. Laurent ran out in a blaze of flashes and explosions.

"Look at my baby boy." Desiree had to yell to be heard over all the screaming and the loud music.

"That's your Uncle Lar," Vicenté yelled to Francois, who was sitting on his shoulders mesmerized.

JP danced around with Perri while Vadé and Martine just screamed. Juliet stood up to dance in her private viewing spot. Laurent lit up the stage in the Magic Kingdom for forty-five minutes before he finished with his latest single.

Goldie was waiting for him with a towel, his robe, and Juliet when he walked off the stage.

"Thanks, man. Where's Claude?"

"Talking to a few of the guys from the Orlando Magic."

"Great, tell him I took the limo. We'll see you guys later."

Goldie walked Laurent and Juliet to the limo.

"But you're—"

"It'll be fine. Little Claude will understand."

Goldie watched the limo speed off into the night before he could say another word and wondered what Little Claude would say when Laurent didn't show up for the surprise party.

"Where's Lar?"

Little Claude was standing in front of him.

"He left, man."

"He left? You're supposed to be with him. Did you tell him about the party?"

"No, you said it was a surprise."

"It sure is going to be a big surprise when he doesn't show up. Did he say where he was going?"

"No. He just took his lady and left."

"Lady? What lady? I should have known he was with a girl."

"Ms. Bárres."

"Ms. Bárres? He's with Martine?"

"No. It was Juliet. The young lady on the swimsuit issue."

"That's Juliet. When did she get here?"

"I don't know. I was waiting for him in the lobby when he walked in with her."

"Lar is with Juliet and neither one of them knows about the party. This has got to be the craziest thing I've ever seen."

"Ms. Bárres doesn't know about the party either?"

"No. It was a surprise for her too. But the surprise is really on us because they're together and we don't know where they are. Lar was right. Things do go crazy for this family during Mardis Gras."

THIRTY-NINE

The family took the Disney World tram back from the Magic Kingdom to Port Orleans. Meanwhile Laurent had showered and changed into a black designer suit. He and Juliet made a very striking couple. They stood together in front of the mirror admiring each other.

"We look good." Laurent grinned and pulled her into his arms.

"I know." She giggled.

It was hard to believe a twenty-year-old had a body like she did.

"And since we aren't married, we are leaving this room," he said.

"He has character to go along with those good looks. I'm loving this more by the minute."

"It or me?"

"You, silly boy." She kissed him and he thought he had died and gone to heaven.

"I was wondering how long you were going to make me wait for that."

He kissed her until he had to pull away. "Let's go. We're getting married."

He took her by the hand. She looked at him as if he were crazy when he inquired about a chapel at the desk and walked her out to the limo.

"You're serious, aren't you?"

"I told you I was never going to let you out of my sight again."

She kissed him and screamed. "I love you, Laurent Chevalier."

Vadé and Vicenté ushered the family into a private room at the Mardis Gras where the carnival was off the hook. Some people were in wild costumes, others were dressed in evening attire. Laughter peppered the carnival music as the revelers danced and drank.

"This is a great party, little sister. What a way for the family to celebrate the kids' first Mardis Gras. You hooked it up down to the last detail. This has been one of the best times of my life."

"I couldn't have done it without you, Vicenté. You got Papá and Mamá here. This has been one of the best times of my life, too. I'll never forget this day."

"It has been wonderful."

"I just wish Juliet could have been here, too."

"We'll all get together. Maybe at the villa, this summer," Vicenté suggested.

"That's a wonderful idea. It's real romantic with the beach. We had a car the last time I was there and JP used to drive us to Cannes every day to go to the beach."

"We will definitely be at the villa this summer."

"Great, you'll have to stay for a month. But you have to come to my house in Paris, too. It was the home we grew up in and now Perri is going to grow up there, too. It's going to be so much fun taking her to the places where Lar and I used to go."

"That is wonderful, Vadé. Speaking of Lar, where is he?"

"Good question. It's eleven-thirty. They should be here by now."

She looked around the room to make sure the family was comfortable. There was a bartender and a buffet of their favorite Creole dishes.

"Where's your brother, Princess? It's getting late. He is coming to the celebration, isn't he?"

Everyone looked to see her response.

"Yes, Papá. He and Little Claude will be here any minute."

She went over to the bar and ordered the first drink she had taken since the last Mardis Gras when the family was together. *What if Lar is still mad at Papá?* She hadn't taken that into consideration when she planned the party. She assumed her brother would be glad to see her father just like she was. Laurent was never one to hold a grudge. *So where is he?*

JP walked over to stand by her side. "He is coming, isn't he?"

"Of course he is. I'd really be concerned if Little Claude was here."

It was as if he heard his name. Little Claude pushed open the doors and walked into the room with Goldie.

"See, I told you they'd be here."

Vadé and JP reached Little Claude at the same time as Martine and Vicenté.

"Where's Lar?" they all demanded.

Little Claude pulled Vadé out of the room and the others followed. "I don't know."

"You don't know?" Vadé squealed. "What happened?"

"I wasn't there when he came offstage. Goldie said he left with your sister." Little Claude looked at Martine.

"My sister? Juliet is here?"

She and Vadé were screaming.

"She's here . . . somewhere."

In a little chapel near Disney World, Laurent placed the missing part of the heart ring on Juliet's finger and smiled.

"With this ring I thee wed."

They kissed as the clergyman pronounced them husband and wife.

"I can't believe you kept that ring in your pocket all this time."

"I had to keep it handy in case I ran into the finger it belonged on and, see, I did."

"You are so sweet and so romantic. I love you, Laurent Chevalier."

"I love you, too, Juliet Chevalier."

The excitement built to a momentum as time approached the midnight hour in Mardis Gras.

"I should have known they were together." Vadé shook her head and smirked. "Lar could be on his way to the south of France. When's the next show?"

"We're free for the next ten days."

"Oh, no."

"Lar's not in France. But if he doesn't show up for this party, your father's going to kill him," JP warned.

"But how is he going to show up for a party that he doesn't know about?"

"Did you leave him a message at the front desk?" Vicenté looked at Little Claude.

"My bad. I'll go do it now."

"We'll leave one for Juliet, too."

The siblings, cousins, and in-laws headed for the desk as Pierre stuck his head out of the private room.

"Where are all of you going?"

"We'll be right back, Papá," Vadé answered for them.

"Kids." He looked at Perri sleeping in his wife's lap and Francois stretched out on Big Claude. "You have to love them."

While the group was at the desk leaving messages for Laurent and Juliet, they walked into the hotel. They could hear the music from the Mardis Gras.

"Come on, beautiful, let's go dance our first dance as husband and wife before we go upstairs."

Juliet eagerly agreed and they went into the club and found a place on the floor. Vadé and Little Claude slowly led the others back into the club. They stood there watching the dancing crowd as they planned what they were going to use as an excuse for Lar's apparent absence.

"Look." Vicenté pointed to someone dancing on the floor. "Isn't that Lar?"

"Where?" Martine tried to follow with her eyes to where he was pointing, but she saw no one who resembled his brother.

"Right there. Dancing with Juliet. Girlfriend has on that fabulous gold dress that she modeled at the Collections."

Vadé took off running and the others followed.

"Laurent!" She practically jumped on her brother, hugging and kissing him while Martine did the same to Juliet.

"Don't leave me out." Vicenté jumped in between Laurent and Vadé. Everyone was hugging, kissing, crying.

"Come on, you two. There are others waiting to see you."

Vadé led Laurent and Juliet by the hand into the private room.

"Here's your other son, Papá." She smiled as she pushed her younger brother toward their father.

"And his wife," Laurent added quickly. He had never let go of Juliet's hand. "We were just married."

"Married?" Desiree hopped up from the table and came toward him. "What's my baby doing talking about he's married?"

"Mamá!"

Silence filled the room as mother and son hugged.

"Where did you come from? Where did all of you come from?"

"Surprise!" They were all smiling.

Laurent was speechless.

"We've been planning this little soiree for weeks and you two almost messed it up. Vadé put the whole thing together and we all helped." Little Claude pretended to be mad at his cousin. "I know I told you to call the girl, man, but dang, I didn't know you were going to go buck wild."

Everyone laughed as the family crowded around the newlyweds.

"Congratulations, Lar. I hope you two will be very happy. Juliet is so special."

"Thanks, Day." Laurent hugged his sister. "I love you."

"I know. I love you, too." She turned to Vicenté.

"I always wondered why God made us move to America when I prayed for us stay in France. God sent us here to find you. Now everything's perfect." She pulled her eldest brother into her arms and hugged him tightly.

Tears streamed out of Vicenté's eyes. "Thank you, Vadé," he managed to whisper.

Martine walked over with a tissue and wiped his eyes.

Vadé smiled as she watched the family mingle . . . Laurent and Juliet holding Perri and Francois. Little Claude sitting between Mamá and T'Giselle eating a bowl of gumbo. Papá and Big Claude in the corner smoking pipes and laughing. Martine and Vicenté kissing and hugging . . . Goldie talking with Rene and Aubrey.

She smiled even more as JP pulled her into his arms and kissed her.

Chevaliers and Oliviers, the family, were together, once again.

And as time entered the midnight hour, Mardis Gras revelers continued the dance.